RUTLAND'S GUNS

ROGER CARPENTER

AuthorHouse™ UK Ltd.
500 Avebury Boulevard
Central Milton Keynes, MK9 2BE
www.authorhouse.co.uk
Phone: 08001974150

First published by AuthorHouse 8/7/2007

ISBN: 978-1-4259-7311-7 (sc)

Printed in the United States of America
Bloomington, Indiana

This book is printed on acid-free paper.

Rutland's Curse available from www.amazon.com **and** www. amazon.co.uk
Or your local book shop quote

This, the second book in the Rutland series, is for Georgia, Abigail, Izzie and Millie – who are the joy of my life.

Acknowledgment

The picture of the Ehrhardt 15 Pounder gun (negative Q36802) is published with kind permission of the Imperial War Museum, London.

The pictures of the Queen's South Africa Medal and the artillery action from the Medal Year Book 2007 are published with the kind permission of Token Publishing Ltd of Honiton, Devon.

Glossary

Boer = (B)   Cockney Rhyming Slang = (CRS)

Adam and Eve it	Believe it (CRS)
ADC	Aide de Camp
Biltong	Strips of dried meat (B)
BSM	Battery Sergeant Major
Corned dog	Corned beef
CRA	Commander Royal Artillery
Daisy roots	Boots (CRS)
Dag	Hi there/ Day (B)
Danke	Thank you (B)
Donga	Gulley – deep dry watercourse
Dooly	Stretcher slung on pole.
Guidon	Small flag on cavalry lance
Kerels	Companions/ Chums (B)
Kopje	Flat topped hill (B)
MO	Medical Officer/ Doctor
Plates of meat	Feet (CRS)
RHA	Royal Horse Artillery
RSM	Regimental Sergeant Major
Shrapnel	Air exploding shell
Spruit	A small watercourse wet in winter only. (B)
Stick man	Smartest man on guard detail who is excused all duties.
Stoep	Verandah (B)
Tot Siens	Goodbye/ Till I see you again (B)
Veldt	Plains, often desert or scrub (B)
Verdomp	Damned (B)

Chapter 1

15th December 1899.
Colenso, Natal State, South Africa

Like a giant thundercloud, the disaster started to take shape.

"14 Battery, right wheel."

"66 Battery, left wheel."

The command orders rang out over the line of British field guns being pulled by the teams of sturdy artillery horses. As the two Batteries swung off their line of march and away from each other, their Commanders again called out the orders that would bring their guns into action.

"14 Battery. Action left!" shouted Major Bailward. The Battery of 15 pounder guns skidded to a halt and their Gunners jumped down onto the dusty ground. Within a few minutes all six guns were in action positions with their barrels in a long staggered line pointing towards the Boer defended hills. 66 Battery was also drawn up in line thirty yards away.

Neither of these Batteries had served in South Africa before but to the Gunners, now standing beside the field guns waiting for Fire Orders, it was all in a day's work. On each man's cork sun helmet was the badge bearing their regimental motto 'Ubique', which was the Latin for 'Everywhere'. Here they were in part of Natal State in South Africa that was to the Gunners just another bit of 'Everywhere'.

The Tugela River ran by only 1000 yards away; though invisible in the morning mist, it was the demarcation between the two fighting forces. But it was a formidable obstacle for the British to cross; a fast flow of water, edged in most places with steep banks. The only road and rail bridge to cross the river was just upstream at the village of Colenso.

The Boers were on the north side of the river in their carefully dug, almost invisible, trenches placed at the foot of the Colenso Kopje hills. They had also cleverly dug dummy trenches in the higher ground rising well behind them, not just to fool the British artillery but, with their well concealed forward dugouts closer to the river, they could defend the banks more efficiently with their accurate rifle fire. The Boer commander, Louis Botha, was certain that he could lure the British close to the river and then, in the open killing ground, defeat them but it was essential that his men did not fire before he gave the order. He wanted the commanders of the British Tommies to feel confident that they could push forward towards the river – well clear of any reasonable cover.

The British Army was deployed on the south side of the river, and they were preparing to attack across open ground that was broken up by the occasional gulley, called a donga, and an amount of low scrub. Concealment in the face of such a determined and entrenched enemy was almost impossible but once across the river they would be able to attack the trenches that they could see set in the hills, which would have been heavily battered by the artillery.

The two Batteries of Field Artillery had been given some rather vague orders to position themselves at a medium range of about 2,000 yards. But in the early mist the guns had pushed just 1000 yards short of the river, closer than expected and certainly closer than Botha had ever expected or wanted.

The forward and manned enemy trenches were now clearly visible to the Artillery Commander, Colonel Long. He stood, with Lt. Col Hunt RA by his side, at the Artillery Command Post scanning the target area with his field glasses. Against Botha's orders and wishes, the Boers had reacted to the danger of the close proximity of the British guns and were replying with their accurate Mauser rifle fire but, as usual, their first shots were flying too high.

"We're closer to 'em than I intended." Colonel Long said. "Still, our guns'll be all the more effective. Order Battery fire on those forward trenches."

"Very good sir." Hunt turned and walked over to the two Battery Commanders standing close by. "The Colonel wants you to stay this far forward and hit those trenches." He pointed to the thin black lines at the base of the far hills. "And of course knock out any of their artillery you can find." Majors Bailward and Foster, the two Battery Commanders, saluted, mounted their horses and cantered back to their Batteries.

"Battery Fire - shrapnel 1200 yards." Bailward shouted out the Fire Orders which were repeated by the section commanders and obeyed by the field gunners. By now the Boer rifle fire was starting to fly very close to the guns and men. The Gunners took the 15 pounder shells from the limbers, loaded them into their guns and placed the firing charges in the breech. The breech of each gun clanged shut; the friction tubes were inserted in the vent by Number 2 Gunner who, having hooked his lanyard on to it, stood to the side of his gun and waited. The order to fire was given and the Number 2 jerked the lanyard smartly; all the field guns started to slam out a reply to the rifle fire with their 15 pound shrapnel shells bursting above the enemy trenches.

But disaster was slowly approaching.

....

Colonel Long's mistake of approaching too near to the enemy, however, was quick to bear fruit. The Gunners' discipline and training held them steady against the mounting casualties as the Mauser bullets started to find the khaki-clad bodies. But relentlessly the British 15 pound shells screamed out, spreading shrapnel bullets and splinters in the trenches, and slowly they reduced the stinging rifle fire. The Boers gradually started to fall back from their forward trenches; Botha's plan of using their accurate rifle firepower to cover the killing ground, and win a bloody victory, was in tatters.

"There's a pom-pom in those high rocks," called Bailward. "Right section target 1800 yards." The artillery duel swayed back and forth with the 15 pound breechloaders gradually winning as the Gunners fed their ever hungry, over heating barrels.

The approaching disaster was being assisted by their own efficiency.

....

Four large wagons brought in the extra ammunition that was quickly issued to the guns, and almost as quickly used. Within an hour the two Batteries had poured nearly 1000 rounds onto the now almost silent enemy. The stock of shells was swiftly used up.

Major Bailward once again checked his ammunition; he then ran over to Lt Col Hunt and reported. "We're getting low on shrapnel again sir."

"Damn waggoners," exploded Hunt. "Colonel Long and I've both sent off messengers but without success. Keep your fire steady. I'll chase them up again."

Hunt walked over to the Colonel who was leaning against an empty limber; there was blood pouring from a splinter wound in his side. "Are you all right sir?"

"Yes, yes, it's nothing," gasped the ashen-faced man.

"Both Batteries are desperately low on ammunition, and there's still no sign of any more on its way." reported Hunt.

"Send an officer this time Hunt. Tell him to demand immediate stocks. Tell him to shout loud and hard to get it here at once."

"Very good sir" Hunt turned away and called out, "Captain Herbert. Gallop back and demand immediate replacement stocks of ammunition. The Colonel insists on instant action. Tell them we are in a desperate situation."

"Right sir" Herbert saluted and ran over to his horse, mounted and instantly spurred it into a standing gallop. Speed was essential – time was of the essence.

The stage was set for havoc to enter.

....

Away on high ground behind Colenso, named as Naval Gun Hill, General Sir Redvers Buller sat on his horse. The General was a large framed man with a ruddy complexion crossed by a drooping white moustache. He was much loved by his soldiers because their welfare was always on his mind; he was a brave man who had won the Victoria Cross fighting against the Zulus. He was a compassionate man who always worried about unnecessary loss of life - but he was also an indecisive man. Much to his own surprise, he had been chosen, by the authorities at Horse Guards in Whitehall, to lead the British force in South Africa; this decision was against his own better judgment.

On arriving in Cape Province, he found that Lieutenant General Sir George White VC was besieged in the small town of Ladysmith. Buller knew it was vital to relieve the town, as a surrender of this size of British force was not to be tolerated.

His plan to attack the Boers, by crossing the Tugela River at Colenso with an unimaginative frontal assault, was unclearly defined and only hazily explained to his subordinates. From high on his hill he had watched the start of the attack and, through his field glasses, had seen one of his infantry commanders General Hart let his Irish Brigade wander off towards the wrong start position. It was at that moment that Buller began to lose confidence in his own plan of attack but he lacked the conviction to make the decision to either push ahead or cleanly withdraw. Though he could not see Long's guns, he could hear them; he was certain that they were closer to the river than he had wished, and that he had ordered. He sent one of his staff to check and to ensure that the artillery was acting in concert with the infantry. The officer concerned went a short way, looked through his glasses and returned to confirm the guns all seemed 'quite comfortable', and that all was going according to plan.

The trigger of disaster was cocked.

....

The two Batteries of 15 pounders were now down to a handful of shells per gun. "Where the hell are those wagons?"

"We'll have to cease fire soon," said Hunt.

"Damn it. Damn it. Damn it." Col. Long was slumped against a limber wheel. A large field dressing bandaged against his side, his jacket draped across his shoulders.

"Keep six rounds per gun to cover the infantry when they attack across the river." he said. "Fire off the rest then retire the men into that donga behind us." Hunt turned to see a long depression 30 yards behind the guns that would shelter the men from any rifle or pom-pom fire. He passed the Colonel's orders on to the Battery Commanders, and within a few minutes, as the last of the shells were fired, the guns gradually fell silent.

"Detachments rear," shouted Major Bailward. "In sections, take cover in the donga behind us. Move!" The Gunners trotted back to the cover of the donga where their wounded mates already lay. The guns were now left standing deserted and silent.

The illusion had been created.

....

Once clear of the open ground by the river, Captain Herbert RA was riding hard through broken country. He had had difficulty finding the way back to the rear, even losing himself at one time. Eventually he saw some second-line infantry, waiting to move forward as he urged his sweating horse for the final effort. "Come on old lady, only a short way to go now," he called to his horse, spurring her to a canter up the gentle slope leading to Buller's H.Q.

On this approach slope, he saw a Major of the Essex Regiment, who was standing with a group of officers, point excitedly at something near the river. Herbert reined in and, from this high vantage point, looked back at the two Batteries. He could not believe his eyes! The guns were unmanned – abandoned! My God! The Boers have wiped out all the gunners! He wrenched his horse round and seeing General Buller standing on the hill crest, galloped towards him. Leaping from his sweating beast, he saluted and reported.

"Captain Herbert from Colonel Long's force sir. The Boers have killed them all. The guns are deserted!"

"What?" Lieutenant General Clery lifted his field glasses. Taking his time, he carefully examined the position. "The guns are silent and appear to be unmanned," he reported.

It was at that very moment that General Sir Redvers Buller's nerve broke. He pulled the trigger of disaster. "Halt the attack," he ordered. "Withdraw the leading regiments. We must rescue the guns."

"But General," exclaimed Clery, "The Boers can't attack while we have the infantry in their present position. If we withdraw, now they will all be exposed to the enemy fire." He pleaded for sanity to reign; there were still more than 30 field guns unused and three quarters of the infantry had not yet been committed.

"No. Bring them back now," insisted Buller. "We mustn't lose those guns."

"But they are safe while our infantry remain in position."

"Clery. I've decided that we'll withdraw. Order it NOW!"

The sight of the twelve unmanned guns had completely stunned his powers of reasoning. He forgot that on both wings of the attack the infantry regiments were at least safely positioned; his mind was blank to the fact that his other guns were still firing. He was no longer thinking as a General but as a Battery Commander. The guns must be saved!

General Buller's ADC, Captain Schofield, stepped forward. "If I may sir I'll take some volunteers to bring back the guns." Buller looked at the eager young man, and nodded his assent.

Schofield ran to his horse, mounted quickly and cantered towards a support Battery at the bottom of the hill. Two more ADCs, Captain Congreve and Lieutenant Roberts chased after him. The three officers found enough volunteers among the Gunners to make up two gun teams and, in high spirits, they all set off towards the silent 15 pounders.

As they left, nine ammunition wagons were seen moving on their way to Colonel Long's guns, but Buller stopped them – it was all too late.

Buller's orders were then sent out to the forward infantry, with strict instructions that they were to be obeyed to the letter - and immediately.

In the small town of Colenso, the only place of interest to Buller, was the railway which crossed the Tugela River on its way to Ladysmith. Buller was convinced that the only way to relieve Ladysmith was by his force following the railway up to it. The Boers therefore knew exactly where he was going and what line he would follow. Buller did not have the imagination for a flanking attack as he had every confidence in the British army taking on an inferior foe by sheer guts and the bayonet.

Close to the railway bridge, British infantry had used their expertise with their new Lee Enfield rifle to swamp and totally silence the Boers on the far side of the river. Their officers scanned the far banks and planned the attack. To cross the bridge was going to be difficult and dangerous but with good artillery support it should not be too costly, but then the messenger from Head Quarters arrived.

"Withdraw! Dear God, we've only just fought our way here." The Colonel of the Queen's Regiment was aghast. His men had taken their objective almost without loss. His regiment with their deadly rifle fire had sent the Boers scurrying back to the trenches in the high ground.

"General Buller wants you to retire sir." The messenger was emphatic.

"I've lost only two men taking this damned town, now I'm told to retire across open country. It'll be suicide."

"General Buller wants you to retire sir," was the repeated message.

"Dear God. No artillery support and I'm told to withdraw in the face of the Boer without any cover. I'll wait until dusk."

"General Buller is insistent that you retire at once sir."

So, on General Buller's orders, the Queen's withdrew without any support, over recently won ground – and they died, or were wounded, in droves.

In the forward donga, Captain Jones of 66 Battery, who was peering over the edge watching the Boers re-invest the cleared trenches at the foot of the hills, suddenly exclaimed "What the hell!"

He turned round and called out "Major Bailward!" The Major, who had been sitting down with a wounded sergeant, rose and scrambled up the bank; he lay down beside the Captain. "What the hell?" repeated Bailward. There in front of his disbelieving eyes, two dozen British soldiers with horse teams were milling around his guns trying to limber up Left Section.

The Boers, who had by now crept up to the banks of the river, instantly started firing into the circling group. As Bailward watched, two of the men were hit by the rifle fire and one of them fell to the ground obviously dead. The Major rose to his feet. He was about to scramble out of the donga and ask what was happening, when both teams, with guns limbered up, galloped off towards Buller's H.Q.

Bailward slithered back into the donga and ran along the bed towards Colonel Long, who was lying on a stretcher and was now in a state of delirium from his wound. Lt Col Hunt was standing halfway up the donga side also watching the two teams cantering off with the two 15 pounders.

"They've damned well taken two of my guns."

"So I see. Can't imagine what that's all about."

A voice shouted from further down the donga. "The Devons are pulling back." Hunt twisted round and peered through his glasses. He could see a line of infantry getting up from their well-concealed positions and, ducking and twisting, start to run back.

"Oh my God! They're being shot to pieces. They're running back without any cover. What on earth is happening?" Major Bailward pointed back at his Battery and shouted out. "There're more teams at the guns." Another two teams of horses were swinging round to limber up more of the guns but now the Boer rifle fire was like hail. Men and horses fell and died, while a Boer Nordenfeldt Quick Firing gun thumped Shrapnel shells onto the line of 15 pounders.

"God! They'll be wiped out!" yelled Hunt. "Pull back you fools." But the brave fools stayed – and most of them died. Eventually the survivors, wounded and dying, limped away to cover; they had achieved absolutely nothing.

"Should we pull back as well sir?" queried Bailward.

"No. We'll stay here 'til dusk. If we try and move before then we'll be shot to pieces." replied Hunt. It was the only sensible alternative, one that the Devons and the Queen's would have welcomed. But these two noble regiments had been decimated by the pointless retirement over open ground.

Buller's weakness had left the two Batteries of guns and men isolated, and unprotected by any other artillery.

The Boers now reversed the tables. Under the cover of the 2lb shrapnel shells from their Quick Firing Nordenfeldt pom-poms, they crossed the river and stealthily surrounded the gunners.

"A white flag!"

"Where?" called Hunt.

"Right front. A man on horseback." Hunt peered over the donga edge and saw a large framed man with a heavy beard, wearing a slouch hat and holding a rifle in the air to which was attached a white cloth. Behind him more horsemen were strung out in a sweeping curve.

Col Hunt called out to Bailward. "I'm going forward to talk to the Boer. You are in command 'til I return."

"Very good sir."

Hunt scrambled out of the cover, dusted down his trousers, adjusted his sun helmet then strode out towards the horseman who was slowly approaching. Hunt stopped when he reached the line of 15 pounders. "What do you want?" he called out. The Boer walked his horse closer until he was only ten yards away from the guns.

"It's the end of the fight for you Englander. You're surrounded." He leaned his rifle butt on his hip and smiled.

"Nonsense." said Hunt. "We are fully supported. You may surrender your horsemen to us and you'll be given good treatment."

"Look around you Mr Gunner. Everyone's gone." Hunt had no intention of peering over his shoulder but he noticed that the ground near to the river was swarming with mounted Boers. The Batteries had been deserted, not even left with artillery cover. Why?

"Mr Boer," Hunt replied with sarcasm. "If you do not surrender to us, I will allow you to withdraw across the river. We will also retire with our guns." The horseman did not answer; rising in his stirrups, he gave a sweeping wave to the men behind him. At a canter they swarmed over and within a few seconds had surrounded the guns and the donga.

"I protest at this misuse of the flag of truce," shouted Hunt.

"Don't be a blind fool." The Boer leader pushed his horse forward and, with a chopping action, struck Hunt on the head with his rifle butt. It was over.

Bailward, seeing Hunt fall and the donga wall lined with armed men, knew it was finished. The Boer leader rode forward. Bailward walked up to him, saluted and said, "We surrender."

The Boer nodded. "Bring your men out of the donga."

"What about our wounded?"

"They can stay there with your medical orderlies. The rest of your men will march with us." Bailward, a career soldier for fifteen years, felt the depression settle on him. They had been deserted and betrayed.

On Buller's hill the surrender was watched without any further attempt to rescue the Gunners. From the two Batteries of twelve guns, only two pieces had been saved. The cost was the deaths of fourteen officers and men.

Three Victoria Crosses were to be awarded for the action to save the guns. One of these medals was to be awarded posthumously; it was given to Lieutenant Freddy Roberts, the much loved and only son of General Lord Roberts of Kandahar, or 'Bobs' as he was known to an adoring nation.

Chapter 2.

A few days later an explosion occurred in London late on a winter afternoon in the year 1899. To some people it was not unexpected but, for all that, it was just as terrible.

On that fateful afternoon there were about 30 members in the Pall Mall Club. Most of them were in the spacious high-ceilinged reading room, either scanning the daily paper or using it to cover their heads while they slept. Two of the members, who were seated in large leather winged chairs by one of the large windows, were engaged in a subdued-toned conversation. The balance of the members were similarly occupied in the foggy atmosphere of the adjoining smoking room. All were in a relaxed mood; they were encompassed by the soft warmth of their leather chairs, coddled by the silently moving stewards and protected in the womb of the thick-walled antique club.

The murmur of a raised voice in the main entrance hall gently crept into the almost silent room - but few members took any notice. Then gradually, without any details at first being discernible, the sound of a strong, loud voice was to be heard on the stairs leading to the inner sanctum. Now newspapers were lowered, books closed and heads raised; such a background interruption was not expected nor was it acceptable. Some members made a written note of the date and time to ensure that this disturbance was reported at the next committee meeting, and the culprit reprimanded.

The approaching sounds grew louder until the double doors burst open followed by an engulfing roar from the red- faced man who strode through the portals. Of heavy build, he was dressed in a black suit; a bushy white moustache cut across his furious crimson countenance. "Another disaster!" he roared. "The third this week!" He waved the half-opened newspaper above his head showing the banner headline. "BULLER ROUTED."

By now the reading room was a throng of members all on their feet and congregated around the shouting figure, who was obviously the bearer of bad news. "The damn fools couldn't organise a picnic at Henley, let alone handle an army."

The smoking-room members had now joined the group by the door; all were asking the questions. Who? Where? Then a steward appeared with a dozen copies of the evening papers all bearing the same headline, and spread them out on the large central table. Decorum was lost among the members as they scrambled for a copy to read.

There it was! A Reuter report cabled from Durban by their reporter with the British Army in South Africa. General Sir Redvers Buller had attacked, with a frontal assault, a well-defended Boer position at Colenso on the Tugela River. The enemy had dug efficient and well-concealed trenches from which they had decimated the advancing British infantry with deadly accurate fire from their Mauser rifles. First reports told of heavy British casualties and of up to ten guns being lost!

That it was a disaster there was no doubt but the cutting point was that it was the third such disaster to be reported that week. First there had been General Gatacre's fiasco at Stormberg where his attack was repulsed; he had withdrawn too quickly and the Boers had captured more than 500 British troops who had inadvertently been overlooked and left without orders to retire.

The second reverse was Lord Methuen's ill-conceived frontal attack at Magersfontein which had been repulsed by the entrenched Boers, with severe loss of British dead and wounded. And now this! Buller is given a bloody nose and also loses his guns. The three defeats were appalling in themselves but what truly hurt the traditional imperialist British was that their army, arguably the finest in the world, had suffered these defeats at the hands of some disorganised, untrained farmers who happened to be very good shots with a rifle. It was so humiliating that Sir Arthur Conan Doyle was to call it the 'Black Week' in British History.

In the Pall Mall club the jostling crowd around the table read the latest report; they discussed and criticised, then roared their anger and woe at the ineptitude of the British commanders. This same scene was being re-enacted throughout the country on that fateful day.

The two members who had been quietly seated at the large window overlooking Pall Mall remained where they were, occasionally looking at the swirling group around the centre table. Both men, dressed in formal black suits, were elderly, in their late 70s and though obviously still mentally and physically active, they showed no inclination to join in the general hubbub. Colonel Charles Tailby and Major Arthur Rutland had been discussing the war going on in South Africa for most of the afternoon.

"Buller," puffed the Colonel. "A brave man, an excellent second-in-command but never a commander." He leaned closer to his neighbour. "I've heard that Buller tried to refuse the C-in-C appointment when he was given it. Had no confidence in himself."

"Do you think the powers that be will let him stay?" asked Major Rutland.

"Arthur, I don't know," shrugged the Colonel. "But I do know who I'd replace him with if I could."

"Roberts," smiled Rutland.

"Bobs. Absolutely right. But he'll be counted out 'cause he's from the Indian Army. They'll forget all of his previous excellent record and exclude him just because he's Indian Army," repeated Tailby in disgust.

An elegant long-case clock close by chimed and then struck six o'clock. "Goodness is that the time?" Colonel Tailby sat up in his chair to peer round at the timepiece. "Well Arthur, I must be off. I'll see you at dinner this evening. About eight o'clock?"

"Thank you Charles, eight will be fine." Both men rose and together they walked down the stairs to the entrance hallway where the Colonel collected his hat, coat and cane. Then he strode off into the busy street.

Arthur Rutland returned to his seat by the window, ignoring the hubbub behind him. He was deep in his own thoughts. He was staying a few nights at his club having come up on one of his occasional trips to London from his farm. He liked to look in on the office of his timber importation company, talk to his solicitors and visit some business acquaintances. He enjoyed these infrequent short stays in London but his main love was always his farm in Chellingham on the North Downs near the Surrey and Kent border.

Arthur ordered a whisky and soda while he waited for his son Peter to arrive; they would then both go to Colonel Tailby's dinner party.

Colonel Tailby's son Tim had married Arthur's daughter, Tessa. Tim was a good friend of Arthur's son Peter from when both had been Majors in the Royal Artillery. Tim had received a shoulder wound serving in the Sudan, and had decided to retire. He had bought the farm adjoining Arthur's, where he and Tessa now lived with their twin daughters Abigail and Alice.

Arthur's mind turned to his own son Peter. He was still a Major after 20 years! It was about time he got promotion - or left the Regiment. Arthur snorted – 'damned silly thing to think, of course he shouldn't leave the Regiment but -'

Peter's wife Beatrice had died only a few months ago. Their six-year-old son Harry, was being cared for by Tim and Tessa. Would Peter feel that he should look after the lad? Arthur looked out through the club window. The gas lamps in the street below were being lit. A light drizzle was gently falling; it glazed the surface of the road and the hooded hansom cabs as they trotted by. Arthur pulled out his gold hunter watch, looked at the time, and decided that shortly he must wash and change for the dinner tonight. Charles Tailby had promised a small but interesting gathering at dinner: a couple of industrialists, a Member of Parliament and some serving army officers. Arthur looked forward to a stimulating evening.

He heard the reading room door open and close; he turned in his chair and saw, with heart-warming pleasure, his son walking towards him. Peter was six feet tall, of slim build and upright bearing, his bronzed face and blue eyes capped with dark brown hair. Moustached, and wearing full mess uniform for tonight's dinner; he looked a fine figure in his blue mess jacket and scarlet waistcoat.

As he walked across the room, Peter still slightly favoured his left leg due to an old wound he had received in Afghanistan in '78. The line of medals on his left chest showed that he was a much travelled and war-experienced officer.

"Hallo Father." Peter leaned over and shook Arthur's hand.

"Nice to see you my boy."

Peter sat down in the chair opposite his father and asked, "How are you?"

"Fighting fit. The entire better for seeing you. Were you able to visit Harry?"

"Yes. I reached Tessa's and Tim's yesterday at midday and spent the afternoon with them all. Their

21

two girls certainly make a fuss of Harry – and keep him in order."

Peter leaned forward and put his hand on his father's knee. "I know Tessa is caring for him but I am so grateful to you and Mother for all you've done."

"Nonsense Peter. You know that your mother and I think the world of the lad, but Tessa loves having a boy about the place. She says it keeps the balance. The way he's talking he'll be in the Gunners before you leave them."

Peter gave a wry smile. "I know. I hope he doesn't feel under any pressure to join the Regiment just because his fore bears did."

"You're getting damned maudlin," exploded Arthur "Harry's the same as you at that age. Sometimes when he sees me in my study, he'll come and ask me about the places I've served in and about your actions. Don't worry Peter. He'll make his mind up without any pressure from you or me."

"Thank you Father. You're as good for Harry as you were for me; he admires you greatly. He was telling me how you'll stand no nonsense from him and how you keep his nose to the grindstone of school work."

Arthur smiled and changed the subject. "Now tell me, what's happening with you? In your last letter you said that the Battery you're commanding is being split up."

"That's correct. All the men and equipment are being sent out to Durban as replacements. The Section officers have all been posted; I'm off to Bisley for a few days' rifle shooting at the County Meeting, then I'm high and dry."

"High and dry!" repeated Arthur. "You must have some idea where you're going and what's afoot?"

"It's all very strange. Officially I've heard nothing but when I spoke to Colonel Smytheson the Regimental Commander, he implied that something had been decided and that I'd be told about it soon."

"Damned nonsense." puffed Arthur. "You can't be left dangling on a string. Get pushing and find out."

Peter smiled. "I knew you'd say that, so when I return from my Bisley shoot, if I haven't heard by then, I'll get pushing."

Peter reached to his waistcoat and pulled out his fob watch. "Isn't it about time you changed for dinner – or are you going in those shoes that've still got mud on from the farm?" Arthur snatched a quick look at his gleaming shoes, and gently punched his son on the shoulder. "I'll go and brush the straw out of my hair." Pulling himself out of his chair, he strode off to his room to change.

Peter sat back in the deep leather chair and stared out of the window into the damp darkness studded by the warm glow of the street gas lamps. It was the first time since leaving his Battery that he had been able to sit and think without being pressured to take a decision or sign an order. The club atmosphere was warm and comforting – but once more sadness washed over him as he thought about the loss of his beloved wife Beatrice. They had been through so much together; she was such a strong personality and so very generous. In fact it was her devotion and generosity that was the cause of her death; she had dedicated an amount of each year to working in the London slums, and eventually she had succumbed to the myriad of diseases in the area.

Peter thought of her every day, even though she had died some eight months before. The void left in him by her death was still deep and very painful. He sighed and made himself think of his son Harry – there was the future.

A steward leaned over him, "Can I get you anything sir?"

"Yes," replied Peter, "a whisky and soda please."

He rubbed his left thigh where it still occasionally ached. It reminded him of his time in Afghanistan some twenty years ago when he had first met Beatrice.

Again the thought came to him; maybe he should hand in his commission and retire to the farm. It was a recurring thought ever since Bea had died – but each time he had put off the decision. Act in haste, repent at leisure – as his father had always told him. He loved his career in the Artillery but he wondered if he should act for the future of his son. He smiled to himself. He knew that he was trained to act quickly when a decision had to be taken, yet here he was dithering about his personal life. The club servant placed a glass and a soda siphon on the tabled beside him. He squirted a dash of soda into his glass and took a sip. In that short time, subconsciously, he had made his decision. Harry was being well cared for and not really missing his father.

Chapter 3

In Colonel Tailby's house in Belgravia, the elegant dining room, with its high ceiling, was lit by two large cut-glass electric chandeliers which sent sparkling light around the pictured walls. On the wall flanking the fireplace were two large portraits. One was of Colonel Tailby in full regimental dress uniform, painted when he had just retired, while on the other side of the fireplace there was a picture of his lady wife in a strikingly beautiful scarlet dress. The two pictures balanced the wall and framed the mantelpiece perfectly.

There were ten men seated at the long table, the Colonel at one end and Major Rutland at the other. The scarlet or blue uniforms of the officers contrasted vividly with the black tailed jackets of the industrialists and the MP. The silver cutlery and the crystal glasses sparkled and glowed in the yellow electric light. A butler and a waitress stood patiently at the end of the room.

With the meal finished, and the cheese board having been removed by the waitress, the butler offered the table humidor around dispensing cigars to those who wished to smoke. Two candelabras holding five candles each were placed in the centre of the table to reduce the cigar smoke in the room. The port glasses were filled and the decanter placed at the head of the table to move gradually, but inevitably, clockwise around the table. Cigars were cut, lit and appreciated, while the candles guttered as the cigar smoke was blown through the flames. Conversation spread across a number of subjects but then inevitably settled on the war in South Africa.

Arthur Rutland noticed that the Member of Parliament was not as jingoistic at the dinner table as he was known to be in the House, or in the public arena. He seemed to be genuinely worried about the loss of men despite the knowledge that the British Army could swamp the Boers by sheer numbers.

"What I don't understand," queried the M.P. "is why our men are out-shot by these Dutch farmers. Why can't our troops match them, bullet for bullet, kill for kill? The Boers use rifles all the time but presumably our troops have had adequate training and inspection."

"I am told that the British rifle is inferior to the German type that the Boers are using," commented Mr Boynton, an industrialist with a large steel works in Sheffield. "The ammunition being used in the new Lee Enfield rifle is supposed to have a lower muzzle velocity and so is less accurate at the greater distance."

"I find that hard to believe," said Colonel Passmore, one of the regular soldiers at the table. "In my Regiment the men can put down a good covering of fire at a range up to 2000 yards."

"Then why are our casualties disproportionately high relative to the Boer losses?"

Colonel Passmore rolled the cigar backwards and forwards between his fingers and thumb as he carefully thought of the wording of his reply. "Ah well, casualties are not only caused by superior weapons," he said.

Here was an implied criticism of poor leadership. Heads nodded at this statement. But rather than let the subject change, Colonel Tailby turned to Peter who was looking studiously at his port glass. "Peter, you do an amount of rifle shooting. What's your opinion of the Mauser and the Lee Enfield rifle?"

"I agree with Colonel Passmore. I've shot both weapons and I find very little difference in their accuracy, though I think it's a shame that the Lee Enfield five round magazine has to be loaded by individual rounds rather than a clip of five or six bullets."

Peter looked up at the industrialist and continued. "I've not been in South Africa during the recent fighting but I spoke to a wounded infantry Captain who had just been shipped home. He made an interesting comment that when his unit had advanced to their attack position, he saw a boulder with the side facing towards the enemy that had been painted white. Obviously the Boers use these as distance markers for the range. The Captain said that he was hit by a bullet before his men could even find the distance of the enemy lines."

"Aha, that's very interesting." Passmore wagged a finger. "Also the enemy are in trenches or lying down waiting for the attack while the British infantry have to fire, often out of breath, having advanced across rough ground."

27

"Not helpful to accurate shooting," agreed Peter.

"Do you think our soldiers should have protection against rifle fire?" asked Boynton. No one answered the question that caused a few frowns.

"Do you mean armour?" queried Colonel Tailby.

"No. I've invented a shield that is about the size of a tea tray that has a 4 inch oval shaped hole cut in the centre. The rifle is placed through the hole and the shield attached to the rifle by clips. A prone rifleman would have incoming bullets deflected by the shield."

After a pause, Colonel Passmore was the first to comment. "I don't think that would work Mr Boynton. All bullets fired over a long distance drop very steeply as they approach their target. A bullet travelling over 1000 yards has to climb to about 80 feet before it descends on to its target. So your shield would not protect against falling shot." Boynton shrugged and accepted the obvious criticism.

"That's very interesting though that you should suggest that idea." Peter looked towards the industrialist. "I hadn't thought about shields for the individual, but I'm surprised that we Gunners don't have shields fitted to our field guns. Now that they're all breech loading, almost all Gunners could be protected behind a shield."

"Wouldn't the weight be a drawback?" asked Boynton.

"That's where you come in; you must manufacture a very strong metal that doesn't need to be thick and heavy."

"There you are." Colonel Tailby beamed at Boynton. "You and Major Rutland can now patent a good idea and retire on the proceeds." With a general laugh the conversation at the table broke up into two or three groups.

At Arthur Rutland's end of the table, the Artillery officer seated beside him was a Colonel Bridport. He and Arthur chatted about their travels and actions with Bridport also asking about the details of Peter's career.

"Your son sounds like a man after my own heart," he suggested. "I think that there are a number of important improvements that the Gunners could use but it seems the antiquated past holds us back."

Arthur raised his eyebrows at this statement. "Antiquated past? That sounds a bit strong."

The Colonel smiled, "You're right. But I'm frustrated when new ideas like the shield your son has just mentioned are blocked." Arthur wondered why this Colonel should want to push forward new ideas. Most Artillery Colonels were only interested in peak efficiency of their regiments plus their smooth running – unless ...

"What unit are you with Colonel?" asked Arthur. Bridport gave no reply to this question. Instead he asked another one. "Did you say that Peter was on leave now?"

"Yes. He's shooting at Bisley. There's a County Match being shot next weekend, and he's in the Surrey team. I think he also hopes to shoot for England."

"How long is he down there for?"

"He comes back in about a week."

"Is it possible to contact him down there?"

"Yes. You can send a letter or telegram to the Surrey Hut. That'll always find him." Arthur leaned closer to Bridport. "Colonel, you didn't say where you were stationed."

Bridport smiled. "No Major I didn't. I hope I can meet your son some time soon. Would you mention it to him? It'll mean that my message to him won't come out of the blue."

"May I know what you want to see Peter about?"

"I regret Major that I can't tell you. I'm not certain I can even tell Peter yet. I hope you understand."

Arthur rolled the ash from his cigar into the silver ashtray. "Of course, of course." he replied.

Bridport looked at the fireplace clock. "I'm afraid I must be off." He held his hand out to Arthur. "It's been a real pleasure meeting you Major Rutland." He rose from his chair, went to Colonel Tailby and apologised for the need to leave prematurely. He bid goodnight to the rest of the guests and left the room.

After dinner Arthur hailed a hansom cab for Peter and himself. It wound its way through the gas lit street towards Arthur's club, then going on to Peter's hotel. In the cab's leather-clad interior, partly lit by the outside bullseye lantern and the passing streetlamps, Arthur mentioned to Peter about Colonel Bridport's interest in him. "I had a feeling that he knew an amount about you already."

"That's interesting," mused Peter. "Colonel Tailby mentioned that Bridport was in some way connected to the testing grounds at Shoeburyness."

"I wonder why he wants to see me." Peter gazed thoughtfully out into the shadowed streets. "Maybe I won't have to do any pushing after all."

As the hansom trotted along Peter noticed that his father was lost in his thoughts, gazing out of the window.

"Penny for your thoughts father."

"I was just thinking about the possibility of you getting a posting to South Africa."

"It's quite possible. Do you have any worries?"

"No, I was just thinking about my younger brother Edwin. Maybe you could find time to visit him and your Aunt Ellen and their son John. They have a farm in Verster in Cape Colony. Ellen is of Dutch descent and, from what I can glean from their letters, your cousin John is possibly a bit sympathetic towards the Boer farmers. I haven't heard from them since this trouble began. I know they're not in the area where there's fighting but I still wondered how they were."

"If I get a chance, I'll call on them."

"This is not quite a civil war but there is a matter of similar people who have different opinions fighting against each other." said Arthur. A silence fell between them as the cab carried them along.

Then Peter had an unexpected recollection. "Father I know all about your exploits in India and Afghanistan but I remember Mother once saying that you'd been in the American Civil War. It's one period of your service that you've never spoken about."

Again a silence fell between them. It was not an uneasy silence, just a pause in their conversation. Then Arthur said, "That was a bittersweet time of my career.

The American people are welcoming, enterprising, good-natured, all that you would ever want of friends. The countryside is so -," he paused "large. So magnificently beautiful; hard in winter and bountiful in summer. It is probably the most ideal place I know of other than England. That was the sweet part of my time there. The bitter part was the fighting. It was as bloody and terrifying as any normal battle, but eventually I was sickened by the killing - not of an enemy – but almost of one's friends. I was involved in the killing of men who I could have talked to and agreed with on most subjects but because of a difference of ideology I was helping to slay them." He paused and looked out of the window. "In the end I could stand it no longer. All wars are bad but a civil war is probably the worst. I'd like to go back there, I have a lot of fond memories of America – but it is too late now."

"How did you get out there and whereabouts were you?"

"I was a young Major with great hopes of a Colonelcy. You were about four years old and Tessa was only two. I was offered a position as a military attaché or official observer for the Royal Artillery to report on how the Union was using their field artillery in modern warfare conditions. We had supplied them with a number of Armstrong breech loading guns.

"I arrived in '62 and left in '63. I was there for about a year and ended up at Gettysburg. It was then that my heart was broken. To see so many brave men, who I could so easily have been friends with, being smashed into oblivion in such numbers was too much for me. I asked for my posting to be ended – and that was the end of my military career. Maybe one day I'll tell you all about it. It's an unusual tale."

Once more silence fell on the two men. Peter let it be as he waited for his father to continue. Eventually Arthur said, "I just worry that this conflict might end up with family fighting family."

Peter turned his head towards the rain-smeared window. 'Might I be asked to fight against my cousin?' he thought. 'It must be very likely that John supported the English but what if he was actively supporting the Boers?'

The cab stopped outside Arthur's club. Peter got out and held open the cab door for his father.

"Thank you my boy," said Arthur. "It has been a very pleasant and interesting evening."

Peter held out his hand to shake his father's. Arthur took it and then, to Peter's surprise, he put his other arm around Peter's shoulder and gave him a light embrace. "Take care, my boy. Take care," he murmured, then turned and, without looking back, walked into the club entrance vestibule.

Peter got back into the cab, closed the door and leaned back onto the leather seat, his mind a buzz of thoughts. 'The Old Man is worried about me. Obviously he thinks I will be sent out to South Africa and he thinks I might be fighting against John. But it was more than that. There is something in the Old Man's time in America that is causing these worries. I must ask him to tell me that story.'

Chapter 4

Peter pulled the collar of his dark blue Artillery cape higher around his neck, and rammed his side hat firmly on his head. The horizontal rain driven by an easterly wind was running down his neck and making him feel even more disgruntled.

The Royal Artillery dogcart jolted over the uneven road leading to the School of Artillery at Shoeburyness. Even without the rain inside his shirt collar, Peter was not at all content with his current situation. Two days ago he had arrived at Bisley, settled into the Surrey Hut and found to his pleasure that he had been selected for the County Team. Then a messenger delivered a telegram telling him that he was wanted with all due haste to report to the Royal Artillery ranges at Shoeburyness. A scramble ensued during which he deposited his rifle, collected his kit and, with a rush, just managed to catch the train to London and then a connection to Southend-on-Sea. None of this was conducive to a good state of humour.

The telegram containing his orders was brief. He was to report to a Major Gurney at the ranges and then to report to Colonel Bridport at Woolwich with all due dispatch. What did this all mean? What was expected of him? Then the old army question - why me?

After half an hour the dogcart pulled to a halt by a Royal Artillery guardhouse. A sergeant came out and saluted.

"Major Rutland to see Major Gurney," Peter said.

"Yes sir you are expected. Please go to the main office." The driver twitched the reins and the two horses trotted over to the doors of a single-storied wooden building.

"Here we are sir"

"Thank you," replied Peter. "Do you know which door I go to?" The driver pointed with his whip. "That one's the Regimental Orderly Office, sir."

Peter pulled his bag off the dogcart and walked over and opened the door. A clerk seated behind a desk, jumped to attention. "Good afternoon sir"

"Good afternoon," replied Peter; the water dripping off of his cloak onto the shiny wooden floor. "I am Major Rutland and I wish to see Major Gurney."

"Yes sir." The clerk quickly walked over to an internal door and knocked, then entered and closed the door. Peter could feel the warmth of the office fire creeping into his cold uniform. He was looking forward to a warm drink and a place to dry out. The door opened and a spruce looking officer with a smile on his face strode across the office. To Peter's amazement the officer was also dressed in a heavy cloak.

"Major Rutland, good to see you. I'm Phil Gurney. I have been told to look after your every need."

"Thank you Major. At present all I want is a place to warm up and dry out."

Gurnley laughed, "All that can be arranged - but not just yet. I have strict orders to take you at once out onto the ranges where a demonstration gunnery team is standing by waiting for you."

"For me?"

"Just for you, but first I have to show you something. You can leave your grip here. The orderly will take it to your quarters. Please follow me." Gurney opened the office door and, walking very swiftly ahead of Peter, entered an adjacent long low building. Inside, unheated but at least out of the rain, was a large room in the centre of which was a table some ten feet wide by thirty feet long.

Gurney did not remove his cloak; he simply swung back the front opening to leave room for his arms to catch hold of a sheet that was covering the table. He pulled it back to reveal a large detailed and contoured landscape map, showing valleys with some tree covered sides and hills.

"Look at this," said Gurney. "If you had a line of guns behind these hills and received a report that an enemy target was beyond them in this valley, completely out of sight but within range, how would you attack it?"

Peter looked at the three dimensional map and replied. "I would find it very difficult. I assume that the reports of the enemy are absolutely certain, in which case I would send out a reconnaissance galloper to see if I could get at least two guns up this track that looks as though it will reach the target."

"The target is a group of enemy ammunition carts and preparing to move. If you don't fire on the target within five minutes, they will be gone."

Peter again looked at the plan. 'What am I missing?' He decided to think out loud.

"I assume it is impossible to take the guns up this slope. I have no time to find a route to bring them into line of sight – I suppose I might try and lob some shells over the hill in the hope that I could hit some of the carts and slow them down for proper action."

"Very good. I won't weary you with more questions for suggestions because I can show you the answer," said Gurney. "We have found a way to fire sighting shots at an unseen enemy, and for correcting the sighters, until a hit is scored. Furthermore, there is now a method whereby when one gun is hitting the target, there is enough information to get the rest of the Battery firing on the same line and elevation and so all six guns can hit the target.

"First of all," continued Gurney, "an observer climbs to the top of the hill until he can see the target and be in a position so that he can signal back to the guns. I will show you how he communicates with the guns later when we are on the ranges. He signals that the target is 100 yards to his left and 1800 yards from the guns. With a six gun Battery, the Number 1, right hand gun, fires a shell which the observer spots. He signals back that it has fallen 200 yards short and he thinks the target is about 5 degrees to the left of the flight of the shell.

The correction of the range is simple but the alteration of line is not.

"We are now using a piece of equipment called a gunner's arc. This is a machined piece of wood that has a line of holes drilled in it on the top. The arc is fitted on the barrel and a peg is placed in one of the holes to line up with the rear sight and an aiming point object some distance away in front of the guns - say a lone tree some distance off, or a chimney on a farm house. When the observer signals an alteration of 5 degrees, the peg is put into the measured hole 5 degrees from its first position. The gun is then layed so that the peg is lined up with the aiming point again and the next round fired.

"If this doesn't hit, then a further alteration to either range or line is made until the ranging gun is hitting the target. The rest of the Battery, who've already got the same original peg position as the ranging gun and are all layed on the same aiming point, will then place the aiming peg in the same hole as the Number 1 gun, aim at the same aiming point and then commence to fire. All the shells will land in more or less the same place. If the target moves, then the observer signals a new range and line of fire. It means that we at the guns can fire at targets that we cannot see."

"This is one hell of a break through," said Peter.

Gurney smiled. "Is it big enough to get even wetter out on the ranges to go and see?"

Four days later, Peter, wearing his blue frock jacket with Sam Browne belt, plus sword and blue dress helmet, walked sharply along the corridor at the Woolwich Depot wondering why the military authorities always painted every wall and door, green and cream. He stopped at a door marked 'Office. Colonel Bridport. R.A.'

As he entered a Bombardier clerk stood up and said. "Good afternoon sir."

"Good afternoon. I am Major Rutland reporting to see Colonel Bridport."

"Thank you sir. Will you take a scat?" The clerk went through a heavy door to the office beyond. Peter decided that he would stand and wait.

The door opened and the clerk said "Will you come this way please Major?"

Peter marched into the office, drew himself to attention, saluted and said. "Major Rutland reporting sir."

The man at the desk stood up and Peter immediately recognised the Colonel who had been at Colonel Tailby's dinner.

"Hallo Major. Pleased to meet you again. I think you might remember me from the dinner at Colonel Tailby's house."

"Yes sir, I do."

"Sit down." He gestured to a chair in front of the desk. Peter sat down, making sure his sword rested by his side. He took off his helmet and held it on his lap.

"It is Peter, isn't it?"

"Yes sir." Peter smiled at the courtesy of Bridport suggesting that he might not actually know Peter's name

"I very much enjoyed your father's company that evening. He's a much travelled Gunner – who has some definite opinions about the Regiment."

"Very strong opinions actually," replied Peter. "I think he'd still like to be serving."

"Once a Gunner, always a Gunner – as the saying goes," smiled Bridport. "Now I expect you had a bit of a surprise when you visited Shoeburyness ranges, and especially wondered why you were given this information. Well, I've some more new facts for you that I think will surprise you even more and also explain why you were sent to the ranges.

"You've been in the Regiment long enough to know that we've not progressed much in the past number of years. Especially, we have seriously fallen behind in Quick Firing artillery. As you are fully aware, because of the recoil after every shot fired, a 15 pounder has to be repositioned and re-layed each time. This causes a great deal of delay before the gun is ready to fire accurately again. Axle spades have been fitted to the trail of all guns going to South Africa in an attempt to reduce the recoil. These spades dig into the soil behind the guns to hopefully reduce the physical movement of the gun backwards.

"We are informed, however, that the French have a true Quick Firing gun which can fire 20 to 30 rounds per minute without having to return the gun to its original position. But we have no idea how it works and they certainly are not going to tell us.

"The newly appointed Director General of Ordnance Sir Henry Brackenbury has been instructed by the Government to enquire into all current Quick Firing guns that are being used by other countries. The Nordenfeldt 'Pom-pom' used by the Boers has been around for some time but it only fires a 2 pound shell which is completely inadequate for our purposes. However, Sir Henry has found a new gun that seems to answer most of our requirements, and could possibly be modified to make it perfect for our use. It is the Ehrhardt 15 pounder made in Germany. The principle is that, instead of the recoil being instantly transferred to the trail of the gun, the barrel is attached to a powerful spring. When the gun is fired, only the barrel recoils and this recoil is absorbed by the spring, which then returns the barrel to its original position. A Royal Artillery observer, Major Turner, who has seen these guns being fired actually placed a coin on the wheel and it did not fall off.

"We are obtaining a number of these guns and equipment for trial. Amazingly, someone high up has had the courage and foresight to decide that two of these guns should be tried out in South Africa under battlefield conditions. I'm not absolutely sure that the powers that be know of the scheme but I have it on high enough authority to put it into effect.

"Right now, two complete pieces with limbers and all necessary equipment are, or soon will be, on the high seas bound for Cape Town in South Africa. A skilled, responsible and reliable team headed by a Lieutenant Colonel has been found to run this trial. And you, Colonel Rutland, have been chosen to be in charge."

Peter raised his eyebrows in surprise. He had been listening intently to the details as they emerged. It was a ground-breaking venture that would effect, and hopefully benefit, the Royal Artillery for years ahead. To be told that he had been chosen to head the team was an honour that astounded him. The fact that he was to be promoted to Lieutenant Colonel was obviously necessary for the situation.

"However," continued Colonel Bridport, "though your Colonelcy was dated from last Tuesday, it will not be gazetted until you have completed the trials and return to England - until then you will appear as Major Rutland. The reason for this is that to have a half Colonel in charge of just two guns would be incongruous, even top heavy. So you will act as a Major, but should it be necessary for you to use your higher rank, you may do so.

"You will be designated as 172 Battery, Royal Field Artillery having two gun crews. We can only spare one Lieutenant but the team will include an experienced Battery Sergeant Major, two gunnery Sergeants and gun crews. You will also have a trained signals section headed by a Sergeant. Most of these men will soon be on their way to South Africa. Though all are competent gunners, none will have been trained on the Ehrhardt gun.

"You must never lose either gun; that obviously will be your first priority - your career depends on it. You will be given handbooks on use and maintenance before you leave England. You've got a very big job ahead of you in training two crews, and then you have to put them to the ultimate test of trial by battle. I am certain that I am not doing you any favours in giving you this venture but I do feel that from what I have read of your career and what I have heard of you, you are the right man."

"Thank you sir, this is a great opportunity. May I ask what type of artillery opponent will we be up against?"

"The Boer Artillery are the only professional soldiers they have. They are very efficient and trained by German officers. They have good quality pieces, being the Quick Firing Pom-pom plus heavy guns made by Creusot and Krupp. Treat them all with very great respect."

"You mentioned that I would have an experienced BSM. Could I request one I know?" asked Peter.

"The short answer is no because there will not be time to find any specific person though I'll ensure that the crews will all have good records." Bridport held out his hand. "I wish you luck Peter. I think that you are going to need a great deal of it but remember the Regiment will benefit considerably if you can prove that these are the right guns for us."

"Thank you sir" Peter stood up, drew himself to attention and turned to leave the office.

"If you leave the details of your chosen BSM with the clerk, I will do what I can," added Bridport

"Thank you sir"

The next few days were spent in a blur of action. He had to obtain a summer field uniform plus getting all the details of transport timing and method of travel, where to go, when to be there and when to leave for the next place. There was no time for him to visit his son Harry, or his father and mother. Eventually, hoping that he had done all that he should, he boarded the train for Southampton.

Chapter 5

23rd December 1899; it was a cold, wet day as Peter pushed his way through the crowds that were wandering away from the quay at the Southampton docks. They had just seen their hero Lord Roberts, 'our Bobs', off to teach the Boer farmers a lesson. They all had complete confidence in this small figure of a man who was a giant in their eyes. Bobs would be the answer to the problems of handling the British Army; he would show the Afrikaners and the world how powerful Britain was, and how invincible the British Army was. He would be the answer to all their prayers.

It was just two hours before the Castle Line mail ship 'Dunottar Castle' sailed for Cape Town. All the other passengers, including Lord Roberts, were already on board. Peter showed his passport, papers and details to the shore officials. He climbed up the ramp to the ship's main deck and reported to the Purser who gave him the number of his cabin. A uniformed steward was instructed to show Peter the way to his cabin and carried his travelling cases.

The cabin, number 147 on the second deck, was about ten feet square with a bed, desk, chest of drawers and a wardrobe. One round porthole was the only source of natural light to his living quarters for the next two weeks. The steward helped him in with the luggage that he wanted on voyage and offered to unpack but Peter decided to organise it all for himself. His field uniform and mess kit he hung in the wardrobe, and then he distributed the rest as he wanted in the drawers available.

One security problem for him was where to hide the ten copies of the Ehrhardt instruction manuals. He must have one to read on the voyage but the rest had to be kept secure from prying eyes; maybe he could put them into the ship's safe. He pulled out the bottom drawer of his desk and found a three inch gap in the space below which he decided would do for the single copy that he needed to study and learn on the trip out. A knock at the door surprised him He quickly placed all the copies into the bottom drawer, then stood up and opened the door.

"Major Rutland?"

"Yes."

"I'm Captain Paul Jordan, ADC to Lord Roberts. He sends his compliments and asks if you would come and see him."

"Now?"

"If you would sir." Peter was very surprised at the invitation but instantly buttoned up his uniform jacket, put on his Sam Browne belt and reached for his side cap.

"There's no need for the cap sir. 'Bobs' is not that formal – well not right now."

Peter smiled, "Lead on Captain." He locked the cabin door and, as he followed Jordan down the corridor, he had time to collect his thoughts. He had no idea why he was being summoned. Bobs was a Gunner. Did he know of Peter's orders? Bobs had just lost his son, who had been awarded a VC at Colenso. Do I mention it? Peter decided that this would not be the right time. In fact by the time Peter reached Lord Robert's cabin, he was still at a loss as to the reason for the call.

He entered the cabin and for the first time saw the great man. Bobs, who had been sitting at a desk, stood up. "Good afternoon Major. I hear that you only just made the ship." He was a surprisingly small man with white hair and piercing blue eyes. A bushy moustache hung on his upper lip. He was dressed in a simple khaki uniform without rank or decoration; certainly no sign of the purple ribbon to show he had won the Victoria Cross in the Indian Mutiny. On his left arm he wore a black armband in memory of his recently lost son. "Wondering why I asked you here I expect," he said.

"Yes sir." replied Peter.

"Well, once upon a time I was a Gunner," Bobs smiled, "as you may have heard, and I got wind of your venture. If I was many years younger, I would have given my eye teeth to have a command like yours."

Peter smiled. "I know sir. I am very lucky."

"I don't think luck comes into it. You were selected because you were the best for the job. I might not have been up to it," he said with a twinkle in his eyes. "But then I might be better at other things.

"If I was in your position," continued Bobs. "I would be worried about the security of your manuals. Unless you have made other arrangements, you can sign them over to Captain Jordan here for safe keeping if you wish."

"That's very good of you sir. I was very concerned about their safety but your suggestion answers the problem."

"Right. Contact Paul when needed for that or anything else I can help with."

"Thank you sir." Peter drew himself to attention ready, to leave the cabin.

Bobs sat down at his desk again. "I've arranged for a mess table in the First Class dining room. It's for all officers on board. Please use it as you want." he said.

"Very good sir."

Peter turned and left the cabin. As he walked back to his own cabin, he realised even more how important his mission was. Bobs had obviously been told of it and was in complete agreement with it. Back in his cabin he organised his kit and the papers, and settled down to the job in hand which was to learn how this new gun worked and how it was to be used.

Peter heard the dinner-bugle call but he decided to stay reading the manual of the new gun. Gradually his stomach told him that he was very hungry, so he hid the booklet in his desk, checked that there was nothing that could be found by any intruder, casual or illegal, and left the cabin locking the door behind him.

On entering the First Class dining room, he found that a long table had been laid for the use of the officers on board. There were some smaller tables set around but these were obviously for the civilian passengers. The officers' table was only half full so Peter sat down close to a young lieutenant sitting alone, who had chain mail on his shoulders that denoted he was in a cavalry regiment.

"Goods evening," said Peter.

"Good evening sir." the young man replied as he stood up.

"I'm Peter Rutland."

"Franklin Goodman. Nice to meet you sir." Peter gestured to him to sit down.

"I beg your pardon. I'm very new at this. I only received my commission last month."

"Congratulations. What regiment are you with?" asked Peter.

"19th Dragoons. Colonel Crumpton Smythe is our Commanding Officer."

"And I expect you are looking forward to some excitement and action in South Africa," Peter said with a smile.

"Rather. I do hope it isn't all over before we get there."

"Don't be too eager to get into the thick of it. When you do, pretty soon you will be very pleased to get a break."

Franklin looked at the medal ribbons on Peter's chest. "With your experience do you find it all a bore."

"Bore! Never. If I did I'd get out of the Army. No, to me this is a job that I like doing but unfortunately people get killed, enemy – and friends."

While he was waiting for a steward to serve him, Peter saw two men walking towards his part of the table. As they got closer, he had a feeling that he recognised one of them from long ago.

"Oh Lord," murmured Franklin, "Here comes the CO."

A tall thin man with gaunt and sunken cheeks, and smoking a cigarette, came up to the table.

"Ah. Goodman, isn't it?" he said, "Go and have dinner with my wife. There's a good chap." He sat down and looked at Peter. "Crumpton Smythe."

"Peter Rutland."

"This is my 2i/c Ramsay."

Then Peter remembered. "Nick Ramsay. Whitgift, Tates, '73 to '77 or something like that."

"Damn my eyes – yes. You must be," Ramsay paused struggling to remember. "Rutland – yes, Peter Rutland but I haven't the foggiest which house you were in."

"Crosses," replied Peter

"Oh bloody hell, are we going to have boring stories of your old school days?" said Crumpton Smyth very loudly.

"Not at all," said Ramsay, rolling his eyes to the heavens for Peter to see.

"Goodman, haven't you gone to my wife yet? She's sitting over there on that table by herself."

"Very good sir." Franklin got up and moved round the end of the table towards a round double table where a lady sat. Peter could not see her face but she was wearing a dark blue dress with a high collar; her dark brown hair draped down in curls at the nape of her neck. She turned her head as Franklin arrived at her table, smiled and waved her hand at the empty seat. Peter had a feeling that, with the current company, his own meal was not going to be a very enjoyable one, and he rather envied young Franklin having a meal with a lady.

He was right. The Colonel seemed to be a grumpy bore who did not really eat anything but drank whisky all the time and just picked at his food. Eventually Peter felt that he could leave without appearing impolite saying that he wanted to have a cigar after the meal. He decided not to go into the smoking room but instead went up to find a lounger in a covered place on the upper deck. Here, with a glass of port and a cigar, he watched the fluorescence bouncing off the waves.

"Another coincidence." Peter heard a voice coming along from behind him. It was Nick Ramsay.

"I just felt like a cigar with a whisky away from the rest of the herd," said Nick, "and who do I find but you – again."

Nick sat down on a lounger alongside Peter and lit his cigar. "I'm sorry about the CO. He can be a bit of a bore."

Peter said nothing; he was not going to make any criticism of a senior officer.

"It's rather sad really." Nick looked around him to ensure that they were on their own. "He is very ill. I suspect he has cancer, and I think he's even dying of it."

"Really!" exclaimed Peter.

"Over the past year or so he's gradually changed from a cheerful, efficient CO to a gaunt alcoholic; he hardly eats anything, he smokes all the time, plus the fact that his marriage is falling apart. The trouble is he's such a professional soldier that he's certain he can handle everything and won't ask for help or assistance from anyone – doctors, friends, not even from his poor wife. He's only seen one doctor to my knowledge, and that was about six months ago. I'm sure he thinks that this campaign is his last, and he wants to go out with a bang. I just hope he doesn't take too many of us with him."

"It sounds as though you've a very difficult job handling him," said Peter.

Nick nodded. "In the regimental base it's just hard work but I'm truly worried about when we will be relying on his military judgement in a fighting situation. Confidentially, when we're at home and he gives an order that I think is crazy, I just let it slip by. He rarely remembers to check, and mostly I manage to get away with it. But, as you know, a battle order has to be obeyed there and then, however mad it might seem. Poor old Crumbly Smith."

"Crumbly Smith?" said Peter.

Nick laughed. "Yes, that's what he is called in the Regiment. It used to be an endearment – 'Old Crumbly Smith', now it's 'Bloody Crumbly Smith'."

"His wife looks a nice woman," said Peter."

"She's marvellous. He married her about three years ago. She's an American, and is a real charmer. She knows what the reasons are for him being rude - even to her. He's bloody lucky to have someone like her." Nick sipped his whisky. "So what are you out here for?"

"I'm just another Gunner who will stand by his gun to get shot at I expect."

"Ever been to South Africa before?"

Peter shook his head. "No. North Africa and India have been my areas."

"Pretty damned large areas, I must say," smiled Nick. "Well, you'll like South Africa. The country is stunningly beautiful - that's assuming you have time to look around while you are being shot at."

He threw his cigar end over the handrail into the sea. "I'd better be getting back to old Crumbly. He always has something for me. See you later."

"Good night," said Peter.

Initially the weather had been good and the sea reasonably smooth, but when the Dunottar Castle reached the Bay of Biscay, she did her fair share of pitching and rolling.

Peter, who had always found he had a good stomach on board ship, decided that he had read enough of the manual and went out on deck to the lee side of the cabins. The wind was still strong but he was able to walk back and forward the length of the cabins.

He had turned and was starting his walk to the stern, when a cabin door opened and a lady, well wrapped up in a travelling cloak and with a scarf around her head, came out onto the deck. The ship rolled and, taken by surprise, she tottered away from the cabin wall towards the handrail. Peter ran over and caught her by the arm.

"Oh my goodness," she gasped. "I wasn't ready for that. Thank you so much."

"Let me help you back to your cabin." said Peter.

"Oh no. I'm not going back in there. I'll stay close to the cabins and hold on to the rail. I want some fresh air."

Peter realised that she was the Cavalry Colonel's lady.

"I think you might be Mrs Crumpton Smythe."

She turned and looked him full in the face. "Yes you are right. How do you know that? We haven't met before, have we?"

"No. My name is Peter Rutland, and I was at school with your husband's second in command."

"Nick Ramsay? Such a nice man." She leaned against the cabin wall and steadied herself by holding on to the rail. "What a coincidence, you both meeting here." Peter was entranced by her soft New England voice. It was a delight to listen to.

Suddenly the cabin door that she had just come out of crashed open and the Colonel, looking like death warmed up, looked out, saw them both and shouted out over the wind. "For God's sake, Georgia. Come inside."

She turned to Peter and said. "Goodbye Mr Rutland. It was so nice meeting you. Perhaps we will meet again on the voyage."

"Thank you, that would be very nice." he replied.

But the fates had other ideas. During the prolonged voyage Peter studied his manual on the new guns so that he virtually knew the actions and instructions by heart, while Mrs Crumpton Smythe seemed always to be with the Colonel or in her cabin.

Eventually the Dunottar Castle made her way into Cape Town harbour, where General Roberts and his entourage disembarked.

Peter decided that he would not leave with the main rush. Though he had tried, he had not even been able to see Nick Ramsay, who was obviously up to his ears with his duties. Peter presumed that Mrs Crumpton Smythe was travelling with the Colonel.

Eventually when the departing passengers had mostly left the ship, Peter gathered up his belongings and made his way to the R.A Transport Office on the quayside. There the Transport Officer told him where he was to be stationed until further orders; Peter presumed that this meant until the guns and the crews arrived. But Peter decided that he might as well live it up because he knew he was going to rough it when out on active service, so he booked into the Mount Nelson Hotel, Cape Town's new and best hotel.

Chapter 6

It was early evening by the time that Peter had moved all his baggage into room 32 at the Mount Nelson Hotel in Orange Street. It was Cape Town's most prestigious and luxurious new hotel that reclined elegantly at the foot of Table Mountain.

He indulged himself by having a deep bath of very hot water and soaking for a full hour. For the past couple of weeks, whilst on board ship, he had only been able to wash in a shower of salt water, and he knew that when he was out on active service, he would not have a bath for weeks – so now was the time to spoil himself.

It was nearly seven o'clock before he left his luxurious soak and started to get dressed. He decided that, though he would have to wear uniform, it would not be up to the level of mess dress. His field service uniform was new and so still smart. In a few months' time he would look like a scarecrow in it but now it would suffice.

He checked himself in front of the mirror and subconsciously stroked his moustache – he smiled at himself. 'How I hate that blasted growth of hair on my lip but I must go with convention.' 'All officers will have a moustache.' At least it was not the large bushy General Roberts or Buller style. Realising that he felt hungry, he decided to have a drink at the bar and eat at the hotel.

He closed the door of his room behind him, and walked towards the stairs. A bedroom door along the corridor opened and the Colonel's wife came out.

"Good evening Mrs Crumpton Smythe."

"Good evening Major." Again her soft New England accent was so attractive to his ears. He watched as she locked her door and turned to face him.

Peter expected the Colonel to appear. "Is your husband here? I thought the Regiment had gone inland."

"Yes, it has – and no, he is not."

"Are you dining in the hotel tonight?" he asked.

She smiled. "All these questions." And then she said, "Yes I am, and I am feeling very hungry."

He looked at her soft features surrounded by her brown hair that seemed to enhance her beautiful brown eyes. This was too good an opportunity to miss, to have this lady as company for the evening, he thought. "Would you do me the honour of dining with me this evening?"

"What a lovely offer, that would be delightful. Thank you very much. I do so dislike dining alone." They walked along the corridor towards the wide staircase.

At the top of the stairs she said, "May I take your arm? I'm always nervous of catching my shoe in my dress and descending the stairs in one enormous tumble. Spectacular but not very ladylike."

At the entrance to the restaurant Peter spoke to the Head Waiter. "Mrs Crumpton Smythe will be dining with me this evening."

"A table for two, certainly sir."

The Head Waiter led them to a table and held a chair for the Colonel's lady. A waiter offered them a menu each and said. "I will leave the menus for you to make your choice."

Peter sitting opposite her said. "May I order a drink for you?"

"That would be lovely but firstly I would be grateful if you'd call me Georgia. Mrs Crumpton Smythe is so longwinded."

Peter smiled "My name is Peter."

"Then, Peter, I would very much like a dry white wine. I believe that the Stellenbosch wines are delicious." Peter smiled again; he felt that this was going to be a very enjoyable meal. "Are you staying in this hotel while your husband is away?"

"Oh no. I've a sister who lives at Dieput just outside De Aar, who has asked me to stay with her. Her husband's a doctor. I haven't seen her for over eight years so we'll have a lot of catching up to do. I'll then return to England with Gerard or, if he's going to be here for more than a few months, I will return on my own."

"I assume from your accent that you are American and I guess that you are from New England. Am I correct?"

"How clever you are." she smiled at him. "Yes, I come from Vermont. In fact a little town called Castleton just outside a town called, surprisingly, Rutland. It is in the Green Mountains. Have you ever heard of the Green Mountain boys?

"No." Peter shook his head.

"I'm not surprised. But the Green Mountains are a very beautiful area with many streams and lakes. Lake George and the Hudson River are close by. I presume that you have never been there."

"Regrettably no, but my father was in America during your Civil War, and he holds it in high affection."

"Really. Which side was he on?"

"Neither, he was a military attaché acting as an observer for the Royal Artillery. He's never really told me much about it but just before I left, he mentioned that he couldn't stand the terrible slaughter of men who he felt he could have been friends with."

"Your father sounds to be a man of very gentle character."

"He is, and a very good father. I owe a great deal to him."

"I hope that some time in the future you'll be able to visit New England especially in the fall."

"The fall? What's that?"

"Oh, I'm sorry. You call it autumn, when the leaves fall off the trees. The main type of tree we have is the sugar maple and in the fall their leaves turn into a mix of colour ranging from butter yellow to pillar box red. It is truly breathtaking."

Then she said. "That's enough about me. Now tell me about you. Can I ask where you are going to in South Africa?"

"Firstly, I am going to visit an uncle who has a farm in Verster. I am rather looking forward to it. Apparently he has cattle, though he also has just started farming ostriches."

"Ostriches!" exclaimed Georgia. "What for? Their feathers?"

Peter laughed, "I don't know. That's why I am interested."

"They must be very hard to catch. I understand that they run very fast."

He laughed. "I assume that my uncle can run faster."

"Peter, may I ask you a question?" Peter looked puzzled, wondering what was coming next. "Certainly," he replied.

"I have only just realised that it seems all the officers I know have a moustache. Is it compulsory in the British Army for all officers to have one?"

Peter laughed. "The answer to that is, no and yes. No, it is not compulsory for us to all wear a moustache but yes, in that it is expected that we'll all wear a moustache. Most commanding officers will insist that their officers are so adorned. I wear one because it is the done thing. Personally, I don't like it but I shall continue to have one until I'm certain that I've reached my maximum seniority in the service then, with great pleasure, I will shave mine off. I will then tell any of my junior officers that they needn't wear one while they are under my command."

"Are you serious?" she asked.

"Yes, you can see that I'm not being very brave about it all but simply going along with convention until I can get away with being clean shaven."

"Why not rebel and have a beard?"

"Oh no. That'd be too much. Bushy sideburns are popular with some officers but that's the maximum any of them can have on his face; but never a full beard, that's only for the Navy."

"I never realised that one of our generals had started a fashion."

"Started a fashion? Who do you mean?" Peter said with surprise.

"Why, our Civil War General Burnside. He had very bushy whiskers on his cheeks and so gave the name to the sideburns you mention."

"Really. Well, I never knew that."

They continued chatting through their meal, very much enjoying each other's company. At one point Georgia threw back her head to laugh; Peter laughed with her but as he did so he looked at her. He saw a beautiful woman in the full bloom of her life who had wit and culture blended with charm and intelligence. He felt a moment of jealousy of her husband, Colonel Crumpton Smythe, old 'Crumbly Smith'. What a lucky man he is, he thought. I wonder if the Colonel appreciates what a gem he has for a wife.

....

Eventually at the end of the meal, having had coffee, Georgia said. "Are you married?"

"Yes - no, my wife died eight months ago." He dropped his eyes to look at his hands. "I haven't got used to being a widower yet." He paused. "She was so beautiful and so generous. She was a qualified Doctor but every year she went to work for a month or so in the East End of London. It was there that she contracted cholera." There was a silence. Then, to his surprise, he said. "Oh God I miss her so much." His throat constricted, and he felt the tingle of tears in his eyes.

Georgia looked across the table at Peter's bowed head; she reached out and touched his hand. No words were needed to show her sympathy for this gentle-natured man. She quietly waited until he had regained his composure.

"You say that your wife was a qualified doctor?"

"Yes."

"She was obviously a very extraordinary lady. I don't know of any other lady who has broken through the male prejudice in medicine. Where did she qualify?."

"Barts." Said Peter

"Where's that?" Georgia asked.

"I'm sorry, I mean St. Bartholomew's. It's a teaching hospital in London."

"What an amazing lady."

Peter nodded again. "I first met her in Afghanistan where she'd just lost her father. She came to stay with my parents while I was away and then she moved to London to be able to attend Barts."

"Was it hard for her there?"

"Incredibly hard. She had to stand up to abuse and even physical bullying but she was so strong. She decided that there was a place for a female doctor to attend to ladies who would rather see her than a male physician."

He wiped his mouth with his napkin. "She was very successful in building up a clientele of a number of well-to-do ladies who she looked after for all their personal ailments. However, she never forgot that her father had been a missionary in Afghanistan and so every year she spent a month tending the poor in the East End of London. She tried bringing pressure on the City authorities to improve sanitation and especially the supply of fresh drinking water." He paused, then in a low tone he said, "Eventually the disease got her. I suppose it was only a matter of time, but I never expected that I would lose her."

There was a silence, then Georgia asked, "What was her name?"

"Beatrice." said Peter.

"Hearing you talk of her makes me feel very humble and insignificant. Your wife gave her life for strangers while I've never done anything in my life that I consider truly worthwhile." Peter looked at her with surprise but remained silent.

"My life has been that of a carefully nurtured and well-educated young woman who eventually married well, as was expected of me, but I've never done anything where I have thought that someone has benefited rather than me."

Georgia had her head bowed and was looking at her gloved hands. "I married Gerard and happily became the Colonel's lady but I've done nothing for the Regiment." She raised her head and looked at Peter, "In fact I know none of the men and only a few of the officers, and then only Captains and upwards. What a snob I've been."

She paused, and Peter did not feel he could say anything. "When I see Gerard again," she continued, "I'm going to make sure that I get to know the men of his regiment. They must have worries about their wives and family at home. I must be able to help."

Peter smiled. "You're right. The ordinary soldier, be he a Gunner or a Trooper, is very lonely when he is on active service abroad. Some can't read or write so they can't communicate with their family back home."

For a few seconds there was silence. Then Georgia looked Peter straight in the face and said, "Your lady wife's example has greatly touched me and you can feel proud to know that I am going to do something worthwhile because of what you have told me." Peter smiled but could not think of any comment he could make to such an amazing statement.

Georgia placed her napkin beside her coffee cup and said, "It's late. I'm afraid I must go to bed now as I have a great deal to do tomorrow." Peter stood up and went round the table to pull back Georgia's chair as she rose.

They walked from the dining room and up the stairs to the corridor leading to their bedrooms.

At her room door, Georgia stopped and turned to Peter. "I'm very grateful to you, Peter, for asking me to dine with you. I would've been so bored on my own but now I've had a memorable evening. I do hope that we meet again at some time in the future." She offered her hand that Peter took.

"So do I, Georgia," he said.

Georgia closed the door behind her and leaned her back against it; her mind was in turmoil. It was racing with the thoughts of the past couple of hours. During that time she had been moved in more ways than she had ever been moved before. She had been made to personally question her lifestyle, her responsibilities

- even her reason for existing. She was a privileged and wealthy married woman who had just realised that her situation was shallow and not enough. Being a Colonel's wife gave her a position of respect and even grandeur that she had easily accepted but now she was being made to question her worth. What was she doing to have earned this respect other than being married to Gerard? She was riding on an unreal wave of self-esteem. She was now aware that this flattering attention only came from the wives of the other officers in the regiment, just because she was the Colonel's lady.

But Peter had cracked her mirror of smug self-satisfaction by telling her of his wife's dedication to unfortunate people who needed her help and expertise. Georgia knew that she must earn any respect, and Peter had shown that she could by accepting the responsibility of caring for the welfare of the men of the regiment. Men who needed her help with the simple act of communication. She was going to be of worth! It would be for her own sake, as well as for the men.

She walked across the room and started to take off her dress. As she prepared for bed, her mind sped off along a different track that she knew was not right, and it had a worrying theme. She thought of Peter; how he had showed the emotion he felt towards his lost love. He was such a gentle and lonely man. Lonely? No, because he was so much involved with the men of his part of his regiment. He cared and he acted, but the heartbreak of his loss was there regardless of what he was doing or where he was. One day he would meet someone who he would love and care for. What a lucky woman she would be, to have such a dedicated husband – and lover.

It was then she realised she had a pang of envy. No, she thought, Gerard is a loving man who I love, who is suffering but, oh, if only he would open his heart and talk to me, like Peter did.

She changed into her nightdress and put on a negligee. Then she sat at her dressing table and started the ritual of brushing her hair. As she used the brush with long strokes, her mind again turned to Peter – to have him caress her hair and rest his hands on her shoulders - No! Gerard did that when we were first married, and after this war when he is well once more, he will do it again and we will make love and have the feeling of being one.

She stopped and looked at her reflection in the mirror and allowed her thoughts to wander again - to Peter brushing her hair, kissing the top of her head and holding her in his arms.

Tomorrow she must check with the rail booking agent that the arrangements to travel to the farm were in place. With that thought forced into her mind, she retired to bed.

Chapter 7

Peter woke very early and dressed into his field uniform but with a side cap not a cork sun helmet. Civilian clothes were not an option. He would be travelling to his uncle dressed as a British Army officer.

He made his way, carrying a small grip, to Cape Town station which was near the Castle. Luckily, Verster was on the main line to De Aar which was a medium sized rail and road junction. It was well before dawn when he boarded the train, and it was still dark when train pulled out of the station but after a while, as the sun started to climb in the sky, the train reached the magnificent Paarl Mountains. The slopes were shaped by the sunlight to great beauty by the contrast of shadow and fierce sunlight against the defining hills. Then gradually the landscape became more barren and flat as it crossed the southern part of the Great Karoo Desert.

The train's first stop should have been the junction at De Aar but the station master had arranged for Peter to be let off at the small station at Verster. The last few hours of the journey were repetitive as it was all through the dusty barrenness of the Karoo. Eventually he saw the train guard gesturing to him, and then he felt the train begin to slow down. He took his grip from the luggage rack and made his way to the train door.

Descending the train steps, he walked across the small empty platform and stood for a while wondering if anyone would be there waiting for him. The area behind the small station was deserted but he could see a rough track leading into the hills. After a few minutes he saw a dust line on the road showing that some vehicle was coming towards the station.

Eventually a Cape cart stopped just short of the station and a man climbed out of the horse drawn cart and walked over towards him.

"Peter Rutland?"

"Yes, that's me."

"Hallo Peter, I'm Edwin, your uncle." Edwin was a bronzed man with light brown hair bleached in the sun. He was wearing a leather jerkin and cord trousers, and was of similar height to Peter.

"I'm sorry I'm late but I've only just received your telegram saying that you were coming."

"I'm sorry. Is it convenient for me to visit?"

"Of course it is, my boy. Is this your baggage?"

Edwin bent to pick up Peter's grip but Peter took it himself.

"Come along. We're all ready for you." Edwin walked to the Cape cart that was being turned round by the black driver.

"Put your grip at the back and then in you get," said Edwin. The two men sat side by side with the black lad sitting on the front seat.

"I'm afraid we'll be walking the horses for a bit so that they're not overstretched. I trotted them here because I wondered if I was going to be late."

"Fine," replied Peter, "it gives me more time to look at this amazing countryside."

The driver tossed the reins on the horses' backs and they started their steady walk towards the farm. The land was still on the edge of the Karoo Desert and looked very arid and burned out.

"I'm surprised that anything can be grown here. It all looks so dry," said Peter.

"Nothing can grow here," said Edwin.

Peter looked at him in surprise. "That's not the full answer is it?" he said.

"No. Boer farmers can't grow anything here because they live off the land. They use large areas for cattle or sheep, mainly in areas where there's some surface water. They only grow a few crops close to their homes for their own use."

"Do you do something different?" asked Peter.

"Oh yes," replied Edwin with a chuckle. "There are a couple of streams on my land which would just support a small herd of cattle but I dammed them both up to create a storage of water for the very dry months. I also made channels so that I could water a much larger area and grow grass for hay in the dry season." He pointed up at some cliffs a mile or so away. "You can just see where there is a small stream coming off that face over there."

Peter shielded his eyes to look but the gentle rocking of the Cape cart made it difficult to focus. Edwin tapped the driver on the shoulder and told him to stop. The lad gave a long low whistle and the two horses gradually stopped.

"Now you can see the water streak over between those cliffs."

"Oh yes, I see it now," said Peter.

"If I owned that land I'd harness the power of that falling water and then dam it for use later, but surprisingly the current owner just lets it all go to waste."

Edwin told the driver to start up again. As the horses now slowly trotted along Peter said, "Just now when we stopped, the driver whistled and the horses came to a halt."

"That's how the Boers train their horses. Their mouths get very soft even for snaffles, so the Boers always give a long whistle that tells the horses that they're going to be stopped shortly. They slow down immediately. There's nothing you can tell a Boer about horses and live stock."

After about an hour the farm house came in sight. It was a large spreading building with a veranda running along one side covering a wooden walkway or stoep. Fenced off paddocks and barns surrounded the building to give it almost the appearance of a small village.

As Peter got out of the Cape cart and picked up his grip, his aunt Ellen came out of the house. She was exactly as he imagined. She was dressed in a long blue skirt and blouse, all covered in the front with an apron on which she was wiping her hands. Her suntanned and friendly face was surrounded by her hair that was parted in the middle and drawn back into a bun.

"Hallo Peter, it is lovely to see you."

"Hallo Aunt Ellen, I've waited a long time for this meeting. Uncle has told me a lot about the area and I can see why you decided that this was where you wanted to stop."

"Oh yes, it's beautiful at all times of the year," she beamed. "But come inside. I expect a long drink is what you really want."

For the rest of the afternoon Peter was shown around the house and the gardens that Ellen tried to keep as close to an English garden as she could. Then, as the heat of the day slowly lessened, Edwin suggested that Peter and he sat in cane chairs on the stoep and had a drink before dinner.

Having poured them both a large whisky and soda, he asked, "Have you met any Boers yet?"

"No. I saw some farming men on the train coming up but I didn't speak to them."

Edwin paused, obviously in thought, then he said. "The South African farming Boers are very different from probably any type of men you've met before." He took a sip of his whisky. It was obvious that he was having difficulty in deciding how to make his explanation. Possibly it was because his wife, who was in the kitchen, came from Boer stock.

"The large central core of these people are hard working, scrupulously honest, trustworthy and very religious in the Old Testament way. They're also narrow-minded, almost to the point of bigotry, unimaginative, and have very little sense of humour. They are totally dedicated to this country that they call 'Ons Land'. This simply translates into 'Our Land' but it means much more than just that. It means our homes, our family, our way of life, our God. They are firmly of the belief that they are the chosen people for this land and that they have every right to it."

He paused again. Peter did not interrupt, as he knew there was more to come.

"As you know, my wife is Dutch and obviously has sympathies towards the Boers. Her maiden name was Pieters and her father came from Eindhoven in Holland. My son John, who now calls himself Jan Pieters, also supports the Boer attitude and way of life. Even I can see virtues in their thinking and love of this incredible country but I'm torn between my roots in England and what I have here."

Edwin sipped his whisky again. "I'd like for things to remain as they are. The British to stay in control of the Cape area and to come to some sensible arrangement with the Boers for the Orange Free State and the Transvaal. But I fear that greed and intolerance on both sides will start tearing this country apart." He turned his face to Peter and looked him straight in the eyes. "I don't want you to think I am anything but a true and loyal Englishman but you'll see that it is not all a clear black and white situation."

Both men sat in silence watching the sun sink behind the hills to their left, giving a deep golden hue to the fields and trees.

"Peter, I'm always hesitant at giving advice, so call what I'm about to say - a tip."

Peter laughed. "I need all the advice and tips I can get about this country."

"Well, I assume that being in the Artillery you have a large number of horses doing the towing and carting."

"Yes, my Battery will certainly use a large number and hopefully have a goodly number of extras," Peter replied.

"I'm not going to tell you how to keep them in good trim, but in England there is one element you never have to worry about and that is water. Here water is life itself, as I told you with my increasing the size of the farm. With your horses, especially as they'll not be acclimatised to the hot conditions, you must make water your first requirement. Before you start off on a journey, water your horses, not too much as you know they don't like to travel with a lot inside them but give them as much as is sensible. It's wise to let them just wet their mouths, even if they don't want to drink. That'll keep them content for an hour or two extra. When you stop anywhere, get them a drink however small or poor the quality of water. Keep them in the shade whenever you can and carry as much spare water on your wagons as you have room for. Without water they will die like flies."

A black girl walked down the stoep and called out "Dinner's ready, Baas."

"Come on Peter, time to feed the inner man."

The food was typical farm fare in that there was a great deal of it, and it was wholesome with plenty of cream and butter. Peter, who had had very little that day, ate well and felt truly full at the end of the meal.

Edwin offered Peter a cigar and, despite Ellen jokingly moaning about the smell of stale cigar smoke next morning, they settled down at the table. A tumbler of whisky and soda was the perfect accompaniment to the cigar after a large meal.

As they smoked, a dog barked outside. Ellen, who had been in the kitchen having cleared the dishes, came back into the dining room. "Edwin, kom," she said, obviously agitated. Edwin frowned, rose and went into the kitchen. Then Peter heard him open the back door and go out into the dark. He could hear voices, just talking; nothing loud, simply voices communicating. Gradually they got closer and whoever it was entered the kitchen, together with Edwin and Ellen.

Edwin came back into the dining room. "A surprise visitor. It's John." Ellen then came back into the room and she was obviously very worried, even agitated. She was followed by a man of thirty or so years, bronzed with sun-bleached hair, almost blond. Dressed in a very dusty, long riding coat, he was holding a slouch hat and had a broad smile on his face. He walked around the table to Peter, holding out his hand. "You are the last person I expected to meet here but welcome."

Peter rose and took his hand. "Good to meet you Jan," he said.

Jan laughed. "I expected you to call me John." He turned to his mother. "Well Ma, I must have a bath, I smell like a hyena. I mustn't offend the nose of a Rooinek." He looked at Peter with a chuckle.

"Jan, that's enough." said his mother.

"What's a Rooinek?" asked Peter.

Edwin with a frown on his face, said, "It is a Boer term for a British soldier. It means a red neck because you all have short hair and get sunburned necks."

Peter laughed. "No, I'm not a Rooinek, I haven't been out here long enough yet to get sunburned so I'm still pearly white, and I've smelt worse smells than you Jan so don't wash on my account."

Jan laughed outright at this. "Danke Piet," he said and then turned and left the room.

"I hope this isn't awkward for you Peter," said Edwin, "I didn't know he was coming back."

"Don't worry, Uncle. I'm sure we'll get on well, and anyway he has more right to be here than me."

Ellen came back into the dining room and started to clear away the dishes. She was obviously very worried about the situation. Peter leaned forward and touched her hand. "Please don't worry, Aunt. It'll be all right; just two cousins meeting and having a chat." She gave a thin smile, but she did seem slightly more relaxed.

As Peter had predicted, the evening went very smoothly. He and Jan got on well with a great deal of leg pulling. Edwin joined in the general chit-chat but Ellen went to bed well before midnight.

Jan talked about South Africa and asked about England. He did say to Peter, "I won't ask where you are going if you don't ask me." Peter agreed and this was the only time that they agreed that they were on different sides of the problem but they would not let it come between them.

At around midnight, Jan said. "I must go to bed. I am truly worn out. See you both in the morning."

Peter and Edwin chatted for a short time longer, then they also went to bed.

Peter woke to a sharp tap on his bedroom window. He threw off the sheet that covered him and opened the shutter to see Jan standing outside on the porch. He was dressed ready to ride and wearing his slouch hat.

"I'm going now, Peter."

"Wait a minute, Jan."

Quickly Peter pulled on a shirt, trousers and shoes and climbed over the low window sill onto the porch. The early morning sun threw a golden light across the background of the far hills. Jan stood a few feet away looking at the beautiful sight. Peter stood beside him in silence.

"Do you ride Peter?"

"Yes, I do."

"I mean really ride, up and down the side of these kopjes and gallop across the veldt?"

"Yes, and I'd like to ride this beautiful country with you when all this nonsense is over."

"Is it just nonsense?"

"No," said Peter, "I didn't mean that. It's all of great importance to you but I am just a professional soldier hoping that my government is doing the right thing."

Jan still looking at the gentle sunlit countryside, nodded and pushed his hat to the back of his head. Peter noticed a tulip-shaped badge clipped to the crown of the slouch hat. "What is the badge, Jan?" he asked.

Jan smiled "My uncle in Holland grows tulips and he sent it to me when I was 12 years old. I've always worn it. I consider it as my good luck charm."

He turned to face Peter. "I hope we never meet again Peter, until we can both ride and hunt together on these hills." He held out his hand that Peter took.

"I look forward to that time, Jan. Take care."

Jan smiled. "Tot siens." He turned to walk along the porch and across the yard to the stables.

Peter climbed back through the window into his bedroom and got fully dressed, and then he walked down the corridor and into the kitchen where a young black woman was tending a large oven. "Coffee Baas?" she asked.

"Yes. Thank you." She poured strong black coffee into an earthenware mug and added cream.

Peter picked up the hot coffee mug and walked out through the kitchen door into the garden, where a large ancient thorn tree stood a few yards away. Peter walked into its shade and leaned against the trunk. The sweetly perfumed flowers of the ancient thorn were abuzz with bees.

He sipped his coffee feeling the strong flavour cross his tongue and warm his empty stomach - and then he saw Jan was standing by the kraal gate with his saddle horse and beside him his fully laden pack horse, ready to go. He was talking to his mother who held his arms; then she kissed him on the cheek. Jan mounted his horse and looked down at his mother, who had her hand on his leg.

Jan started his horses to the gate, then turned and, looking at his mother, called out his thanks, "Danke Ma." and then came the Boer farewell "Tot siens." "Till I see you again."

As the two horses walked away, a haze of reddish dust rose gently in the morning air behind them. Jan did not turn round again even though his mother continued to watch him. She stayed there until his figure disappeared in the gentle swirling cloud of dust. Eventually she turned away, a handkerchief to her eyes, and walked back to the kitchen door. Just short of the house she lifted her tear-stained face and saw Peter; she did not stop but entered the house in silence.

Peter drank his coffee, and made a decision. He must leave. He must leave at once. He could not stay here when his aunt's son had already left.

Peter loaded his grip onto the Cape cart and walked over to his Aunt and Uncle, who stood by the gate.

Peter held out his hand. "Goodbye Aunt Ellen." She took his hand and looked up at him, her eyes still red and moist with tears.

"Goodbye Peter." The tears were not for him but for her son riding away to fight, maybe to die. He released her hand and putting his arms around her, he gently embraced her. As he held her to his chest, he felt her sob; softly he kissed the top of her head.

He turned and held out his hand to his Uncle. "Goodbye Uncle."

"Goodbye Peter."

Peter climbed into the Cape cart alongside the black servant who tossed the reins to start the horses into a gentle trot. He did not look back; he did not wave. He did not know if his Uncle and Aunt watched him or if they had walked away. He was going back to his war.

On that day, two cousins rode away from the farmhouse. One was wearing a slouch hat with a tulip badge, and led his laden pack horse to the North – the other, dressed in a khaki uniform sat in a Cape cart which trotted steadily to the South. Both men, with the dust of their travelling hanging in the still air, looked at the beauty of the country around them, both wanted so badly to return – but both had heavy hearts.

Chapter 8

The day after his return from the farm Peter heard that he was to report to the Royal Artillery Depot. The office of the Commander Royal Artillery CRA told him that the guns and all extra equipment were at shed number 87. The office also told him that the Gunners, NCOs and Officer of his Battery would arrive the next day. He asked at the office where shed number 87 was, and then walked out to see the new guns for the first time.

As he approached the shed, he saw a number of British soldiers in shirtsleeves playing football. Peter got closer and called out. "Who is in charge here?"

A tubby man, with three stripes on his shirtsleeve, gave the ball a last kick and said. "I am sir." He walked over to Peter. "Can I help you?"

"I'm looking for shed number 87."

"Oh yes the one with the guns in. It's over there." The Sergeant pointed to a storage shed with large sliding doors in the front. In the sliding doors was a hinged entry door. Peter walked over to the entry door and saw that it was unlocked.

"Sergeant," he called.

"Yes sir."

"Put on your jacket and helmet and come over here."

The Sergeant got dressed with slow bad grace and walked over to Peter, who saw from the badges he was wearing that he belonged to a county militia.

"This door is unlocked."

"Yes sir, the warehouseman's inside. I let him have the key."

"Had you seen him before?" asked Peter.

"No but he knew all about the guns."

"Where is the officer in charge of this guard?"

"In the office over there."

"Sergeant, you will double over there and tell the officer to run back here at once. Then you will call out the guard."

"What do you mean?"

Peter put his face close to the Sergeant's and said, "Do exactly as I say or by the end of the day you will not be a Sergeant."

"Yes sir" mumbled the Sergeant and trotted towards the office.

"At the double, Sergeant," shouted Peter. The tubby figure stumbled into a run towards the office.

The soldiers had stopped playing football and were watching this encounter. Peter shouted out to them. "All of you, get your rifles and surround this warehouse – at the double. Move!"

Instantly they grabbed their jackets and ran to where their rifles were stacked. In some confusion they each grabbed a rifle and started to run down the sides of the warehouse.

An officer came out of the office and followed by the Sergeant walked towards Peter. "At the double, both of you!" shouted Peter. The lieutenant arrived in a bit of a fluster. "You wanted me sir?"

"Yes, the incompetence of you and your Sergeant have allowed an unauthorised person into the warehouse. I am going inside and I want to know that the outside is secure. Do you understand me?"

"Yes sir," mumbled the Lieutenant.

Peter opened the door into the warehouse as quietly as possible and stepped inside. It was an enormous area, at the end of which Peter could see a number of canvas-covered shapes. Presumably they were his guns and limbers. He walked towards them, trying to make sure his boots did not make much noise. He looked down the first line but there was no sign of anyone. Then he heard a scraping sound. At the next line he saw a man lifting one of the covers. He was holding a broom in one hand as he held up the tarpaulin with the other.

"What are you doing?" called Peter. The man jumped and dropped the canvas cover.

"Nothing. I'm just the warehouse man and I'm checking that everything is all right."

"Get away from those covers," said Peter as he walked towards him.

"There's no reason to get uppity," said the man. "I'm only doing what I'm paid for." Peter lifted the corner of the canvas that the man had been under, and then turned towards him just in time to see a broom handle swinging down to smash him on the side of his neck. He fell to the floor stunned and gasping for breath. He struggled to stand and looked up the line but the man had disappeared.

Peter looked again under the tarpaulin and saw that there was oil of some sort dripping from the front end of the gun. It seemed that a plug bolt had been loosened and was allowing the oil to leak out. Peter tightened the plug up with his fingers until it stopped dripping.

"You wanted me sir?" Peter turned to see the Militia Lieutenant standing behind him.

"No. Why?"

"The warehouseman said that you wanted to see me."

"Are you holding him?" asked Peter.

"No sir, did you want to see him?"

"You are a bloody fool," said Peter "Get outside and make sure your men totally surround this warehouse and wait for me to come out."

Peter rubbed the side of his neck where the broom handle had hit him. He cursed the stupidity of the officer and the incompetence of the Sergeant then gave himself a good kick in the pants for the way he had handled the whole matter.

Quickly he lifted the ends of all of the tarpaulins to check if there was any other sign of sabotage but nothing was readily apparent. Still rubbing his neck, he walked to the entrance door and stepped out into the bright sunshine, where the Sergeant and Officer stood talking to each other.

"Sergeant," called Peter.

"Yes sir," he replied and ran over to stand at attention in front of Peter.

"How many men have you?"

"Sixteen sir."

"You will post two men at each end of this building, and four men down the sides. The rest will stay in a squad in the front. When you have done that, report to me in the office over there."

"Very good sir," replied the Sergeant and ran over to the squad of men and started to post them as instructed.

"Lieutenant," called Peter. "Follow me." He strode towards the office, entered and saw a room with two desks and chairs He walked over to the larger desk, took off his helmet and sat down. The lieutenant followed Peter into the office and also took off his helmet.

"Put your helmet back on Lieutenant, and stand to attention. What is your name?"

"Dunbir sir. Lieutenant Dunbir."

"Well Dunbir, you have made an idiot of yourself today. You have been incompetent, ineffective and thoroughly stupid. You have allowed your guard to be incompetent also and in doing so endangered a very important venture. Your Sergeant is the epitome of everything a Sergeant should not be."

Peter leaned forward and with his arms on the desk, looked Dunbir straight in the eyes and said. "Go outside and tell the Sergeant to come in. When you return you will stand at the side of the desk at attention until I say otherwise. Do you fully understand?"

"Yes sir"

"Right, do it now."

Dunbir left the office and closed the door. A few seconds later the door opened, he came in and stood beside Peter's desk. The Sergeant followed him in, stopped in front of Peter, and saluted. He stood stiffly at attention.

Peter looked him up and down for a few seconds and then said. "Sergeant, you have acted disgracefully and irresponsibly. You were clearly instructed to maintain a guard on the warehouse to ensure complete security. You did neither of these things. You did not check my credentials and incredibly you allowed a civilian inside the very area you were meant to keep secure."

Peter paused to allow this all to sink in. "I will give you one last chance. Tomorrow at some time, my Gunners will take over guard from your section. Until then you will ensure that every minute of every hour there is a competent and instructed guard on the warehouse. You've plenty of men to have a relief system which you will ensure works. If you fail in this task it will not simply be a bad report to your Commanding Officer. It will be a Court Martial. Do you fully understand?"

"Yes sir" was the instant reply.

"Go now and organise it. You will be in charge of the guard until my men arrive – whenever that is. Dismiss."

The Sergeant saluted and marched out of the office.

Peter turned to Dunbir. "You Dunbir, are as guilty as the Sergeant. All that I said to him applies to you. Go out there now and ensure that the guards' eating and sleeping arrangements are properly organised and carried out. My men will arrive sometime tomorrow until then you will be responsible for the security of this area. Just one slip up Dunbir, and I will break you."

The young lieutenant was visibly trembling. "Very good sir. I'll see that your orders are fully carried out."

"Dismissed," said Peter. Dunbir saluted and left the office.

Peter stood and picked up his helmet and put it on. Though he was very keen to examine the new guns he knew that firstly he must go back to the RA Depot office and find out what arrangements had been made for his men's accommodation.

As he was about to enter the Depot office, a Colonel came out of the office door. The Colonel stopped. "Are you Rutland?" he asked.

"Yes sir."

The Colonel turned around and said, "Come with me." Peter followed him into an office marked 'Colonel Davenport'.

"Sit down Rutland," he said, "I don't normally personally attend to officers wanting goods from the Depot but you – or rather your guns – are a bit different."

He offered a pack of cigarettes to Peter. "Cigarette?"

"No thank you, sir."

Davenport took one and lit it with a lighter. "I've had strict instructions to hide your guns away until you came. Haven't even seen the damn things meself. Don't worry, Colonel Bridport has filled me in with the details." He stood up and went over to a cupboard and unlocked the door. He took out a folder and brought it back to the desk.

"Now, what have we here for you?" He opened the file and took a number of papers. "Here's a list of the equipment that's in shed number 87. For just two guns it seems one hell of a lot." He handed some papers to Peter. "Amazingly you have also got sixty five horses coming for you."

"Sixty five!" said Peter.

"Fifty two would be the normal allotment but someone up there is looking after you by letting you have the rest as spares. Take my advice and tell no one. Sound horses are in great demand because so many have been lost through poor horse management. Water is the answer, plenty of it at all times."

"I've been given that advice already."

"Well, make sure you use it. And keep a good guard on them especially in 'friendly' areas - like here."

He handed over some more papers and said, "This is the number of men you will be getting. I haven't got names and details yet but they'll come with all the waffle tomorrow morning. I've arranged for you to have a tented camp just one mile from the warehouse. You'll be able to take the guns and wagons over there, and it'll be reasonably remote. Don't quote me on this, but I shouldn't be too fastidious about keeping them carefully covered up. They're going to be seen anyway and it's almost more noticeable if you go around with guns under canvas. I think it's the details of the gun and the knowledge of how to use it that must be secure."

"Thank you sir, that sounds good advice. I think I'll bed down for the night in the office close to the warehouse and be ready for the men tomorrow."

"By the way," added Davenport. "I can tell you that luckily, for ammunition, the ordinary 14 pound shrapnel fits your guns - or so I am told. If I were you, I'd fire the first one off and be at some distance just in case it fouls up."

Peter gave a laugh and stood up. "I hope to see you after I've fired the first one then sir."

"I'll come and see you and the guns when you've settled in your new camp. If you want any help, give me a call. And also, a personal tip, I suggest you don't wear your Sam Browne belt any more. In the field we're all using the Slade-Wallace belts. It'll keep your appearance and your officers the same as your men. These Boers are sharp enough to sort out the officers and pick 'em off.

"Thank you very much sir." said Peter, "I'll take that advice." He picked up his helmet, came to attention and then left the office.

With the papers tucked under his arm, he walked back to the warehouse where the militiamen were slowly moving around the outside on guard. The Sergeant was standing in front of the entrance door. He saluted as Peter approached.

"Open the door please, Sergeant"

"Certainly sir." He pulled out a key and undid the padlock and then opened the small swing door. Peter entered the warehouse.

Again he could see the long bulky shapes that were covered in green tarpaulin sheets. He walked over and lifted up the first covers so that he could peer underneath. He pulled the canvas right off and looked at a squat limber, very similar in shape and size to the usual 15 pounder limber but the wheels were very unusual; they were extra thin and light, and made totally of metal.

He pulled off the next cover to reveal the new Artillery piece that he had seen earlier. He pulled the canvas well clear so that he could see the gun completely and clearly. This was so very different from the 15 pounder pieces that he knew, and from any gun that he had ever seen before.

He had only ever known guns that were basically a gun barrel fixed to a cross axle that had a wheel at each end. This was all balanced and towed by the gun's trail. This Ehrhardt gun he was looking at had the same two wheels as the limber's, which were very light and made entirely of metal. These wheels were fixed to an axle that was attached to a trail for towing but the barrel sat on a long oblong box; it was this box that was attached to the axle. The barrel, which was slightly longer than the box, lay on top. Peter walked round the piece carefully examining each part.

From what he had read, the long box housed the buffer system that absorbed the recoil. When the gun was fired, the barrel would be thrown back against the buffer system that consisted of a number of baffles inside the long box forcing glycerine oil against them to reduce the recoil. Having recoiled, the spring recovery system would bring the barrel back to its original position. Colonel Bridport had said that it was reputed that this system was so effective that a coin could be placed on the wheels and it would still be there after the gun had fired.

The trail had a towing eye at the end, plus a foldaway handspike attached to the trail to move the gun onto the target.

Peter felt the excitement coursing through his veins. This was a fantastic weapon. With a swift recovery system and with no need to relay the gun onto the target after it had fired, it meant that the one gun could throw as many shells as the current Battery of six guns.

He walked around the other wagons, most of which were uncovered, and checked them off against his list.

2   Ehrhardt 15 pounder guns complete
6   Limbers for above.
4   Ammunition Wagons
1   Forge Wagon fully stocked
4   Wagons General Stores etc.
1   Signals Wagon complete

There was a list of all harness and saddlery required. The number of horses showed that there were enough for officers, Battery Sergeant Major and the Sergeants plus about eight spares.

Peter stepped back through the small swing door and closed it. Lieutenant Dunbir was standing outside; he saluted Peter.

"Lock it up, please Sergeant." The Sergeant again pulled out his key and locked the padlock back.

"Come with me, please Lieutenant," said Peter and walked over to the office.

Inside Peter took off his helmet and noticed that Dunbir did not remove his. Peter took a piece of paper off the desk and wrote an address on it and gave it to the Lieutenant.

"Will you please order two of your men to go and get all my kit, which is at the Mount Nelson Hotel and bring it to me here. Then arrange for a camp bed for me to use in this office with a few home comforts such as some water and a bowl."

"Certainly sir," said Dunbir, and turned to leave.

"When you have done that and when you have personally checked that all arrangements for the overnight guard are correct, you can go back to your mess and have a meal. Make sure you inspect the guard late in the evening and make at least one surprise nighttime check. Also make sure that this office is included in the security area for the guard to cover."

"Yes sir,"

"When my men arrive tomorrow, report to me."

"Yes sir." He turned and left the office.

Chapter 9

Next day Peter managed to find a Regimental mess nearby where he was able to have some breakfast. As he returned to his office, a runner from the RA Depot reported that his men were on their way and would arrive shortly.

Peter settled down with his papers that he had been working on last night.

He was worried that there did not seem to be adequate spares and servicing material. In the notes it said that, as the guns were made individually and not mass-produced, the parts would not be interchangeable. It also showed that the extra hydraulic glycerine oil necessary for topping up the buffers had not been included with the current delivery. That did not matter as long as there was no excessive spillage. They only had a small amount that would be taken with them into action.

Outside he heard the shout of orders and stamping of feet that told him a number of Gunners had arrived. There was a knock at the door.

"Come in," he called.

The door opened and a slim, tall, very smartly turned out Royal Artillery First Lieutenant entered. He saluted. "Lieutenant Julian Stevens reporting, sir."

Peter stood up and held out his hand. "Hallo, Lieutenant. Glad to meet you. Sit down and tell me a bit about yourself."

Stevens took off his helmet, to show light sandy-coloured hair. He sat in the chair opposite Peter, and then casually crossed his legs. He was obviously completely at his ease and totally self-confident.

"Well sir. Done the usual training at Woolwich and the usual range firing but so far no luck in seeing any action."

"Have you seen any of the men outside before? Do you know any of them?"

"'Fraid not sir. They came on a different ship to me. I only met 'em an hour ago. The BSM looks a good man though. Don't know his name."

"God, I hope he is good. I'm in bad need of a sound senior NCO."

Peter leaned his elbows on the desk. "Have you done any training of men before?"

"No, not really, but I think it's all a matter of organisation to get it done properly." Peter's heart sank. This was not the experienced officer he expected, one who could take on the main training. Stevens did not inspire confidence at all. Then Peter decided to throw him in the deep end.

"Julian, I want you to go to the RA Depot office, which is close by, and get the details of where we are to set up a tented camp. I think that the tents and equipment are all there already. If not find out about it and then get the men over there and start to organise the whole camp."

"Very good sir," Stevens rose smoothly, put on his helmet, saluted and left the office.

Lieutenant Julian Stevens did not impress Peter at all. His record sounded all right; he must have a technical brain, he had a pleasant manner but how would he under pressure? Stevens had never seen action – but that applied to all of us initially – there was just something about him that made Peter feel uneasy. It might be that he seemed to be too casual, as though he was not taking anything too seriously. But he is the only officer I've got, he thought.

Peter went to the hand basin and poured in some water from the large jug standing in it. He splashed his face to freshen himself just as he heard a knock on the door. "Come in," he called with his back to the door. He put a towel to his face to dry it.

"Good morning sir."

Peter spun round. "Hills!" The stocky figure, immaculately turned out, saluted with a smile on his ruddy cheeked face.

"Very nice to see you, sir."

"And to see you, Sar'nt Major," said Peter eagerly, and put out his hand with warmth to shake hands with the man who Peter knew instantly would be the rock he could always rely on. There was no need to give second thoughts about trustworthiness here.

"You are a sight for sore eyes," he said. "We have a hell of a job ahead of us and you're just the man I want. I did ask for you but was told that it would be impossible to make a selective posting." He reached forward and placed his hand on Hills' shoulder. Peter regarded this man with great affection – not just because Hills had saved his life in '79 but also because he embodied all of the finest qualities of the Royal Artillery.

Peter turned and sat on the edge of the desk. "Have you met the Gunners yet?"

"Yes sir. Two full crews with a few extras. Sergeants McCann and Hazzer are the Numbers 1. Both men with good records and all Gunners experienced and trained in field artillery drill. Sergeant Piper is in charge of the Drivers. He's a good man who really knows his horses. I've been with them through the trip out, so I got to know them a bit. "

"Sar'nt Major, you'll learn that we've been given a difficult and highly responsible assignment. I want your absolutely honest opinion of these crews at all times. I must be able to rely on them completely. Do you have any doubts now - however small?"

There was a moment's silence before Hills replied. "Sgt Hazzer's record, in and out of action, is good – but there is something about him that I can't quite explain. There's also something wrong between him and Bombardier Kirkby."

"What do you mean, wrong?"

"Well sir, twice I've heard them arguing, and I found out that Kirkby's wife had left him for Hazzer." He paused. "Don't worry sir. Basically they are both good men; I'll make sure they pull their weight."

Peter smiled. "I've no doubt about that, but we must have good security. You will understand why when I explain all to the Battery. So if you think or even feel something is not quite right, let me know."

"Very good sir."

"I want to see you and Lieutenant Stevens this afternoon at 1400 hours when I can fill you both in with the details. In the mean time, you and Lieutenant Stevens have got the enormous job of organising a tent camp."

"Don't worry sir. I've done it all before."

"You have indeed. It really is good to have you here Sarn't Major."

Hills smiled. "Thank you, sir." He saluted and left the office.

At 2 p.m. when Lt Stevens and BSM Hills reported to his office, Peter was delighted to learn that the camp had been set up and the Gunners, with their kit, all properly billeted in their allotted tents.

With the two men sitting in front of his desk, Peter gave them the full details of what they were expected to do in the trials of the new gun. Peter knew that Hills would not make any show of amazement or excitement at the project but Peter was surprised that Julian seemed to take the whole matter as quite usual, and almost of no interest. Then he astounded Peter. "Would you like me to organise a training programme for these new guns, sir?" he asked.

Peter was very surprised at the initiative and replied, "I haven't had time myself to even address the situation but I think it might need all three of our brains on that job."

"I don't see it as a very big job sir," replied Julian in a very casual tone. "All the men are trained Gunners so they know how to handle the horses, the limbers and ancillary wagons, so the only training is on the actual gun itself. Even that cannot be too different from a breach-loading piece. The only major difference will be in the maintenance of a system that none of us have any experience."

Peter looked at Julian who was almost lying in his chair. It was amazing. It seemed that this man could be at ease and comfortable even on a hard office chair.

Peter leaned forward, his elbows on the desk top. "You're quite right, Julian. You've got it in a nutshell." He took out two of the training manuals and gave one to each man.

"Julian, this afternoon will you order the two Sergeants to assist Sgt Piper to lay out the lines for the horses, which will arrive shortly. Get Piper and the Farrier to check each horse carefully."

"Right sir."

"Sar'nt Major, will you get three sets of Slade-Wallace equipment for the three of us. I've been told that all officers and senior NCOs should wear it so that we can't be picked out from the men."

"Very good sir."

"The three of us'll learn how to use the guns tomorrow morning, then we'll start training the men. Now any other suggestions from either of you?" Peter asked.

"Messing, Sir?" asked Hills.

"Julian and I to have separate tents in camp, and we will mess together. We'll share a tent when in action and then we'll mess with you and the Sergeants."

"Shall I choose batmen for both of you?"

"Yes, but we only need one between the two of us. He'll be excused all other fatigues."

"I'll also try and find out if one of the men can cook."

"Oh God," groaned Julian. "Battery cooking."

Peter gave a laugh. "Well, I've got to see the CRA now, but tomorrow the three of us will learn how to handle the guns. I think we'll then bring in the Sergeants and their Bombardiers, and finally the rest of the gun crews can be taught."

Julian and Hills rose, saluted and left the office.

The next few days were a blur of activity as the officers learned the new drill, then taught the Sergeants who, in turn taught their Bombardiers, and then finally their gun crews. The drill was repeated over and over again until each man knew his own post duties plus most of the other positions.

The horses arrived, were checked, and then had to be exercised to train them up to acceptable fitness. The long sea journey had made them very soft but Sergeant Piper was the man to handle that job.

"How are the horses, Sar'nt Piper?"

"Bloody marvellous if you'll excuse me. After the long sea journey I thought they'd be almost dead but they've come back real good sir."

"They're going to have it very rough shortly, with little or no water and poor food while working to the utmost," said Peter.

"No food sir? Blimey, they won't be much good without their short feed and oats sir."

"So do your best to keep them fed and watered. It's going to be a tough job but I am relying on you."

Julian even found a signwriter from the RA Depot and suggested that the two guns should be numbered.

"Good idea," said Peter "Obviously Number 1 and Number 2."

"Well I thought of that but it's rather plain. I think it should be RG1 and RG2" suggested Julian.

"RG? What's the RG for?" asked Peter.

"Rutland's Gun No 1 and No 2."

Peter let out a laugh. "On your head be it. You can explain that to the CRA if he asks."

A Gunner, with leather equipment in his arms, stamped to the halt in front of Peter saluted and said "Gunner 'iggins sir."

"Iggins?" replied Peter.

"No 'iggins sir."

"Oh Higgins," said Peter.

"Yes sir 'iggins."

"Well Higgins what are you here for?"

"The Battery Sergeant Major 'as made me your bat man sir, and for the Lieutenant, sir. And 'e told me to give you this Slade equipment."

Peter took hold of one set of buff leather belt, shoulder straps and two ammunition pouches and started to put them over his shoulders. "Right, Higgins let's see if this fits."

"Are you goin' to wear this sir?" asked Higgins in amazement. "What about your Sam Browne?"

"We've been told to wear the Slade equipment and not our sword belt."

"Well, I can't Adam and Eve it. Don't seem right to me, sir. Hofficers should wear Sam Brownes. Sir, then we knows they is hofficers."

"So does Mr Boer," replied Peter. "What do you mean 'Adam and Eve' it?"

"Oh, sorry sir. That's Cockney slang for 'believe it'. The Sar'nt Major told me not to use it but it comes sort of natural like. I'll be more careful from now on sir."

Peter smiled. "I think you're going to find that difficult but make sure you give me a translation."

With a very straight face Higgins replied, "Very good sir." He had been watching Peter struggle to get the equipment on, and now off. "Shall I clean them both up for you and the Lieutenant Sir?"

"Yes but no better than the rest of the Gunners. I don't want to be as smart as a stick man on Guard duty. Understand?"

"It's a shame sir. I could get you off a lot of duties," quipped Higgins.

"Buzz off, Higgins before I give you extra duties,"

Higgins stamped to attention and threw an impeccable salute. "Right sir."

Peter turned to Julian, who was standing beside Number 1 Gun. "I think we've got a bit of a character for our batman."

"As long as he brings me a cup of Earl Grey each morning, I shan't complain."

"Oh God, another comedian," moaned Peter.

Eventually the Battery was as trained as it could be in the time allowed. Hills kept a beady but fatherly eye on every man. They were all timeserving regular Gunners, who had travelled the world. They were the best of their type and need very little chasing or help, but even so, he was always there.

On one of his tours Hills walked around No 1 Gun's ready ammunition towards No 2 Gun. He saw Bombardier Kirkby kneeling by the limber and Sergeant Hazzer bending over him. Hazzer stood upright and walked forward to the gun. Hills heard Kirkby call out "You foul mouthed sod!" Hazzer turned, smiled and wagged his finger in mild reproach. Hills knew he had to act – this matter was getting out of hand, and it was now too bad to leave. He waited a few seconds then called out "Sergeant Hazzer, here please."

Hazzer strolled over without haste as Hills moved further away from the guns. He did not want to be overheard. "You wanted me?" asked Hazzer.

"You've gone too far now, Sergeant," said Hills.

"What do you mean?" queried Hazzer.

"I know the problem between you and Bombardier Kirkby but you will never do again what you just did."

"What do you mean?"

"You know full well." Hills voice showed firm authority. "Just once more and I'll have you off this gun site immediately. But because you know about the guns, you'll be sent back to a dead end job in England with a black mark on your record."

"You couldn't do that," exploded Hazzer.

"Just one word to Major Rutland and that is exactly what'll happen, and from now on, and every time in the field, you will call me 'Sir'. Understand?"

"Yes sir."

"Right, get back to your gun and remember my warning." Hazzer turned and walked back to his gun.

Hills decided he would tell the Major; he had a feeling that Hazzer was not going to take his advice.

While Peter learned about his new guns, and trained his men to the efficiency he wanted, his cousin Jan gently rode north towards the Boer line.

When Jan left the farm, he rode for some time with his mind full of what had happened during the past few hours. He had always seen the Rooineks, or the Khakis as they were also called, as his enemies – as his country's enemies but he now had a problem. Peter was not the red-necked bullying soldier with big boots suppressing our land; he was – human, friendly – 'my cousin'.

'I could ride and talk with him, Jan thought. 'But – what if I see a British officer in my rifle sights? Do I shoot, or do I think that he might be Peter?' He bowed his head and his eyes focussed on his horse's mane as it plodded slowly on. His hands, holding the reins, were folded on the pommel of his saddle as he tried to settle the problem in his mind. 'Damn it, why did I have to meet him now?"

He forced his mind away from the present problem and reminisced by recalling the beauty of this wonderful land; a land that he had adopted and made his own. He thought of the times he had ridden out into the veldt

– alone with just horse and his rifle. He recalled the sounds of the wild cry of a flying crane; the roar of a male lion in the evening dusk; the heart-stopping sight of a herd of elephants moving slowly through the bush; the wonder of the enormous cream-of-tartar tree – and of course the sweet scent of the flowers of the ancient thorn tree, especially the one at the home farm.

Jan was returning to his commando at Magersfontein, which was just south of Kimberley over 200 miles away. He was taking his time; he did not want to wear out his horses and he wanted to talk to farmers and locals who showed sympathy to the Boers. He would take back information to his commando. Where were the British forces? How many did he see? What condition were they in?

He had to take great care not to be noticed by any troops in the area for, though he was claiming to be a hunter heading for Bechuanaland and so uninterested in the current situation, he looked to be the typical fighting man.

It took over two week's riding for Jan before he saw the camp where the Boer army was. As he rode towards them, he looked around for any of his friends, and then he heard a shouted welcome. "Dag Jan. Had a holiday?"

Jan stopped his horses and replied. "Dag Henk." He smiled at the welcome sight of the sun-tanned face of his good friend and main fighting comrade, Henk Willems. Henk and Jan had been together from the very start and together they had fought the Khakis at Magersfontein

the previous December, when they had defeated Lord
Methuen, at the second battle of Black Week.

Jan eased himself out of the saddle, slid to the
ground and leaned against his horse.

Henk slipped off his slouch hat and smacked it
against his corduroy trousers to create a cloud of dust.
He ran his hands through his long black hair. He put his
hat on the back of his head, and patted the bundles on
the packhorse. "Coffee?" he asked.

Jan nodded. Henk patted again and said quietly,
"Tobacco?"

Again Jan nodded. "But keep it quiet."

"I've never heard noisy tobacco," said Henk as he
put his nose close to the bundles. "Smells like biltong
to me."

Jan laughed. "That's as well, you can chew the
'baccy and smoke the biltong."

Henk slapped him on the shoulder. "Kom. Our tent
is over there."

"Tent!" exclaimed Jan.

"Ja, we've been here so long, we have tents. Unless
someone gets their blood moving, we'll stay here and
grow mealies for all the good we are doing."

Jan followed Henk as they walked through the Boer
encampment, which was now five miles from end to
end and where about 6,000 Transvaal burghers were
gathered together all waiting for orders. As he looked
over the enormous spread, Jan could see a number of
flags. All were the Vierkleur of the Transvaal. It was
an amazing sight, the largest group of men he had ever
seen - so many shaggy men on shaggy horses. Then he
noticed there were numerous wagons and also women.

"What're all these women doing in the lines?" asked Jan in amazement.

"It's crazy," replied Henk, "but the General wants to keep the families together."

General Piet Cronje, commanded this army. He was a large framed, slow-moving man who was very set in his ways; a God-fearing farmer who was not a soldier and knew little of military matters.

His second in command was General Christiaan De Wet, a completely different character, who had a natural basic understanding of what was wanted militarily, and had an adventuresome spirit - but he was continually being overruled.

Chapter 10

Peter stepped inside Colonel Davenport's office.

"Ah, Major Rutland. Just the man," said Davenport. "Sit y' down." Peter sat on the wicker chair in front of the Colonel's desk.

"Now somewhere I've got some specific orders for you. Ah, here they are." Davenport sat back in his chair and went though the papers. "Did you know we're all going up country to Ramdam?"

"No sir." Peter said with an element of surprise.

"Well, we are. Just about everyone." He thumbed through the papers again. "Here are your details for transport." He did not give the copy to Peter but started to read from it. "Full Battery – blah blah - complete with wagons – blah blah – to go from - Ah here it is. Day after tomorrow from the south siding. A train to carry you and two companies of the Green Howards. Doubt if you know where the south siding is do you? Well I'll have a stores Sergeant show you." Davenport looked up and handed the paper to Peter.

"Can the Sergeant show me straight away sir? I'd like to have my BSM involved."

"Certainly, I'll get him now." He stood up. "Guns suitable?"

"Yes sir. You never had a chance to see them though."

"I will. I'm coming up country too. Hope to see some action." He walked to the door. "Now let's get you a guide."

With characteristic efficiency, and only a little assistance from Peter, Hills had the Battery ready for moving to the rail siding at the required time. It was obvious that the gun crews that Peter had been given were very experienced.

To load the guns, limbers, wagons, horses and then men plus tents and equipment was a complex and time consuming job. The more efficiently it was done, the sooner it was completed. Eventually all were on board and the detachment of Green Howards also entrained.

The journey was slow and tedious. Peter reflected on the fact that he had travelled most of the track before, when he had visited his Uncle but this time it was much slower and not anywhere near so comfortable.

The railway travelled almost due north, directly towards besieged Kimberley. At last, after two days the small railway station of Graspan was reached, some 60 miles south of Kimberley. The Battery detrained and instantly started on a march to the small town of Ramdam. On their arrival the Battery was shown its position to camp, but they were warned that they would be moving in a day or so.

To Peter's surprise, there was not a very big encampment as apparently the main part of Lord Roberts army was about 30 miles further up the line at Modder River Station just below Magersfontein and the Boer position.

The Boers were absolutely certain they knew where the British were going to attack next. They were sure that the British Army would only advance along the track of a railway so that their mass of supplies could be easily transported to the frontline troops.

Roberts, with his army, was due south of Kimberley on the railway that pointed north to his next object. The Boers knew he would relieve the siege of Kimberley. Then he would turn due east and follow the railway to Bloemfontein, the state capital. The Boers, confident that this was Roberts' policy, started to prepare strong defensive positions, as only they knew how, in this barren and broken countryside.

But Roberts had no intention of doing what the Boers were certain he would do. He decided to feint at Kimberley by using Lord Methuen's command to move aggressively north along the railway while the main force moved south and east. He ordered the cavalry, supported by the Royal Horse Artillery, to proceed ahead of the force and swing swiftly to cut the road and rail link between Kimberley and Bloemfontein. This cavalry attack would be consolidated as quickly as possible by pushing the infantry across an arid landscape to ensure that the Boer forces at either town were completely separated.

This was an incredibly risky move as it meant that all the arms of the British Army would be carrying their own supplies across an arid and unforgiving landscape. Also, if the Boers learned of this attack, and were able to move a strong enough force from either Kimberley or Bloemfontein to meet the British, they would have the advantage of short and good supply lines, while Roberts was right at the end of his very slow and vulnerable line of supply. It was therefore imperative that secrecy was maintained right up to when the cavalry left Ramdam. Only the most senior commanding officers were informed of the plan of attack, so the individual commanders of the RHA and Cavalry did not know where they were going to when they set off at 2am on Monday 12th February 1900. Their first march out of the camp would be due south and eventually northeast. They were going to head for Waterval Drift, a crossing of the Riet River, then they would aim north for Klip Drift and so cross the Modder River just short of the road that joined Kimberley and Bloemfontein.

Speed and secrecy were of the essence.

No one at Ramdam knew any details of Roberts' plan to trap Cronje, so any orders that arrived were thought to be mysterious if not downright stupid. On February 10th, Peter was informed by Colonel Eustace, the Commander Royal Artillery (CRA), that 172 Battery were to be attached to the Royal Horse Artillery and move with the cavalry when it moved out of Ramdam; he was not at all pleased

"But though our guns are fast moving, they are not light enough to keep up with the RHA, sir," he firmly commented to the CRA.

"I'm fully aware of that Major, but when the cavalry next move out of Ramdam, Bobs wants you with them to give speedy and concentrated fire. No arguments!"

"Very good sir." Peter saluted and returned to his Battery position.

Peter explained the situation to Stevens and Hills.

"I suppose Bobs'll get the cavalry to strike off the rail to Kimberley and they'll want heavy artillery support as quickly as possible," suggested Julian.

"That sounds very likely," replied Peter "but that doesn't help us – we aren't horse artillery. Also we're too damn far south."

He paused then said, "I'm going to split the Battery. We can't possibly travel with the cavalry with our entire backup. Julian, you and I will take the two guns with two extra limbers and some spare horses. Sar'nt Major, you will have the main task of following us with all the Battery supply wagons and signals." He looked at Julian. "On the first action I'm not going to get involved with the new tangent sights. It's going to be tricky enough on a first time using the new guns without any extras."

"How about using some of the extra horses to tow two more limbers loaded with water?" suggested Julian.

"Excellent," said Peter. "That'll stop anyone trying to commandeer any of our spare horses, and we can always dump the limbers when the water is used up. Work out a way to carry the water, will you, Julian?"

"Right sir."

"I want this split to be done right now," said Peter. "I think we might be called at any time." As Julian left, Peter turned to Hills. "Sar'nt Major, you are left with the lousiest job of all."

Hills smiled, "Don't you worry sir, I'll manage."

"I know you will, but as a mere BSM in charge of a Battery supply chain you will be in a weak position. I'll ask the CRA, Colonel Eustace, to give you all the help possible and I will give you a written order showing my true rank as a Lieutenant Colonel."

"Really sir," said Hills, "Lieutenant Colonel, congratulations sir."

"Thank you," Peter smiled, "but keep it under your hat, I am only meant to use it *in extremis.* Now get as much organised as possible and if you think you'll want anything, then let me know quickly."

"Very good sir," Hills saluted.

The next day Peter was told to have his Battery ready to move the next night on 12th February. They were to be provisioned with food and water for three days. General French was taking a force supported by the RHA on a sweeping journey to attack the Boers where they did not expect to be hit.

At midnight, by the lights of handheld lanterns, Peter gave his two-gun Battery a final check before the long march. The two artillery pieces were in line with horses standing ready but not harnessed in. The Drivers were standing by their pair of horses, each man holding his short-handled whip; on their left hip they wore the newly issued revolver, fixed on the end of a lanyard, but in an open holster. Each man had a metal leg guard on their right leg that made them look uneven and cumbersome, but with the limber towing pole hard against that leg and in between two galloping horses, the guard was a vital piece of equipment however awkward it felt.

At each limber Peter saw the Gunners standing at ease. As he passed each one he did a final check on catches and locks. They had all been checked before but they were of such vital importance that they were checked again.

A junior staff officer trotted down the lines and said to Peter. "Guns to move off in thirty minutes' time, sir."

Peter nodded an acknowledgement and gave the instruction to lift the poles onto the horse harness. When completed the Sergeants, who were the guns Numbers One, checked the straps and hooks. Peter and Julian rechecked. Nothing was being left to chance.

Peter stood beside his horse. In the moonlit gloom of the night he could see his guns and limbers ready to go. He smiled to himself when he saw the six limbers as expected but also the extra two carrying water. No one had queried the extra number of limbers but he felt a smug satisfaction at having the extra amount of the life saving liquid. It also gave a reason for bringing along some of his spare horses

The night air was still warm, and along the line of Battery horses he could smell the tang in the air of the neat's-foot oil used on the leather and horses hooves. Each horse was in its prime, well groomed and fitted with harness that was in perfect condition. The Gunners in their khaki uniforms merged into the gloom even with their drab white Slade Wallace equipment straps. Peter had given orders that this equipment was not to be scrubbed or cleaned; he had seen that the infantry were all too conspicuous with their immaculate clean strapping.

There was a stirring ahead and the soft words of command to the cavalry, "Forward!"

Peter turned and called the order. "Mount." Drivers and Sergeants mounted their horses and the Gunners mounted the guns and limbers. With a wave of his arm, Peter started the Battery on the march to its first action. General French was taking them on the first move to cross the Riet River.

Jan lay on his back. The warmth of the late afternoon sun was still warming the air. He had just had some food with the rest of his commando and was now relaxing while the tough meat hopefully digested in his full stomach.

"Wake up Jan!"

Jan lifted his hat that had been shading his eyes. Henk was kneeling over him.

"De Wet is moving." Henk spoke quietly so that only Jan could hear.

"Where? Why?"

"Get your bedroll and come with me."

Jan ducked into the tent and picked up his bedroll, plus rifle and all the extra kit he would need. It had been ready for the past few days – ready for De Wet to take some action. Outside the tent he saw Henk striding towards the horse line, carrying his kit plus a saddle. Jan picked up his saddle and followed.

He caught Henk up as he was putting the saddle on his horse.

"What's this all about Henk?"

Henk put his finger to his lips to signal silence. "Get your horse ready," he said. When both men had their horses saddled up and all their kit tied on, they walked down through the camp towards the stream. No one made any comment or took any notice of them. It was not unusual to see a couple of men setting off on a scouting trip or going hunting.

Once clear of the camp they mounted, and Henk moved alongside Jan's horse.

"That old woman Cronje still wants us to stay here," said Henk "but De Wet is certain that the Khakis are going to move. He doesn't think they're going to follow the rail track. He wants to take a strong scouting force out to the east where he thinks Roberts is going to try and split us from Bloemfontein. Cronje says 'No', but De Wet is going anyway." He wriggled in his saddle and reached down to tighten up the cinch strap around his horse's belly. "I was told that we could go with them but only if we kept quiet about it."

Ahead, close to a cluster of trees, Jan could see a group of a hundred or so horsemen. They were standing still just, waiting for their leader, the imaginative and perceptive soldier, De Wet. When the two men joined the group, they were acknowledged only by the odd nod of the head. There was almost silence as the group waited for the leader.

After a short wait, a group of four men could be seen cantering across the veldt towards them. In the lead was a stocky man with a trimmed brown beard, wearing a dark jacket and waistcoat that sported a gold watch chain across its front. His dark hat was unusual in that it had a curled brim, and around the low crown was a light coloured band. This was De Wet. He would be easy to see in a crowd.

He rode straight into the centre of the gathering and started to speak in a deep but very clear voice. "The British are fighting up the railway to Kimberley, but I think that the crafty old fox Roberts is going to try to swing around us." He paused. "I'm going to ride out east along the Riet River towards Fauresmith. If you want to come we may see the Khakis – if we don't, we'll have had a good ride."

He twitched the reins of his horse to ride further through the gathering; he was going east. It was as simple as that; it was the start of the ride. All the men slowly fell into a double line and followed this charismatic leader. They were eager to fight the British and they trusted De Wet to lead them.

Chapter 11

The British force left their camp in the middle of the night with all their tents still standing just in case someone was watching. The Line of British cavalry and Mounted Infantry, accompanied by RHA guns, plus 172 Battery, travelled south for almost two hours. Then it turned due east to cross the dried veldt. There was nothing ahead but inhospitable country interspersed with scrub and cut across with dongas. Undulating open country with the occasional kopje, those small flat topped hills so common on the veldt, that were an ideal place for a lookout, be he Boer or British.

Gradually the column swung towards the north and, as the sun climbed higher in the sky, a green smudge on the horizon told the column that they were close to the vegetation along the banks of the Riet River and the crossing at Waterval Drift.

Peter riding at the head of the Battery heard distant rifle shots. The Boers were obviously defending the crossing.

He could see an officer galloping down the line. "Major Rutland?" the rider called. "Yes," replied Peter.

The officer, a Captain from French's staff, rode close and spoke in lowered tones. "The crossing ahead is defended but the General feels that it's only a small force. Never the less, he's going to put a stopping force against them and ride a couple of miles up steam to cross at Dekiel Drift. He'll then attack this force from the flank and rear. You will be the right hand flank artillery for the stopping force, which is the 2nd Cavalry Brigade under Colonel Broadwood."

His horse sidestepped a boulder and bumped into Peter's. "If you will come with me sir, I will show you where the 10th Hussars will be taking up an attacking position on the right and where you are to come into action."

Peter waved to Julian, who came at a canter. "Julian, bring the guns on. I'm being shown where we're to come into action."

"Right sir."

Peter turned to the messenger. "Lead on, Captain." Both men cantered down the column for a short while and then the Captain stopped and pointed. "There sir. You can see the line of scrub bordering the river; the Boers are probably on both sides but Colonel Broadwood thinks they are only on the north side."

Peter nodded. "Where's the cavalry force?"

The Captain stood in his stirrups and looked around. "Over there sir." Peter could see a line of skirmishers lying down firing at the scrub line, at a distance of almost 1000 yards. They aren't going to do much good there, he thought.

"All right Captain, leave this to me and the Hussars."

"Thank you sir" The Captain turned his horse on a sixpence and galloped back to the column, which was now moving further east towards the second crossing. They were hoping to get there before the Boers.

Peter looked back and could see his Battery trotting up to his position. He was pleased to see that Julian had not stretched the horses by cantering up. He looked again at his target area and decided that the guns could come into action right here. They were far enough away to be almost out of rifle shot and yet could cover a large length of riverbank.

He faced towards the river and waved his arms to Julian, at the same time calling out, "Action Front!" The two guns came into action with a speed that greatly pleased Peter.

A horseman could be seen cantering up from the cavalry position. "Guns?" he called out.

Peter looked at a Lieutenant Colonel. "Yes sir."

"Bloody hell, just two?" exclaimed the Hussars commander.

"But specials, sir" replied Peter.

"Look Major, with just two guns we could be in a sticky position. As you can see we're meant to be a screening force just to hold the Boer attention on this flank but if he decides to attack in force, my men with carbines and only two guns aren't going to stop them."

"I think we will sir."

Peter dismounted and waved to Higgins to take his horse. He ran across to the guns. "Number 1 Gun ranging, shrapnel 1500 yards. Fire."

The Number 6 adjusted the fuse indicator and handed the shell to Number 4 who pushed the round, followed by the brass cartridge, into the breech; Number 2 slammed the breech closed. "Ready" called the Number 3 sitting in the layer's seat, his hand on the firing handle. "Fire," called Sgt McCann. BANG!

Peter watched through his field glasses and saw that the shell was slightly short. "1600 yards."

Again the drill of loading and firing was completed. This time the puff of shrapnel showed it was over the target area.

"Number 1 Gun, 5 rounds gunfire. Number 2 Gun, 5 degrees left, 5 rounds gunfire," shouted Peter.

The two guns started to punch out their rounds at a speed that was truly amazing. The instance a shell had been fired, another was being placed into the breech. It was almost fired before the previous one had hit the target.

"Bloody hell." The Hussar Colonel repeated himself. "That's incredible!"

De Wet had ridden hard and had been closely following the Riet River bank. After some time, one of his scouts rode in to tell him of a dust cloud some way off to the south. It must be the British he thought. But where would they cross?

Jan heard the order being passed down the line to prepare to ride hard and fight at a moment's notice but until then, they were to continue just moving along.

After an hour it was obvious to De Wet that the ford at Waterval Drift was the most likely but he did not have enough men to defend it and stop the British crossing. He sent a messenger back to Cronje telling him of the Khakis moving in force and asked for either more men now or a stronger defence position to be formed further back. Then he told his men to line the riverbank and prepare to fight a mass of British Cavalry as they crossed the river.

Jan slid off his horse, his rifle still slung across his back. He pulled the extra ammunition belt off the saddle and threw it over his left shoulder.

Henk was ahead of him, running crouched towards the riverbank. He waved to Jan to come on his right-hand side. Flopping down in the scrub, together they pulled some branches away from their line of sight and used them to cover their heads and shoulders. The view of the British was not good because there was too much scrub on the other side of the river but the area ahead would make a perfect killing ground as the cavalry charged across the river ford.

The two men lay with the rest of the Boer force in silence; they were certain that they had not been seen and they wanted the Rooineks to come really close before they realised that the ford was defended.

Then some idiot fired a shot! He fired it just to prove he could hit a horse or rider at 1500 yards.

The British column stopped and seemed to spread out, presumably in readiness to attack the river. The Boers saw a detachment of British horsemen ride a little closer. These men dismounted and started to fire from the prone position at the Boers.

"They've got more ammunition than sense," said Henk.

Jan lay with his weight on his elbows and his hands crossed over the breech of his rifle. He rested his chin on his hands and waited. How often had he adopted this position, allowing time to pass, waiting while hunting for an impala buck to slowly move into rifle range?

There was a great deal of dust rising from the British column as they moved about; it looked as though they were going to attack from downstream as the dust moved in that direction.

Then a howl, like a banshee, tore through the air followed by a crash! The British were using large guns at them. Jan and Henk had never been on the wrong end of artillery shells before and the noise made them both jump.

"Yow, Mutti!" exclaimed Henk "I don't like that."

Jan pushed his hat more firmly onto his head as though in protection "I think we're going to have a few more of those soon." Sure enough another howl and crash, but this time it was with the whistle of shrapnel flying through the leaves of the trees.

Henk wriggled lower into the undergrowth. There was a pause. "Maybe they're just showing us that they can fire and now they'll attack," he suggested.

"Maybe," replied Jan. "If so, I'm ready for them." He lifted his rifle, snuggled the butt into his shoulder and worked the bolt to slide a round into the rifle breech.

Then the rain of hell fell on them! Howl, Crash, Howl, Crash. Again and again the deadly metal tore through the undergrowth. A scream went up as one of the men of their commando was hit by a slicing piece of metal tearing into his chest. The Khakis were going to give them a hammering before they charged across the river.

Having fired the ten rounds, 172 Battery fell silent. The Colonel and Peter scanned the river edge for sight of any movement; other than dust in the air, all was still.

"That's given them something to think about," said the Hussar officer.

"Colonel, may I suggest that we try a bit of guile."

The cavalryman put down his glasses and looked at Peter, "What are you thinking?"

"Well, we are certainly not going to attack but if I give them a similar dose of shelling in a few minutes, and in the meantime we get our horses to mill around out of sight back here to create dust, the Boers will think that we are organising an attack. It'll make them concentrate on us rather than the main column, but they won't think of coming over this side of the river."

"Good idea. Our horses are back over there. I'll get them split up and move about towards the Boer left where we could swim the horses over if we were really pushed to it. They just might feel their retreat is going to be cut off."

"Very good sir. I'll move my horses with the limbers to make dust behind the guns. I'll repeat the shelling with different amounts at varying spaces so they won't know when to expect a dose of shrapnel."

The Colonel took one more look through his glasses then rode away to arrange his part in the deception.

"Lieutenant," called Peter. Julian ran over. "Sir."

Peter explained what had been agreed and told Julian to fire two rounds from each gun in three minutes.

Jan lifted his face from out of the dust where it had been pressed all the time the shells were flying in. He looked round at Henk, who still had his head buried in his hands and in the dust. Jan peered over the river bank and he could see some men lying down who were still firing their rifles, but with no effect as far as he could see. He heard a couple of cries from men around him who had been wounded by the shells and were being taken further back. That had been a terrible few minutes – and we had not been able to do anything. He shielded his eyes from the bright sunlight and peered out over the veldt. Where were the guns? Then he saw them. He could only see two of them. Presumably the rest were further round and out of his sight. Tiny figures moved around them and he saw a figure on horseback ride away over to the right. He pulled his rifle towards him and looking at the British guns tried to work out how far away they were. It was more than 1000 yards - 1500 yards? Or even further? He decided to call it 1800 yards and so pushed his leaf sights up towards the 2000 yard mark. I don't stand much of a chance of hitting any of them but at least I'll have had a go at them and they might even notice, he thought.

He gently pulled the bolt of his Mauser part way back and saw that a round was in the chamber. He pushed it forward to close it and lifted the butt to his shoulder. He looked out across the veldt to see how much the wind was stirring the dust. Not much but slightly from left to right. He decided to aim at the left hand edge of the Gunners so that any drift would put the round into their midst. He started to slowly squeeze the trigger - when he heard the howl and crash of more shells exploding above his head.

Peter looked through his field glasses towards the east – was that a cloud of dust from the column? Yes. They were coming up the riverbank, and would be at the Boer position in a few minutes' time. His guns had just finished firing a short pattern. "Lieutenant. Give the target two more rounds from each gun and then the cavalry'll be on them."

"Right sir." Julian shouted out the fire order to the two Sergeants as Peter watched the Boer position. The shells exploded above the riverbank, leaving dust in the air. The column would be on the enemy position very soon.

A few seconds after the shelling stopped, Jan lifted his head again and heard cries and shouts. Henk crawled from the bank and called out, "Jan, the Khakis are coming quick!"

Jan felt the fury in his heart. We have ridden hard, endured their bloody shells and now we must run. He lifted his rifle and aimed at the Gunners about a mile away. They seemed to be standing around having done their job, certain that they had done well and were not in any danger. He fired one shot, worked his bolt and fired again. Once more the bolt flew back and forth and once again with a steady hand he let another round off at the Rooineks. Maybe, just maybe, one of them noticed that a couple of bullets were coming their way. Then pulling the spare ammunition belt over his shoulder again, he picked up his rifle and, in a low crouch, ran as fast as he could back to the horses which were hidden in a depression behind the river.

Henk and a number of other Boers were already mounted and ready to go.

"Jan. Here!" called Henk. Jan pulled his rifle strap over his head and threw himself onto his horse's back, and then they were off at a gallop.

As Peter watched a line of cavalry getting closer to the Boer position, he saw movement of figures getting up from the bank and scurrying away. He could not see their horses; the Boer was too clever to leave his animals in danger.

Peter waved to Julian to bring the guns out of action. All of the Gunners felt pleased with themselves at how they had used the new guns in their first action. Peter knew that the hours of training had paid off and they had all done very well.

In their eagerness to act with speed to get out of action and limber up, Gunner Ash stumbled and fell over - but he did not get up! Sergeant McCann bent over him. "Medical Orderlies!" he shouted.

Peter ran over. "What's happened?"

"He's been shot sir," said McCann. Peter looked at Ash, who was moaning, with a growing bloodstain coming from the top of his trousers near to his hip.

Peter turned and looked back at the riverbank. If the bullet came from there, it was an amazing shot of up to 1600 yards. Or had it come from closer? He stood up and, with his glasses, scanned the ground in front of where the cavalry had been firing, but there was nowhere for a sniper to be hidden. It must have come from the riverbank.

He looked back at the Gunners as they limbered up the guns. We've all learned a lesson there, he thought. Don't be complacent. Those Boers can shoot far and accurately.

Chapter 12

General French, having seized both of the two Riet River crossings, stopped and rested his horses for just one day. He was about to take his force on the most dangerous and hazardous part of the attack. The Cavalry force was going to cross 25 miles of waterless veldt to take the Modder River crossings at Rondeval and Klip Drift.

The British Cavalry horses were strong beasts and, when they started from Ramdam, were very fit. But the weight that they carried totalled about 250 pounds; this was made up of the rider plus saddle, sword, carbine, blankets and coverings plus spare ammunition. These horses were all used to having good amounts of quality short feed, including oats, but now there was virtually nothing. Water from the Riet was welcome but the essential food was well behind the column, being brought up by the wagon train. The cavalry had moved fast but the essential supplies were moving much slower.

Eventually the column's wagon train arrived at 4 a.m., but there was no sign of BSM Hills and the 172 Battery supplies. An amount of feed for man and horse was distributed as quickly as possible, but the time taken for this meant that the dash for the Modder could not start before mid-morning. For the column to leave later into the evening was not an option; the General had strict orders to reach the Modder, and then push on to Kimberley - and he was to stop for nothing. But by noon, after three hours of riding, men and horses were suffering terribly. The sun high in the sky blistered them, while dust storms choked throats already parched.

The Batteries of the RHA had been placed on the extreme flanks of the advancing force but 172 Battery was kept just behind the main body. This helped with a shorter line but the dust created by the horses ahead made a terrible cloud for man and horse to breathe.

Twice Peter stopped and allowed the Drivers to wet the mouths of their horses and clean out their nostrils. The men were only permitted one mouthful of water each; the horses' welfare was the most important. He had spare blankets tied over the horses' backs to try and cover them to reduce the sunburn.

"A patrol coming in from the left, sir" shouted Sergeant McCann. Peter could hear gunfire coming from over to the left of the column.

A Staff messenger galloped up to the Battery. "Those kopjes over there, sir." He pointed at a range of low hills in a half-horseshoe shape to the left and left front. "We want covering fire as quickly as possible."

Peter nodded, turned his head to the guns and shouted out, "Action Left."

The two guns swung round, the Gunners unhitched the guns, the drivers moved the limbers on a few feet and the Gunners unhitched them to run them alongside the guns. The Drivers walked the horses behind the gun position and started to find what shelter they could for the horses in the way of tarpaulins or blankets, anything to reduce the sun's burning rays.

"Lieutenant," Peter called to Julian, "The target is the centre of those low hills." Julian acknowledged with a raised hand.

"Number 1 Gun ranging. Shrapnel 3500 yards. Fire." Peter shouted out the fire order and stood looking through his field glasses, trying to see exactly what the target was. The British column was moving over to the right, away from the hills but there was quite a gun battle going on further to his left. That must be the RHA on the flank, who were up against a Boer gun of some sort.

Bang! Number 1 Gun fired. A puff of smoke from the bursting shell showed slightly short of the top of the kopje.

"3750 yards Number 1 Gun. 5 rounds gunfire." He scanned the top of the hills again but could not see any sign of men or guns.

"Far left sir." called Julian. "A gun has just fired."

"Your target, Julian"

"Number 2 Gun ranging 4250 yards. Fire." As both officers watched for the result, a spurt of dust from the exploding Boer shell appeared in front of the English Cavalry that had been left to screen the guns.

Peter ignored this but scanned the site where Number 2 Gun's shell had flown. "I didn't see that fall of shot," said Peter.

"4000 yards," shouted Julian, and again the two men watched for the result. It appeared close to the place where they had seen the Boer gunfire.

"Number 2 Gun, 3 rounds gunfire."

The Battery slammed out the shells in a few seconds. "Rider coming in sir," called Sgt McCann.

The messenger reined in his horse and called out. "Rejoin the column, please sir," he called. Peter acknowledged and shouted out "Limber up."

Again the Drivers brought their mounts round to the guns, while the Gunners hooked each gun onto its limber, which was then hitched to the harness. The column ahead was moving fast; they were going to bypass the kopjes with the Boer force on and head directly towards the Modder River, which had to be crossed.

After an hour of hard riding, a line of greenery could be seen ahead. It was the vegetation on the banks of the river. Then to Peter's amazement the column seemed to split up with a considerable number moving further over to the right.

A Captain on the General's staff cantered up. "Major Rutland?"

"Yes," called Peter. The Captain came over and said, "We're doing the same here as we did back at Riet River, only we seem to be up against a larger number of Boers. The General's going instantly for the Klip Drift, which is a few miles upstream. The RHA has some guns out to the left and the General is taking the rest of them with him in case he hits opposition at Klip. He wants you to make as much trouble for the forces over there, especially on the right flank so that they won't think of joining the others at Klip."

"I shall want an ammunition wagon extra to my limbers," said Peter. "I can get through a great number of shells in a short time."

"Right sir, I will tell the General, who I am sure will give you what he can spare." He saluted and turned to gallop back to the Staff.

'All he can spare,' thought Peter. 'That doesn't fill me with confidence.'

He waved his arm in the air and circled it while shouting, "Action Left."

"Lieutenant!" he called out, while he pulled out his field glasses to look at the target area. It looked almost the same as at Riet River – except he saw a flash as a Boer gun was fired, then another, then a third!

The guns were almost in position when he called, "Number 1 Gun ranging shrapnel 3500 yards. Fire." Julian arrived as he was shouting the fire orders.

"Same as Riet River, we have to keep the enemy pinned down but they've just fired -" three explosions in front of him interrupted his sentence. It was incoming fire and it had fallen short by about 500 yards. The Boers were using High Explosive shells. "- something heavy at us." Peter completed his sentence.

Bang. Number 1 Gun fired. The two officers waited to watch the fall of shot. It was short. "4000 yards," shouted Peter.

After a short pause, Bang, Number 1 Gun fired. Again they waited and again they both saw the twinkling of the Boer guns being fired. The British Gunners were feeding their pieces that bit faster than the Boers but the shells were on their way and coming in.

"Still short sir" called Julian as he spotted the shrapnel burst. "Yes," replied Peter. "Battery fire, 5 rounds gunfire, 4250 yards."

Crash. The first of the three incoming shells quickly followed by the other two landed only 50 yards in front of the Battery position. Splinters of shell plus lumps of rocks whizzed around them and a cloud of dust rose into the air. The explosions of the HE shells were quite localised. If they fell right on the Battery, they would have a horrendous effect, but this would be difficult for the Boers to achieve.

Then the two guns from 172 Battery started their flow of shells. If they were exploding near the enemy guns, then their Gunners there were in a lot of trouble.

"Julian, with Number 2 Gun keep up a steady rate on that target, I am going to fire slightly more to the right to stop any one thinking of moving in that direction."

"They've fired again," called Julian.

"Hopefully they're still firing blind," said Peter.

But whoever the Boer Gunners were, they were having the difficulty of getting a very accurate fall of shot, so they had played a clever game. They had fired the three shells at slightly different ranges. Crash, the first shell landed as before 50 yards in front; the next landed just to the right of Number 1 Gun but the shell splinters flew mainly forward and so did no damage. The third shell went 50 yard beyond the guns and landed in front of the Battery's horses but not close enough to do harm.

Sergeant Piper instantly ordered his Drivers to move the horses back further from the guns, and to keep them well in hand so that, if Mr Boer did get their range, then his precious horses could be moved to another position very quickly.

Peter had moved to the side of the Battery position to try and see beyond the dust created by the Boer fire. The dusty soil was creating difficulties for both sides except that the shrapnel was not kicking up as much as the HE.

He scanned the area with his field glasses but still could not see any actual enemy. Number 1 Gun completed its fire order and the Gunners stood waiting.

Peter ran over to Sgt McCann and showed him where he wanted the shells to fall, slightly to the right of the present target, then he called out a fire order. "Number 1 Gun, 5 rounds gun fire."

Again the Gunners went into their automatic drill, and the guns banged out their deadly shells at a steady rate. Peter could hear Julian's orders to Number 2 so that they were also pumping the shrapnel to explode over the Boers' heads. Peter suddenly realised that there had not been any incoming shells. Surely we couldn't have hit all of them so that they were wiped out?

He stood behind Number 1 Gun because by now the dust from the Boer shells had settled. He heard horses bring up the next limber with more ammunition. The empty limber was taken away. He was just thinking about how long he could carry on firing if no replacement ammunition came for the column, when he heard the howl of incoming shells. The Boers, finding the shrapnel was hitting them too hard, had moved and, as they knew the range, it was easy for them to hit the Gunners accurately from their new position.

Again the Boer shells were staggered, but two undershot while just one landed smack in the middle of the Battery. Two Gunners were instantly cut down, but the guns were not hit. "Julian, did you see where those shells came from?" shouted Peter. He scanned the area with his field glasses, but it was too late. He would have to wait for the next dose of medicine unless Julian had seen them. Without lowering his glasses, he called again, "Julian, did you see where they came from?"

"Julian!" Peter shouted even louder still scanning the target area.

"No sir, I'm afraid I didn't," a weak voice sounded beside Peter. He turned and saw Julian covered in dust with blood running from a cut on his head.

"Are you all right?" Peter asked.

"Yes sir, just a slight cut. Number 2 Gun is still firing but we are running low on ammunition."

"I'll call up the other limber for you."

As Julian staggered back to his gun, Peter ordered a Gunner to run back to the spare limbers and get the next two brought up. If we don't get more stocks from the column soon, we are going to fall silent. Then he saw the Boer guns fire; they had moved some way over to the left. He ran down to Sergeant McCann. "Do you see those taller trees?" "Yes sir" "Well, aim slightly to the left." "Right sir."

"Number 1 Gun 5 rounds gunfire 4250 yards." Peter shouted. The incoming shells started to arrive still slightly short but one shell fell close to Number 2 Gun. The Number 4 Gunner spun round, his arm smashed by the flying metal, but again the actual gun was undamaged.

Peter thought, they can see us clearly now and they will simply close all three guns onto us. He peered through the dust haze again, when inspiration came to him.

"Sergeant Piper." He shouted at the top of his voice, "Sergeant Piper."

The Sergeant sprinted over as quickly as he could. "Yes sir."

"Get two teams of horses pulling two of the empty limbers with some tarpaulins dragging behind to create dust and get them to gallop about 50 yards in front of the guns but covering a line of some 200 yards. I am going to move the guns back as soon as you put up the dust screen. Understand?"

"Yes sir." Piper turned and ran as fast as he could to carry out the ruse.

Peter ran over to Julian. "I am going to get a cloud of dust in front of the guns soon. Move your gun back and well over to the left as soon as the cover takes effect."

"Right sir, but we've only got fifteen more rounds left."

"Damn it. Well, carry on to the end and then limber up."

Peter ran over to Sergeant McCann. "Keep firing the current order but when I tell you stop, move the gun by hand back about 100 yards and over to the right. Get the limber also."

"That limber's empty sir. Another one is coming up though."

"Bloody hell, that must nearly be our last one! Just keep firing until the dust starts to rise and I tell you to retire."

"Yes sir."

Through the dust Peter could just see that Julian's gun was still being fired and then he turned to see Sergeant Piper with two limbers, galloping from the horse lines out to the far right edge of the gun position. He was riding the lead horse himself and as they turned to run in front of the guns, he made the teams twist and turn so that the limbers skidded over the ground creating an impenetrable screen of dust.

"Cease fire!" shouted Peter. "Guns retire!" Both teams manhandled their pieces around and ran them back to their new positions just as another cluster of Boer shells arrived. Piper and his horses were safe; they were too close to the Boer guns to be effected. 172 Battery was not quite so lucky. One shell landed close to Number 1 Gun and the left wheel had half of the spokes smashed. The wheel would still just turn, but it would not bear the weight of the gun firing.

"Keep coming," shouted Peter. "Bring it back here." The gun team heaved and pulled the reluctant damaged piece back, then turned it to face the target.

"Get that wheel off." Peter ordered. "And use the wheel off the limber."

The Gunners knew what to do and they did it. Peter could see Number 2 Gun as it turned and started to fire again. Piper's teams were doing a great job, the dust clouds hung in the air and got thicker; the only trouble was that the Gunners could not see their target.

Peter ran to the side of the gun position but he had to go a long way before he was clear of the cloud. He shouted to his gun, "Fire one sighter at 4250 yards." But no one heard. He waved his arms and gestured for a Gunner to come over to him. Then he told the man to go back to Sergeant McCann and for him to relay the orders from Peter to McCann. It was crude but it was better than nothing. 'We are going to be out of ammo very soon.'

The sighter was fired and Peter watched for it, and saw the Boer guns fire again. McCann's shot was too far to the right. The Boer shells exploded on the previous gun site and added to the dust – that was the good news.

"10 degrees left," shouted Peter. The Gunner repeated the order. How on earth McCann was going to guess what 10 degrees was like when he did not have the arc? But he had to try. Bang. The shell was flying.

The Gunner relayed a message back to Peter. "Only nine more shells left."

Peter felt a knot in his stomach; what a catastrophe! New guns shooting well, but they would be useless without ammunition.

He looked over towards Number 2 Gun wondering how many Julian had. Then he saw a wagon. It looked like an ammunition wagon, making towards him from the rear. The column had sent some ammunition at last. Peter waved his arms and gesticulated towards Number 1 Gun. There was no time to load the limbers and then transfer them to the guns. It was risky but we must get some rounds direct to the guns to keep them going.

Then maybe if other wagons were behind, they could load up the empty limbers.

McCann fired again. It was almost on target. "5 degrees further left," shouted Peter. The Gunner passed the message on and again McCann fired. As he did so, Peter saw the Boer guns fire again, so shells were flying to them and from them. Which would be on target?

Peter saw his sighter explode just where he wanted. "5 rounds gunfire." he shouted just as the Boer shells arrived, as before, on the old gun site creating more dust.

Peter ran over to Number 1 Gun and the ammunition wagon. Two men were moving cases of shells and cartridges to behind the gun. "That'll do," said one of the men. Peter could not believe it. "Hills!"

The dusty, sweating man stood up and saluted. "Yes sir, looks as though we got here in the nick of time."

"Dead right. Take some over to Number 2 Gun."

"Right sir, then I'll unload the rest back there and fill the limbers. Sorry we're late."

Peter could not resist it. He smacked Hills on the shoulder. "Good to see you at any time, Sar'nt Major."

Julian staggered up to Peter. "Thank God Hills turned up. I was on my beam ends there for ammo."

"Right, Julian now we're going to give them a good pasting. Keep on aiming for the guns as I will. I'll stop Piper making a dust screen, then we'll both give them ten rounds each that should stop them for some time. I expect that the cavalry will be attacking from the other side soon .At least we've kept the Boers and their guns off the main force."

"Right sir," Julian staggered back to his gun. Peter waved to a Gunner who was back with the horses. "Take a horse and tell Sar'nt Piper to stop his dust making and come back to the lines at once."

"Yes sir."

Peter touched McCann on the shoulder, "Fire sighters on my command until I know you are hitting the target; we have the range so it is just the direction. I will stand away from the dust and direct you." He ran out to the right of the gun until he could see the riverbank. Bang. A pause then – yes, there it was. A good hit.

The dust was starting to clear, so Peter ran back to a position between the guns and shouted loudly "Battery 10 rounds gunfire." And then it started. Once again he was amazed at the rate of gunfire from just two guns. Just imagine what it would be like with a full six gun Battery.

As the fire programme went along, he could see that the Boer gun area was being badly hit – and then he heard a shout, "There's the Cavalry."

He scanned over to the right and sure enough a large group of horses were cantering down towards the Boer position. There would just be time to complete his fire programme before they arrived.

"Battery limber up."

The now weary Gunners lifted the guns by their trails and swung them round to hook them onto the limbers. They stood exhausted, while the horses were hitched on. Then they mounted, ready to start the move towards the column.

Peter walked back to the horse line and then over to where the rest of the Battery wagons were now standing. Hills saluted and handed Peter a pad. "Here's the casualty list sir."

Peter took it from Hills' hand and said, "Did you bring extra water?" "Yes sir, not a lot but enough for a cup of tea."

Peter smiled, "No, just a mouthful for each man, the rest for the horses. We will be stationed by the river shortly. We can drink then."

"Right sir."

Peter looked at the list. "Two dead. Five wounded - two of them badly." He saw that Julian's name was not on the list. He lowered the pad and looked around as the Battery, having limbered up, started to move off.

This part of the veldt where the guns had been in action showed the litter and detritus of battle - a lopsided limber, a broken wheel, scattered brass cartridge cases, and of course the ephemeral stains of blood where wounded men had lain or dying men's lives had drained into the dust. He walked over to his horse which was held by his batman Higgins. He took the reins and nodded to the Gunner to go and take his place with the Battery.

Mounting his horse, he again looked around at the magnificent and dramatic countryside; no wonder his cousin Jan thought it was the only place to be. Turning his horse to catch up with the Battery, he wondered if he would ever be able to ride and hunt with Jan up and down the kopjes around his father's farm.

Chapter 13

Twice in quick succession General French had outflanked the Boers and crossed two hazards that might have been used defensively by the enemy and caused the British a great deal of trouble. But his orders were that he still had to get to Kimberley, yet his horses were completely done in. They had ridden hard for over twenty-five miles of arid veldt at a very sharp pace under a scorching hot sun; they had then been used for two attacks within a couple of days, having only had the minimum of food and water.

Now French had to wait for the infantry to come up with the wagon train to hold the crossings he had won.

Peter found a reasonable place for the Battery to camp with some shade for the horses and yet not too far from the river and water. He was worried about the condition of the guns as they had not had the full maintenance done on them. In the gun park Julian and BSM Hills were catching up on it plus repairing the damaged wheel on Number 1 Gun.

"Well, Sar'nt Major, you certainly joined us at the eleventh hour. I take it you had a rather rough trip."

"Reasonably rough, sir" said Hills. "I was very lucky to have the extra few horses. I managed to get two more wagons and then I met up with Major Hoskins of the Green Howard detachment; apparently they hadn't had any transport vehicles given to them so I suggested that they could put their kit into the spare wagons if they would work along with us. He was delighted and we made a good team."

Hills paused and shook his head. "Without them I'd have had a very hard time crossing the Riet River. There was absolute chaos with horse-drawn wagon behind ox-drawn wagons behind infantry columns – it was a real mess. The Green Howards found a ford that I was able to use just above the normal drift. It was deep but we got ahead of the rest. If we hadn't, I wouldn't have arrived yet. If the Boers had turned up while the column was crossing, there would have been a complete disaster."

Peter looked at the recoil carriage on Number 1 Gun, which was open for greasing. "Is it all looking all right?" he asked.

"Yes sir, but did you know we only have a gallon of the glycerine oil. There's only enough for a few weeks of average use."

"I've sent a message to the RA stores at De Aar but nothing so far. I might have to send a detachment back to get our spare stock." He walked over to Number 2 Gun where Julian, with his jacket off and rolled up sleeves, was working on the recoil system. He still had a bandage around his forehead but no sun helmet.

"Everything all right, Julian?" asked Peter.

"Yes, but I'm having trouble in getting the drain plug for the recoil system to sit properly and not leak. I've used up a pint of oil already in the last lot of firing."

"What have you tried?" asked Peter.

"I drained the whole system down and collected the glycerine then made a leather washer to fit around the drain plug bolt. It stops all the leaking when standing but I don't know how it will stand up to the pressure of firing."

"Right, I'll send another urgent message for the spare oil stocks. How are you feeling with your wound?"

"Oh, I'm all right, sir. A bit annoyed at having a perpetual headache without having had a good party to cause it."

"Wear your helmet as much as possible. In this sun you could be badly hit."

"I'll put it back on when I've finished with this maintenance. It won't stay on over these bandages."

"How have the gun and the crew been working?" asked Peter.

"It's bloody marvellous as far as fire rate. It's jolly easy to move by hand on those wheels but I think they're too light for the normal work on this terrain."

"Yes, I've had to replace one damaged by shell fire but the limber wheels seem good as spares. How were the crew?"

"Good, very good. Hazzer is a good Number 1 but I had to dress him down because he had another go at Bombardier Kirkby. I wouldn't like to lose him so I gave him a right roasting. I hope he'll take notice."

Peter pulled a wry face. "I hope you're right. But if it gets too bad, I'll back you if you want him off the site."

"God, I hope not. He's good at his job and it would be difficult to replace him."

Peter nodded and turned to walk towards the horse line. Sgt Piper in his shirtsleeves was working with the drivers on the horses. All of the men were in helmets with the neck shades hanging down the back.

"How are the horses now, Sar'nt?"

"Bloody awful sir, beggin' your pardon, sir, but I don't think half of them can go on much more. We must have some better food."

"HQ said that we have to manage with what we've got until we reach Kimberley. That's another 30 odd miles with a couple of days' fighting."

"Gor blimey, sir, my old Dad would turn in his grave if he knew 'ow we is working these horses. He was a Huntsman with the Fox Hounds and very proud about how his horses were turned out. I've seen the Mounted Infantry's horses, sir; they are in a terrible state. They know sweet … sorry, nuffink about how to handle and care for them. It's not the men's fault, they should have been trained better."

Peter nodded. "I'll have another go at HQ but I'm afraid the answer will be the same. At least we're in a better way regarding the carrying of spare water, so do your best, Sergeant."

Piper saluted. "I certainly will, sir."

As Peter walked back to his gun park, he saw a line of cavalry riding past the Battery site. It was the 19th Dragoons. He could see Colonel Crumpton Smythe leading them with Nick Ramsay riding beside him. Peter waved an acknowledgement and Nick trotted over. "Good to see you, Peter. Heard about your quick firing guns. They sound pretty damn good."

Peter smiled, "They are bloody marvellous. Have you been in any action yet?"

Nick shook his head. "No, but I think tomorrow looks like the first of a big move."

"How's your Colonel?" asked Peter. Nick looked back at the cavalry line moving by and said, "He's very ill. I think he might keel over any day." He twitched his reins and turned his horse. "Take care, Peter."

"You too Nick" replied Peter as he watched him canter back to his position alongside his dying commander.

What an awful position to be in, thought Peter. Then he remembered the Colonel's wife Georgia, and the lovely evening they spent together. I wonder where she is now.

As he walked back to his tent, he took off his helmet and wiped the sweat from his brow. He put it back on his head and looked up to see the one sight he truly wanted to see; Higgins, his batman, holding a tumbler of whisky ready for him. What a marvellous man.

After five days in Cape Town, Georgia left the Mount Nelson Hotel to travel by train to see her elder sister Isabella, who had a house just outside De Aar. She arranged with the hotel to keep her two large trunks that had not been wanted on voyage but she took three cases for her stay. She was not quite sure about the level of social life her sister had, but Georgia decided to take too much rather than be considered the poor little sister. Having boarded the train with her baggage, she settled down to a long journey.

When she eventually reached the bustling station at De Aar, she felt utterly worn out after the very tedious trip. The coach attendant helped her by taking her cases off the train and stacking them on the platform. She looked around as the group of passengers who had alighted with her departed, but she did not recognise anyone around, certainly not her sister.

On the open platform she stood in the sun's full glare, with her long skirts and full coat, plus naturally her hat, feeling the heat beat down on her. She quickly became aware that she could not stay where she was for much longer – it was just too hot!

A Cape cart pulled up and a woman climbed out calling, "Georgia."

"Izzie," replied Georgia. Isabella put her arms around her sister "Oh, Georgie, it is lovely to see you again."

Georgia hugged her in return, "It's marvellous to be here with you after all these years."

Isabella held her at arm's length. "For goodness sake. Take off that hat and coat you'll bake in all those clothes." She took hold of Georgia's hat and pulled it off, disregarding hat pins and coiffured hair.

"That's better, my girl," Isabella smiled. "Come on take that coat off and let's get your baggage on the cart."

Georgia obeyed her elder sister, who had always been the active one of the pair. Izzie had ignored tradition, and the establishment, by marrying her school time sweetheart, who had decided to become a doctor and practise, not in a fashionable area of New England or Virginia, but on the African continent, which turned out to be in Cape Province in South Africa.

The two sisters loaded the Cape cart, clambered on board and, with Izzie taking the reins, they set off. Within minutes they were in deep conversation and laughing to the point of crazy giggling as they trotted along the dusty road that led to Izzie's house. Georgia gradually became aware of the awesome beauty of the arid countryside. She fell silent as she looked at the dry veldt with occasional clumps of trees but she sensed its grandeur. "This is amazing," she said.

"Why?" asked Isabella.

Georgia paused before she replied. "An hour ago I was the Colonel's lady, all dressed up, accompanied by her necessary baggage waiting for a porter to load it all on a carriage. I would arrive at my hotel where I would be greeted by the manager and taken to my room, there I could slowly undress and prepare myself to meet company. Instead I have to load my own baggage on a cart, my hat and coat are thrown on top and my sister is driving the cart taking me to her house. This is the second time in the past few days that I've been taken down a peg – and I must admit I liked it."

"The second time?" asked Izzie. "What happened at the first time?"

"I'll tell you all about that later," replied Georgia. "Now tell me about your house and about your husband Franklin. I never really got to know him before you left."

Izzie turned to look at her sister. "He's all I ever wanted," she said. "He's so generous of spirit yet strong, and a marvellous father."

"I suspect he's a great lover as well," smiled Georgia.

The house at Dieput was a couple of miles out of the junction of De Aar. It was a large sprawling dwelling house set in farm grounds. Izzie had two boys of two and four years of age.

The sisters sat in the large, cool kitchen while the two boys were playing outside with their black nanny, a bright looking young woman. Georgia could hear the screams of pleasure as the children romped about.

"This looks perfect for you," said Georgia. Izzie got up and started peeling some potatoes. "It is," she replied. "Franklin works very hard. Without the money from his parents and ours we couldn't stay here and live like this. He'll treat anyone who calls, black, white, yellow or coffee coloured. But he's very satisfied with what he does, though some of the landowners around would prefer him to just treat them and not the natives."

She looked out the window. "Well well, here he is." She went to the door opened it and stepped outside to call. "Franklin, Georgie's here."

She stood at the open door until her husband came up and kissed her. He was a tall, almost gangling man with a kindly though gaunt face; he looked just the man you could talk to and trust his opinion.

"How's my favourite sister-in-law," he said as he came over and bending down, kissed Georgia on the cheek. Georgia had forgotten that he had a slow Southern drawl to his deep voice. She understood instantly why Izzie had fallen in love with him and yes, this is a man I could trust.

"I'm very well but tired and in a state of shock."

"Anything I can prescribe to assist?"

"Izzie has already given me some wine for the weariness, but the state of shock is that I am no longer the spoilt English lady but just another American girl with her bossy sister."

"I know what you mean. She bullies me as well." He flopped down into an easy chair.

"This is a marvellous home you have here," said Georgia.

"Sure do," he replied stretching out his legs. "It's all due to this little lady here." He smiled at Izzie. "So no babies yet, Georgia?"

"Franklin!" said Izzie. "That is very pushy, and mind your own business."

Georgia smiled and looked down at her hands folded in her lap. "No, Franklin, no babies yet."

Franklin stretched his arms above his head and said, "I suppose Gerard is up country with Robert's forces. How is he?"

Georgia paused then still looking down at her folded hands, she said, "He's ill. I think he's very ill."

Izzie looked up from her cooking; Franklin slowly lowered his arms and turned his head to Georgia. "What do you mean?"

Georgia, with her head still lowered, spoke softly. "Over the past number of months he has changed so much. He has always smoked cigarettes a lot, but then he developed a bad cough that's gradually got worse.

His chest gives him so much pain; he's lost his appetite and so much weight that he seems to be just skin and bone. He finds that whisky gives him relief - but his personality has changed. He's too proud to discuss anything as mundane as his health with me, or even with anyone. I've seen bright red blood on his handkerchief but I just cannot talk to him, and he can't talk to me."

Izzie looked at her husband and her eyes asked a silent question. He put it into words. "You know the truth don't you, Georgia." She nodded and then closed her eyes and squeezed them tight, but this did not stop the tears from falling onto her hands.

"He's dying, isn't he?"

Franklin nodded. "Yes, and I think he knows it. He doesn't need a doctor to tell him."

Izzie moved quickly across the kitchen to stand beside Georgia and cradled her head. "Oh, Georgie, I'm so sorry." She bowed her head so that both sisters wept together.

Franklin quietly rose from his chair and went outside to his laughing, playing children – he left the two sisters in their sorrow.

That evening as the three of them sat on the stoep after dinner, Izzie said to Georgia, "What are you thinking of doing. You can stay here as long as you like but have you any plans?"

"It all depends how long this campaign is going last," replied Georgia. "If it looks as though it is going last longer than a month or so, I will go back to England and wait for Gerard there."

"Campaign, you call it," said Franklin. "Sounds like an army expression to me. This is a war, almost a civil war. And it ain't going to be over in a month. The British have had one surprise already, and I'm certain sure they're in for a couple more."

"What do you mean?" asked Georgia.

"I don't know about fighting but for certain sure the Boers won't roll over in a few months. They've already given the British Army a bloody nose and they know how to use the country, while the Army doesn't." He looked out at the vast area of land before him and quietly said, "There's a helluva lot more blood to be spilt before it all ends."

"You said the British were in for two surprises. What is the second?"

Franklin sat upright in his chair and leaned forward, his elbows on his knees. "From the little I've learned about the British Army, they've mainly fought campaigns where they're always on the move. They've never spent a long time where they have thousands of men all in one place. And if they have, there's been plenty of good water." He paused. "Here they'll all be on top of one another with poor water and sanitation and they'll start to die like flies with enteric fever and even cholera. When that starts, even the healthy'll start to die."

Georgia was reminded of Peter's wife Beatrice. "When we were on the ship coming over, I met an Artillery officer whose wife was a doctor, but she'd worked in the East End of London and she died of typhoid."

"Yup, that's the problem. Poor sanitation, bad water and too many people together. You said his wife was a doctor?"

"Yes, she qualified in London and spent a number of months each year working with the poor in London, but the disease got her."

"Wow, that's some lady. To become a doctor among all those stuffed shirts with dinosaur brains is one helluva thing to do. And then she died; that's really a bad deal."

"When he told me of his wife," Georgia explained, "it was then I realised I'd been such a pampered individual. I said I was going to get to know the men of Gerard's regiment. He said that it would be appreciated by the men."

"But maybe not by the officers?" queried Franklin.

"You may be right but I think I must try. But tell me, both of you, why did you decide to come to South Africa?"

Franklin leaned back in his chair again. "Simple, because this lovely woman seduced me into it. I wanted to stay in the lap of luxury in New York but, oh, no, 'let's go to South Africa.' she said and here we are."

Georgia looked at Izzie, who smiled but kept silent.

"Well, maybe it wasn't all her fault," added Franklin. "And shucks, I've kinda grown to like it here. You know I don't have a political opinion; I'm an American doctor who treats any one, black or white, Boer or English or anything else. The blacks pay what they can. I get a bowl of dried mealies or a lump of impala from them as a 'thank you'. The Boers give the minimum that they think they can get away with, while the funny old English pay well because they think the more they pay the better treatment they get. I'll never get rich but it's marvellous to be living in this fantastic country. There are the riches of learning about the natives and how they use and adapt to the land. It's incredible."

Georgia watched him as he spoke in adulation of the land. Then she said, "When you next go to see your native patients, may I come with you?"

He turned to look at her and said. "Nope, not if you are wearing those clothes, but, if Izzie'll get you something suitable, you're welcome to come along."

And so Georgia started to learn what life was like when she was not seen as a Colonel's lady.

Chapter 14

Colonel Eustace, Commander Royal Artillery, stood outside his tent with a map mounted on a framework. All the Battery commanders of the Royal Horse Artillery and 172 Battery Royal Field Artillery stood in front of him as he gave the necessary orders for the start of the day's action.

"You'll see that there is a long, wide valley ahead of the force that narrows at the end where the road leads to Kimberley. The end of the valley is overlooked by this horseshoe line of hills that the Boer are occupying. We think that they have a few guns, but there are one hell of a lot of rifles, all well entrenched and ready for the cavalry to charge – which is exactly what we are going to do. The General is going to mass all of his cavalry and Mounted Infantry to sweep across the open country and totally overwhelm the Boer forces in one enormous cavalry charge.

"Our instructions are to supply artillery cover, firing onto the hills here and here." He pointed to the line of hills on the map at the end of the shallow valley. "You will continue to fire until you consider it is dangerous for the cavalry but you must maintain this fire for as long as possible. Is that understood?" The Battery Commanders nodded their acceptance of the orders.

"It is as simple as that, gentlemen. Keep firing as long as you can to give all possible support to the cavalry. Here are your specific positions." He then showed each Battery where they were to be positioned for the coming battle.

The BCs returned to their Batteries and ordered them to move into their allotted sites. 172 Battery was situated to the right of the valley where Peter could see the whole area to be covered but especially the position he was expected to bombard.

"Battery ranging shrapnel 5000 yards," he shouted. Both guns elevated to the ordered range, the Numbers 6 wound the range onto the fuse, and the guns were loaded. Then they waited.

Through his field glasses Peter watched as the whole mass of 6,000 horsemen manoeuvred into their positions, preparing for an enormous charge. It would be the largest charge since the Crimea when only hundreds of cavalrymen were involved. Here there were thousands. Though a number of horses were not fit to gallop the whole way, the sheer number would be overwhelming. The Boers might have a field day in shooting at the incredibly large target but in the end they must be swept away by the wave of lancers and swordsmen. The mounted force started forward. The 9th and 16th Lancers were in the lead, and instantly the two guns that Cronje had sent with the burghers started to fire. The RHA on the wings opened fire to range in on the enemy artillery and quickly silence them.

When he saw the start of the charge, Peter shouted, "Fire!" Both Ehrhardt guns threw their shells towards the enemy position. Julian and Peter watched for the telltale sign of the explosions. They were well short.

"5500 yards. Fire," Peter shouted. Again both guns coughed out their shells and again both officers waited.

"Spot on," said Julian.

"5500 yards 15 rounds Gunfire," shouted Peter, and the Battery started to pour shells onto the Boer positions.

The mounted force was now cantering down the valley but they were almost hidden by the dust they created. The Boers could only see the front few horses while the remainder were in an enormous dust cloud but they started to shoot and the whole line of hills ahead seemed alive with the sparkle of their rifle fire.

Then, with just one thousand yards to go, the buglers of the front regiments sounded the charge and the weary horses drew on their last ounce of energy and threw themselves towards the enemy in true Light Cavalry tradition. There were enemy rifles to the front of them and rifles to the left and right but they did not stop or falter. It was death or glory. Wave after wave of horsemen with their pennants and guidons flying and lances and sabres poised, charged in one overwhelming mass. It was an incredible, impressive, impossible sight never to be forgotten. Peter watched in awe.

The Battery finished their Fire Order well before the RHA Batteries, and before the cavalry reached the end of the valley.

"5500 yards 5 rounds gunfire," shouted Peter while he and Julian watched this amazing charge of the British forces. It was splendid. It was heroic. It was breathtaking. Nothing could stand in their way – and the Boers didn't. They fled, with only a few being caught by the dipped deadly lances and slicing cavalry swords.

The way to Kimberley was open. The Boers were routed, while British losses were amazingly small, just twelve men dead and wounded. It was a British triumph. But soon disaster would strike them where it would hurt them badly.

When De Wet was forced from his position on the Riet River he had only lost four men but he knew that though he would not be in a position to attack the British force head on, they were dependent on their line of supply that must follow behind them, on almost the same line as they had advanced. He decided to wait until the main force had passed him, and then on 18th February he moved with his force which had been enlarged to almost 1,000 men and two guns, back to a crossing on the Riet and there he was going to ambush them.

Jan waited in a shallow donga edged with short scrub, close to the crossing with the rest of his commando. Henk sat on his horse close beside him. They both had their rifles across their laps ready for use. They could see the land sloping down to the Riet River about half a mile away, it was a rocky patch with tufted sword grass and short scrub.

The dust of a British transport column of some 170 wagons showed its progress across the arid veldt. The Boers waited patiently. After some time the leading wagon section crossed the river and the lead oxen were being allowed to rest; they were exhausted after the long pull with poor food and little water. It was as they waited the arrival of the rest of the column, with the river splitting the line that De Wet struck.

The Field Cornet in charge of Jan's commando waved his arm. Jan and Henk slid off their horses, and with other Boers, tied their horses to the scrub. Then, crouching low, they scrambled out of the donga and on to the open veldt where they could see the khakis pulling bales and biscuit tins crates off the wagons to use as a defensive wall. The two men lay flat on the dusty soil in a slight depression and started shooting at a range of about 500 yards. Henk was firing very quickly with little pretence of aiming but his bullets were close enough to keep British heads down. Jan was much more selective. At this range he knew he could hit almost anything he shot at that was larger than a melon. He sighted at a helmet and head that was peering from the side of a bale and, with a slow squeeze of the trigger, knew that he had not only hit the man, he had killed him. He looked for another target and spotted an officer who was crouching behind the crates, directing his men to get more rifle fire at the Boers, but he kept peering over the crates; it was his death knell. Jan squeezed his trigger again and knew that with two shots he had killed two Rooineks.

Henk had slowed his rate of fire as there was little return fire from the British. A howl of a shell flew over their heads; it was not from the Khakis but their own artillery that had fired at the mass of oxen milling around the river bank. Instantly the animals stared to panic and, mixed with a number of mules, they lumbered off in various directions despite the attempts of the native drivers to control them. The beasts either died in lines while pulling the wagons or in clusters where they were standing at rest. It was an ugly scene but it was war.

The British support gradually concentrated their fire and made the Boers pull back to a safer range of 700 or 800 yards. Both sides then took time with their shooting and started to score hits. The Boers were more numerous, while the small British contingent could little afford to lose anyone, so they steadily improved their defensive position with crates, bales and boxes. It looked as though it was going to be a long drawn out fight. The Boers could not afford to take too much time otherwise the British would send strong reinforcements, or would they? When Bobs learned of the ambush, he decided, after some thought, that he could not spare any men to recover the lost goods because he was on the track of his main quarry. Cronje at long last had decided to move; all his burghers and their wives and children were on the move, and Bobs wanted to head them off.

Jan and Henk had been firing carefully and selectively for the past couple of hours; they both reckoned they had killed or wounded at least nine khakis.

"Look, they're moving," called Henk. "On the right, up the river banks."

Jan slithered to the side of the rock he had been firing from and saw that the Khakis seemed to be fewer behind the defences and there certainly was some movement of men on horses over to the right.

"They're leaving the wagons and running," shouted Henk. It was true, the British had had enough and now they were off, leaving a mass of materiel that was essential to them but the actual soldiers were more important to General Roberts.

The Boers watched as the Rooineks retreated behind a mask of rifle fire and then marched off towards Jacobsdaal.

Over the next 24 hours De Wet organised the removal of this incredible bounty while his men found food and the clothing, especially boots that they were desperate for.

A scout came back from a column of 200 Boers led by Commandant Lubbe with a report that Cronje's force had left Kimberley but that Roberts was close behind and might head them off before they reached Bloemfontein. De Wet decided to follow Roberts so that the chaser would also be chased. He hoped to inflict damage on the British that would make them turn, and relieve the pressure on Cronje. For this venture he had some 400 to 500 Boers with two guns, one Krupp field gun and one Maxim-Nordenfeldt.

His horses were well fed, his men rested and also well fed, so he started the chase.

Chapter 15

After supporting the cavalry charge at Klip Drift, the men of 172 Battery all hoped that they would be able to sample the joys of a stay and rest in Kimberley for a few days before moving on – but that was not to be. They were ordered to remain at Klip to protect the infantry who were to hold the crossing until the wagon trains had passed through. The rest of the column had gone on to Kimberley and were hoping to attack Cronje. But Cronje was still convinced that the British would stay with the railway, until he learned of the swing around the flanks and that he would be cut off from Bloemfontein unless he moved now and moved quickly. He did move now but when he did, he insisted on taking his 400 wagons, carrying women and children with him, so he did not move quickly.

At first good fortune was with them in that his 5,000 men and their families moved east for two days without being spotted, and then Colonel Hannay's Mounted Infantry saw a dust cloud and so discovered the main Boer force steadily plodding east towards Bloemfontein.

General French's cavalry, on totally worn out horses, was sent out to stop them. He managed to head the Boer column off at a crossing of the Modder River called Paardeburg. Cronje, again if he had acted with a military mind, could have left his wagons, plus women and children, and made a break for Bloemfontein with his fighting force. But the farmer mentality would not allow him to leave them. They were in fact all their worldly possessions – where they were, he would remain.

At dawn, Peter was standing by his tent looking down the Riet River at the rising sun when he saw an officer walking towards him.

"Major Rutland?"

"Yes." Peter saw that the officer was also a Major but an infantryman of the Green Howards. "Hallo, I'm Geoff Hoskins; I met your Battery Sergeant Major back in Ramdam. We travelled up with him. You've got a good man there."

"I know I have," smiled Peter

"'Fraid I haven't got time for pleasantries. I've just had orders telling us to move at once or even earlier east, keeping one mile from the banks of the Modder towards a crossing at Paardeburg. I've been told to tell you to accompany us as we're about to have a confrontation with our Boer friend Mr Cronje."

Peer nodded. "I'll get moving straight away."

"Sorry about the scramble and also I've been put in command of the column. Are you senior to me?"

"Doesn't matter, Major," said Peter. "I'll be happy to be under your command of the column."

"Many thanks," said Hoskins, "I have two companies of my regiment plus two companies of the 2nd Buffs here. I'd like to start as soon as possible. When can you be ready?"

"I can have the Battery on the move in 30 minutes."

"That's fine. I'll order a start in half an hour."

"May I suggest you say three quarters of an hour? That'll give me time to fill up every container with water that we can carry on the wagons plus limbers."

Hoskins smiled. "Excellent, I'll make it 45 minutes. You seem to be as good as your BSM."

Peter laughed. "Maybe one day." He saluted the Major and turned to call Julian and Hills to tell them the orders.

One hour later the column of artillery and infantry were marching in line, a mile below the banks of the Modder, heading east.

The march was a distance of only about 12 miles and with an early start, they hoped to avoid the extreme heat and the dust and arrive in about five hours.

The infantry marched and the Gunners walked. All the 172 Battery officers and sergeants led their horses knowing that the animals might be needed in emergency and they were certainly not just to carry a man from one area to the next.

As they marched along the Modder valley, Peter was amazed at the number of farms they passed. This was true Boer farming country; here they bred their cattle and grew their mealies. He saw chickens and pigs, heard farm dogs barking and lowing cattle. This was what the Boers were fighting for – to live free from foreign control of thought and religion. Was it all as simple as that? He was not sure.

In fact it was just after four hours, and a mile or so short of their objective, that they first heard firing. It seemed to be mainly rifle fire but the occasional report of gunfire could be heard.

Major Hoskins called a halt. A Green Howards Captain rode up to Peter. "The Major is sending a patrol ahead to find out where HQ is. He doesn't want to bump into Mr Boer just yet. He said that he'll keep you informed." Peter nodded. The Captain saluted and cantered back to the head of the column. The noise of firing was now more intense and getting louder.

"Sar'nt Major," shouted Peter. Hills ran up. "Yes, sir?"

"I think we're going to be in action shortly. Get the support wagons together and find a place to camp when the guns are called away."

"Very good, sir"

A rider could be seen galloping back to the head of the column. He stopped for a second, spoke to the Green Howards Major, then kicked his horse again and rode up to Peter. He stopped his sweating horse and saluted. "Major Rutland BC of 172 Battery, sir?"

"Yes," answered Peter.

"A message for you, sir," The orderly handed Peter an envelope, which he immediately opened. It was an order to report with the Battery to Colonel Eustace, Commander Royal Artillery.

"Do you know where Artillery HQs are?" Peter asked.

"Yes sir. Shall I lead you?"

"Yes." Peter climbed up into his saddle, turned and waved his arm to the guns. The Battery started into a trot behind him as he followed the messenger. After five minutes' riding, he could see a cluster of wagons and a number of tents.

"The RA Head Quarters are in the large tent to the right, sir," said the orderly.

Peter called to Julian "Halt here. I'll report to the CRA." He trotted up to the tent and dismounted. A duty Gunner took his horse's reins for him. Peter entered the tent that was more a marquee than a tent. At the end was a cluster of officers around a large table. Peter approached and saw Colonel Eustace, in charge of all the Royal Artillery in the area. He saluted. "Major Rutland reporting, sir."

"Ah yes, Rutland, 172 Battery," Eustace looked down at the map. "Have a look at this," he pointed to a sketch of the current position showing the Modder River as a wiggly line running diagonally across the page from the southwest to the northeast. Just north of the start of the line was shown a hill named Paardeburg. On the north side of the river were a number of ridges behind the actual riverbed.

"Cronje is entrenched along the northern river bank and in front of these ridges," Eustace explained. "We cannot attack across the river itself as it is too deep, and he is protected by the steep banks in front of him."

The map showed that the south side of the river also had ridges some four miles in length plus a small hill or kopje. "For reference we are calling this hill Kitchener's Kopje. Apparently it's called Stinkfontein," continued Eustace. "I want you to move a mile beyond it and start to bombard the Boer trenches from a position as close to the river as you think is safe."

"My Battery has the Quick Firing guns, sir," said Peter "They are not exactly suited to sheer bombardment."

Eustace looked up at Peter and gestured for him to move to the side of the tent away from the other officers. "I accept your valid comment Major, but for the sake of the infantry, just go and do it. Very confidentially, Kitchener has got a bloodlust on him. Bobs is ill in Jacobsdal. Bloody Kitchener arrived here late yesterday with infantry who had marched in appalling conditions at an incredible speed. This morning he started an attack at dawn and predicted that we'd be in the Boer position by 10.30 a.m. He can't use the heliograph because it's cloudy and so he can't communicate with them properly. As they're not jointly controlled, the infantry are making piecemeal attacks without any real hope of success and they're incurring large losses. The Artillery is not being used to support these attacks that seem to be totally uncoordinated. You're an extra Battery on my list, so go and hammer the Boer position wherever you can from that northeastern position just to help the poor bloody infantry. It's an awful mess, so just do what you can. Do you understand?"

Peter was astounded to hear such outright criticism of the commanding General, replied, "No, I don't understand sir, but I will act as you say."

"Good man, do your best for the infantry's sake. That's the main thing. The Boers have some artillery but I think it's only a few guns, maybe just pom-poms."

Peter saluted and walked quickly to the tent entrance. He mounted his horse and rode over to Julian at the head of the Battery. "Sar'nt Major," he called. Hills rode up in a cloud of dust. "The guns are moving up river about three miles. Make the camp a few hundred yards behind the gun position that I choose when we get there."

"Right, sir," replied Hills and pulling his horse round rode back to the supply section.

"Julian, bring on the Battery to follow me and then join me so I can explain our orders."

Julian saluted, turned to wave the Battery forward, then put spurs to his horse to catch up with Peter, who was trotting well ahead.

The Battery rode over land that was deeply cut by innumerable gullies and channels, all within a mile of the Modder River. Peter and Julian could see the Boer entrenchments along the high steep cliffs that edged the riverbank. The surrounding land had thickets of mimosa and thorn that spread across the land to a depth of some hundred yards. The north bank that the Boer occupied above the cliffs had been fortified with trenches that made the position almost impregnable to attack, and meant that the defenders could use low trajectory fire against the attackers. It was obvious that the infantry would have a very hard time from this angle unless they were heavily supported by the guns. But where would they be attacking from?

Peter told Julian what Colonel Eustace had ordered them to do and the comments he had made about the general. Typically Julian did not make any comment other than letting his eyebrows rise in surprise.

The hill called Kitchener's Kopje, was easily spotted as it was the only high ground other than the ridges. The Battery passed it and, after a mile or so, Peter stopped and, with his field glasses, viewed the river bank. He could clearly see the Boer entrenchments and beyond them, what looked like wagons. The river was about 2000 yards away so he felt safe from rifle fire while he could shell the wagons and camp as he wished.

"Action left." He shouted. The two teams of horses swung the guns in an arc and the pieces and limbers were swiftly unhitched and swung to face the river. Hills moved the wagons to the rear and had the spare limbers in line some two hundred yards behind the guns ready to supply the extra ammunition.

Peter spoke to Sgt McCann telling him to aim at the Boer wagon park. "Number 1 Gun ranging. High Explosive, 2,500 yards. Fire."

Bang! A cloud of dust rose to the right of the wagons and short. "Five degrees left. 2600 yards."

Bang! It looked a very close shot.

"Battery, 5 rounds gunfire." Peter decided to fire short patterns slowly and accurately. The Battery started to spew out its parcels of death and destruction. Dust rose from the target area and then suddenly an enormous flash of yellow shot up and a large cloud rose into the air.

"That must've been an ammunition wagon," suggested Julian, still looking through his glasses. Peter nodded.

When the fire order had been completed he looked around to see where any infantry were, especially those he was meant to support. A great deal of rifle and gunfire could be heard from the left, down to the south of the river. There must be an attack going in there.

It all seemed unreal. The fighting was close but not near to him, yet he was meant to be covering infantry. He again looked through his field glasses to find where the nearest British force was. Maybe he should move back closer to Kitchener's Kopje. Other than the wagons it seemed that the Boers were well entrenched and would not be hit easily with a few guns.

"Lieutenant," he called, "The gun crews can stand down and rest for a while."

Julian raised his arm in acknowledgment.

Peter walked to the side of Number 2 Gun and again swept the area to the south looking for British forces or enemy targets. Where the hell shall I go?

He heard a shout behind him and turned round; Bombardier Kirkby and Sergeant Hazzer were face to face. Kirkby swung a punch at Hazzer that seemed to just hit him on the cheek. Hazzer stepped back and turned to walk away, as Kirkby shouted at him.

"Sergeant Hazzer, Bombardier Kirkby," Peter shouted. "Here at the double!"

Both men ran over, halted and saluted. "What was that all about?" asked Peter. Neither man replied. Then Hazzer said, "Nothing, sir." Peter knew it was time to act. "Bombardier, return to your gun." Kirkby saluted and doubled back to the No 2 gun position.

Peter turned to Hazzer. "Sergeant, I know what that was all about. You have been warned twice but have not listened. You are relieved of duty as Number 1 and will stay with the spare ammunition wagons until I get a relief for you."

"But he hit me, sir!" argued Hazzer.

"He hit you because you taunted him," replied Peter. "You have acted very foolishly while the Battery is in very close proximity to the enemy. Because of your knowledge of these guns you will be returned to England to the Royal Artillery Depot. You have done your service record no good today. Now, report to BSM Hills and say that you are to remain with the ammunition wagons."

"Yes, sir." Hazzer saluted and walked away to the rear – and to disgrace.

Peter turned back to the serious problem of whether to move or not. The Boers were certainly to the front and in a very strong position; it was most likely that they were preparing to make a run for it by charging through the weakest point of the British lines that must be to the eastern flank. But to move the Battery further to the right would leave a large hole uncovered by guns, yet it would range over an area where the Boers might easily make a bolt for freedom.

Suddenly a horse galloped past him from behind and between the guns. Peter looked up to see that the rider was Sergeant Hazzer! He was kicking the horse to even greater speed. He must be heading for the Boers thought Peter. My God, he's deserting!

He ran over to the stack of Lee Enfield rifles by Number 2 Gun's limber. He lifted one out and pulled back the bolt. The magazine was full. Pushing the bolt forward, he felt a round feed into the breech. Hazzer was 200 yards away; Peter raised the rifle, tucked his left elbow into his Slade ammunition belt, and took the weight of the rifle on his left clenched fist. Hazzer was moving away and to the right.

Peter aimed for his back and over the horse's head to allow for the moving target. He took up the first trigger pressure, held his breath and fired! Hazzer jerked his head round at the sound of the shot; he was not hit but his helmet fell off and it bounced along the dusty ground behind him. The bullet must have just passed in front of him; Hazzer slapped the horse's neck with the reins to urge it on even faster.

Peter worked the bolt back and forward to empty the spent round and to push a new cartridge into the chamber. Once more he pulled the butt into his shoulder and rested the fore end onto his left fist, again with his elbow tucked into his belt, then breathing slowly he levelled the sights to the same position over the horse which was now 300 yards away. First pressure, steady breath. Crack!

The horse continued in its galloping flight but instantly Hazzer straightened up then, leaning back, gradually fell off the horse. The .303 bullet had smashed into his spine. The horse slowed down from its wild gallop as it felt its rider slip and then gradually fall from the saddle.

Peter pulled back the bolt and ejected the spent cartridge. With his left thumb he pushed down the remaining rounds into the magazine and slid the bolt over them to close the empty breech. He pulled the trigger, put on the safety catch with his forefinger and returned the rifle to the stack. "Bombardier Kirkby, here," he called. Kirkby ran over and saluted.

"You are now Number 1 of Number 2 Gun and promoted to the rank of Sergeant. Send out two men to bring back Sergeant Hazzer and the horse."

"Yes, sir." Kirkby, his face expressionless, turned and walked back to his gun.

"Smithy and Close," he called to two of his Gunners, "Go and get the horse and Hazzer."

"There's dust over there, sir," called Hills. "Over to the right, on the other side of the river." Peter looked through his glasses and saw three lines of British infantry moving slowly towards the Boer position.

"Lieutenant!" Peter shouted at the top of his voice. Julian ran up. "Yes sir."

"See that infantry? Well we're going to support them. I'm going forward to that large clump of thorn, with the signals section. We're going to use the arc. I will be able to see the fall of shot right up to when the infantry arrive at the trenches."

"Right sir." Julian turned and called out, "Battery targets. Arc sighting. Number 1 Gun ranging."

Peter called out, "Sergeant Line, here with your signals section." The Sergeant acknowledged with a raised arm and shouted instructions to his section.

"Follow me as quickly as you can," called Peter over his shoulder, and he ran forward towards the river and slightly to the right of the guns. He had to find a good observation post that the Boers could not spot, yet where the Battery could see his fire orders. He came to a donga and waited until the Sergeant could certainly see him, then he dropped over the edge and ran along the gulley towards the river. After a couple of hundred yards he saw a clump of thorn hanging over the far edge. Crawling up to its shade, he peered over the edge. This was the place. The heliograph could be set up behind him and in sight of the guns.

The panting signals section scrambled to a stop behind him. "This is where we will stay."

"Adams, put it up there," ordered Line, "and make contact." In a few minutes the signaller said, "Got 'im Sarg."

"We're in contact with the guns sir"

Peter had been scrutinising the target area. He had to put down shells along the trench line in front of the infantry. The wagon park was hit at 2600 yards. He pulled out his pad and sketched the scene in front of him, marking in the target. "3200 yards. Fire," he said. The heliograph machine clacked behind him, catching the sun's rays and reflecting them to the other helio back at the guns.

"Acknowledged, sir" said Sgt Line.

Peter waited, and then he heard the howl of a shell passing over his head. It landed too far to the right, almost on the infantry. "Left 10 degrees, 3200 yards."

A pause, then "Acknowledged sir." Only a few seconds passed and another howl and another puff of dust closer to the trenches. "Left 5 degrees, 3250."

He had an idea. Another howl, another puff of dust smack on target.

"Number 1 Gun target 3250 yards 10 rounds gunfire. Number 2 Gun 3200 yards 10 rounds gun fire." This would give the Boer trench a pounding over a longer area.

"Acknowledged, sir."

"Sergeant, can you turn your helio and try and signal the infantry. They just might have one of your machines."

"I'll try, sir." The shells started to scream over their heads and Peter watched as the Boer trenches were turned into a turmoil.

"Got em. Yes sir," called Line. "They are the Essex regiment."

Peter studied the lines and then called out to the Sergeant. "Say 'We will shell for five minutes before you attack. Indicate your start time.' "

After a short time, Line called out the reply, "'We start in 10 minutes. Many thanks.'"

The guns had completed their fire order and the dust had settled on the Boer site.

"To the guns signal 'Repeat previous. Fire when instructed.' " The signaller had to re-establish contact with his gun helio. Then he sent the message.

Peter and the signallers waited in the silence before the storm. "Signal coming in, sir" said Line. Peter turned to see him writing down the letters from the helio signaller. "Kitchener's Hill under attack from Boers."

"Bloody hell!" exclaimed Peter. "I can't stop the infantry support now."

"Sar'nt, signal 'Cancel previous. Number 1 Gun, 10 rounds gunfire at 3200 then 10 rounds gunfire at 3250. Fire. Number 2 Gun to engage Boers on hill." He peered through his glasses at the trenches and waited. Then the gunfire came, earlier than the infantry expected but it would take a bit longer to complete.

"Line, signal to the infantry 'Gunfire will cease after 20 rounds.'"

The Battery was engaged on two targets at the same time, and the second one might be so close that the Boers could actually attack the guns.

The howl of shells ripped through the sky and he could see dust and earth being thrown into the sky. There was a very short pause and then the gun started 50 yards further up. The result was very impressive, especially as it was only coming from one gun.

The firing stopped and he saw the lines of Essex get up and start to run towards the trenches. They had to go about 500 yards but amazingly they had only moved about 100 yards when they dropped to the ground. They must have been taking heavy rifle fire.

Peter called out "Sar'nt, signal to the guns--." "Sorry, we can't sir, the cloud is over us."

"Damn." Peter looked above him and sure enough heavy cloud obscured the sun. "Pack up and get back to the guns." Peter slid down the donga slope and ran as fast as he could back to where he had entered the gulley. Over the edge he ran in a crouch back towards the guns. He could see Number 2 Gun pointing to the right, slamming shells at a target on Kitchener's Hill. Number 1 Gun was standing silent. Peter ran up to Hills, who was in charge and said "Two degrees left shrapnel 10 rounds gunfire 3200 yards."

The Gunners twisted the range on the shell, loaded it with a cartridge behind, slammed the breech closed and then - bang - off went the first shell.

Peter had got his breath back and was looking through his glasses. "We're firing blind but I hope we're hitting the Boers behind the trenches and possibly the trenches themselves. The Essex are taking a hammering. They'll either get into the trenches or at least we'll have given them some covering fire while they retreat."

Hills heard the explanation but made no comment. He was watching the gun crew. If there was going to be a problem he wanted to be on it at once.

"Next limber," he shouted and a full limber pulled up to be manhandled alongside the gun.

"Oh God," said Peter. "They're pulling back." He could see men of the Essex scampering back to where they had first appeared. Some were left lying on the ground in front of the Boer position. "What a mess."

Number 1 Gun finished its fire order. "Ten rounds shrapnel 3200 yards," ordered Peter. Then he said to Hills. "When that's completed, move this gun to fire on the hill to support Number 2 Gun."

"Very good, sir."

Peter walked briskly to the left to Number 2 which was in the middle of a fire order slamming shells onto the kopje. Julian was standing to the side with glasses to his eyes. "What's happening?" Peter asked.

Julian, with his glasses still up, said, "De Wet has brought up a commando of a few hundred men and taken Kitchener's Hill. We've hit them so that they've gone to ground but they're well hidden and covered."

Peter also peered through his field glasses.

"I'm using shrapnel mainly," continued Julian. "But I think they are settling in."

"Look, to the right," said Peter. "Infantry. They are going to either counter-attack or at least seal off the hill."

"Do I continue to fire, sir?" asked Julian. Peter paused to think. "Yes. The attack is not coordinated with us but we must be supporting them if we keep on spraying De Wet with shrapnel." But dusk was starting to fall and they could not continue to fire for much longer. He looked back at Number 1 Gun and saw that it had completed its fire pattern and was being manhandled to a position behind but to the side of Number 2. "What range are you on, Julian?"

"4500. sir"

Peter ran over to Sgt McCann the Number 1 and waved Hills over to join him. He said to both of them. "The Boers are on that kopje. The infantry are attacking from the right and front that we can see. I want you to aim midway up the front slope where they might be in shallow trenches. I will give you short fire orders probably to be repeated swiftly, .I will start with High Explosive."

Both men nodded. "HE 1 round sighter 4500 yards. Fire," Peter called out. McCann lifted the trail of the gun with the handspike and pointed the barrel towards the aiming point. Number 3 pulled the firing lever and the shell tore through the air towards the kopje.

They all waited. Then Peter saw a puff of dust just to the right of the aiming point, possibly the light wind had taken the shell there. "5 degrees left 5 rounds gunfire. 4500 yards." By the time he had finished speaking, a round was in the breech, and a few seconds later it was tearing its way to the kopje. The next few rounds followed swiftly. The hillside was a cloud of dust; where were the infantry?

Peter shouted over to Julian. "On completion of your fire order, stop." Julian raised a straight arm above his head in acknowledgement.

Two more rounds were fired by Number 2 Gun and then all the Gunners watched – and waited. They might be hitting an advancing infantry line or they might be hitting Boers who were firing at the infantry. Peter decided he could not risk it any further until he could see more.

"A rider coming in, sir!" Peter looked over to the right; a khaki rider was galloping towards the guns. Still at some distance he waved his arm in the air to attract their attention. Peter watched him as he careered towards the Battery.

Pulling his horse to a skidding halt and throwing up a cloud of dust, the rider, a Captain, called out. "Major Rutland?"

"Yes," replied Peter. "Oh thank God for that. General Smith-Dorrien asks you to cease-fire as he is having infantry dig in close to the Kopje and he is worried that you might shell them. Two Batteries of RHA are shelling the Boers now and through the night."

"Thank you, Captain. What is the position there?"

"A bit of a muddle actually, sir. De Wet popped up right behind us with a couple of guns, took the kopje and is possibly hoping that Cronje will make a breakout towards him. We can't box De Wet in but the General is hoping to keep Cronje where he is now."

"How about the attack of the Essex on Cronje?" asked Peter. "We were able to give some artillery support but how did they do?"

The Captain lowered his head. He spoke quietly, "I don't know sir but there's been a number of bad howlers made and the poor infantry have suffered badly." He leaned over towards Peter, "There's even been a suicide cavalry charge and at least one CO has died. It is a terrible mess." He sat upright, "I'm sorry sir. I shouldn't be talking like this but it has been a terrible day with so much blood spilt."

"You're right, Captain. Make sure you control your emotions, despite the circumstances. Please report to General Smith-Dorrien that we will come out of action but we'll be available as he orders. Our Battery station is 200 yards to the rear. Can you also inform Colonel Eustace CRA of that information, please?"

"Certainly, sir, and I apologise."

"You have nothing to apologise for Captain. Thank you." Both officers saluted and the staff messenger turned to canter back to his HQ.

"Battery. Limber up," shouted Peter. The Gunners came out of action – not with great speed for they were all bone weary. It had been a long and hard day.

Chapter 16

De Wet had not been able to harry the British forces as he had wished. Still hoping to bring relief to Cronje, he approached the battle area of Paardeburg from the south and saw that the Stinkfontein hill was the only chance he had of entering the British lines and holding out while a message was sent to the besieged Boers. The plan was audacious with a high risk factor but De Wet did not falter. He was truly a man of courage and vision.

In one mad dash accompanied with his two artillery pieces and a few hundred men, he took the hill and immediately started to entrench. He would stay there until he could get a message across to Cronje and then wait while they disengaged from the Khakis and made the breakout. When both forces were together, they would be strong enough to give the Khakis a good kicking.

Jan buried his face in the dust as the shells slammed into the ground around him. A few minutes before he had heard the whine of the shrapnel flying through the air; every piece seemed to want to end up in his body. Henk had been hit in the thigh of his right leg and had bandaged it up to stop the bleeding. It was a bad gash but it looked as though it would heal up. It seemed as though the guns were just spraying their shells anywhere as the Gunners did not actually know where the trenches were.

Jan peered over the top of his shallow trench looking for an infantry target but the Rooineks were too far away, being very careful and not showing themselves; they had learned a lesson.

He called over to Henk, "If we can't see them to shoot at, then they can't shoot at us." Henk laughed and carefully rolled over onto his back. "I'm going to have a sleep. Shout if I am wanted," he replied.

Jan peered over the trench lip; the gunfire had slowed down and he wondered if an attack was coming in. But there was no sign of movement from the soldiers way off except - "What the hell is that?" he exclaimed. "What?" asked Henk, who rolled onto his front. "Where?"

"Look to the left front. There's a damned great balloon on a rope with," he paused, "a basket underneath and it's got two men in it."

"Bloody hell," exclaimed Henk, "They're lookouts for the guns. They can see us just as we can see them." He slid back down into his shallow trench. "Now we are in for some trouble."

Henk was right, and it would only be the oncoming darkness of night that would give them a break before the onslaught to come.

On the second day of the battle at Paardeburg, General Roberts arrived and took over command. Kitchener had had his day and, though determined to defeat Cronje in a matter of hours, he had only managed to have a great number of British troops killed in uncoordinated attacks against a well dug in foe with modern weapons. He had failed to reconnoitre any part of the enemy lines and had ordered regiments into action without artillery support and even without informing the Divisional Generals. It was one man's ego run amok.

Roberts decided to use his artillery to pound Cronje and also to wear down the Boers on Kitchener's Kopje until at last De Wet realised that Cronje was too stubborn and that he was not going to break out. De Wet then had to look after, and save, his own force. At the end of the second day he saw his chance and with great élan, by pushing through a gap in Roberts' line, he was away.

By that evening more British field artillery had arrived and the exhausted 172 Battery were stood down from the shelling

Peter felt very weary. Even though it was well into the evening, the heat from the midsummer sun still rose from the arid baked soil. He walked back to the Battery tent area and the ammunition wagons; in the dusk he sat on a large rock and looked out at the grassland sweeping down to the river. Higgins his batman appeared beside him. "Thought you might like a whisky, sir."

"You're a bloody marvel, Higgins," Peter said as he took the metal tumbler. "Thank you."

Peter saw Hills marching towards him. "Well, Sar'nt Major that was a hell of a couple of days. But it didn't finish too badly."

"No sir, all's well that ends well."

"I'm having a whisky. Will you join me?"

"That's kind of you, sir. Get the dust out of me throat."

"Higgins, another whisky for the Sar'nt Major," Peter called. As Higgins moved away, Peter said to Hills. "You know, I have no idea how Higgins gets this whisky to me. It doesn't travel in my kit, yet it's always there."

"Ah well," said Hills, "I shouldn't ask if I were you, sir."

"Good Lord, why not?"

"Well. Two bottles of whisky wrapped in cleaning rag fit exactly into a 15 pound shell section in the limber." Peter threw back his head with a laugh. "Gunners! They have an answer for everything."

Hills sat on the rock beside Peter and took off his helmet to wipe the inside sweatband and his own forehead. Higgins arrived with a tumbler for Hills. Peter said to no one in particular. "I only hope we don't run out of ammunition."

Hills with a deadpan face said, "Don't worry sir if we do we can always throw the empty whisky bottles at them." Peter slowly turned his head to see Higgins walking smartly away.

The two men, whisky in hand, sat at ease with each other's company. "I do feel I'm getting past all this excitement," said Peter.

"I know what you mean sir," replied Hills. "I'll be retiring in a few months time. Hopefully, I won't see too much of that type of action before then."

"Retiring!" exclaimed Peter. "Of course I suppose even you must retire at some time. What'll you do?"

"Go back to my family. My wife Mary lives on her father's farm in Kent with our two lads."

"Hills, I am so embarrassed. I rely on you so much yet I never thought to even ask you if you were married, let alone with a family. What are your sons' names?"

"Alfred and John."

"You are an Alfred," said Peter. "Do you always have an Alfred in the family?"

"Yes, sir, always the first son."

"How old are they?"

"Alfred is eight and John is six."

"Will you take up farming?"

Hills nodded, "Oh yes. My father had a small sheep farm in Holling below the North Downs. But in them days there was no future for a boy like me on the farm so I joined up. Dad died a couple of years ago and Farmer Dennett, that's Mary's father, took over our 50 acres that was next to his farm. Farmer Dennett suffers badly from arthritis so I shall run both farms. That's about 160 acres."

"I expect you and your sons will make a great team," said Peter.

Hills laughed. "Even at eight, Alfred likes uniforms and wants to be a Gunner. I don't know though."

Peter gently slapped Hills on the shoulder. "Alfred, there's always room for an Alfred Hills in the Royal Artillery."

Sergeant McCann appeared beside them and saluted. "Excuse me, sir," he said, "but we've found a black man and he is in trouble." Peter and Hills got to their feet. "What trouble?" asked Peter.

"He was down the road a bit, under some brush. One of the lads was looking for fuel for the fire when he came across him." Peter, closely followed by Hills, strode across to a knot of men looking at something on the ground.

"What's happening?" asked Peter.

"We just found him and brought him in here," said one of the Gunners.

Peter knelt down to the figure on the ground. He was a black man, apparently unconscious, who had obviously been badly beaten. His shirt was just strips of rags that were heavily bloodstained. His hands had been bound but were now cut free though they still had raw leather strips around each wrist. His ankles had been tied together, again by raw leather.

"Cut his ankles free and those ties around his wrists, they look as though they're cutting into his flesh." Gunner Bream cut the ankle ties with his clasp knife.

"Get some water," ordered Peter. He felt the man's wrist and found a strong pulse. He was obviously alive but out for the count.

"Here you are, sir." A canteen was put into Peter's hand. He pulled out the cork and poured water over the man's face, then pressed the water bottle spout against his mouth. Gradually the lips parted and he took in some water.

"Sit him up against that wagon wheel."

Two Gunners dragged the man and sat him against the limber wheel of Number 2 Gun. He slowly opened his eyes and dazedly looked around him. He felt his wrists and looked down at his ankles. He was obviously puzzled.

"Who are you?" asked Peter. The man did not reply. Peter offered him the canteen of water. He took it and drank deeply. He stopped and slowly tried to rise. A Gunner gave him a hand. He was obviously very weak. "Lean him against the wagon," said Peter.

"Do you feel all right?" asked Peter.

"I don't think he understands English," said Hills.

"Me know what you say," the man said.

"What is your name?" asked Peter.

" Me mVumbiso. Me Zulu."

"Vumbiso?" said Peter. The man nodded.

"Well, Vumbiso what happened to you?"

"Bass beat me, tied me."

"Why? What did you do?"

There was a long pause before mVumbiso replied. "I looked at Baas in the face." Peter looked at the man: he was at least six feet tall, well built and had a confident attitude. He probably has a strong character, Peter thought and he maybe stood up to his Boer employer. "Was it the first time you had looked at him in the face."

"No, Baas."

"I am not your baas. I am a Major in the British Army."

"mJor." The man gave the native inflection to the rank.

"Yes. You can stay with us until you are strong enough to go where you want to," said Peter and turned to Hills. "Sar'nt Major, will you get the medical orderly to look at him and arrange for the cooks to feed him. See if you can find some clothes to fit him as well."

"Very good, sir."

In the early morning, Peter lay on his camp bed looking at the dawn light shining through the canvas of the bell tent. A shadow appeared at the entrance. "Good morning, sirs." called Gunner Higgins.

"Good morning Higgins."

"For your breakfast, would you like some Rosy Lee before, with it or afters."

"What is breakfast?" asked Peter. "Kippers perhaps?"

"No, sir, but we have some lovely corned dog and hard biscuit just like yesterday – and the day before."

"Well, Higgins, I'll have a portion of the corned beef and I'll leave it to you when we have the Rosy Lee."

"Very good, sir." Higgins turned and pushed his way through the tent entrance flap.

"All this hilarity so bloody early," moaned Julian from his bed. "What the hell is Rosy Lee? Oh, don't tell me, it's Cockney for a cup of tea."

"Your education is coming on in leaps and bounds, Julian."

"My father will be delighted that he only had to pay for me at Harrow when he could've had to pay for me to learn Cockney rhyming slang."

A shape appeared at the tent entrance. "Excuse me, Major Rutland, sir." It was BSM Hills.

"Yes, Sar'nt Major." called Peter as he stood up and pulled his braces over his shoulders. "What brings you out so early?"

"Voomby has gone."

"Voomby?"

"Yes sir, the black man."

Peter smiled; it didn't take long for a British soldier to anglicise the African name. "Well, I am surprised. I thought my judge of character was better than that. Oh well he'd have gone sometime, I suppose the quicker the better." Then he had a thought. "Has anything been stolen. Has he taken anything?"

"Not that we can see, sir"

"Right, thank you, Sar'nt Major. I'll be out shortly."

Peter washed and dressed, leaving Julian who had been up a great deal of the night with the sentries. He then went out to see the gun position before the Gunners had their breakfast. As he got close to the guns, a voice called out, "Over there – he's coming in!"

Peter shaded his eyes against the low early morning sun to see a figure running steadily towards the gun position. It was a black man and he appeared to be holding a canvas bucket in his hand.

"It's Voomby," a sentry called.

"Let him in," called Peter. Voomby, running steadily, approached the guns and ran, without slowing, up to Peter. He placed the canvas bucket, which he had obviously taken from the horse lines, gently at Peter's feet.

"For you, mJor." said the black man. The canvas bucket appeared to be full of straw but as Peter carefully pulled back the top layer of straw, he saw there were about five or even six dozen chicken's eggs all stacked in a lining of straw.

"I don't think I'll ask where these came from," said Peter quietly. Obviously a Boer farm not far away was short of a number of hen's eggs that morning. He looked at Vourthy with smile on his face. "Will you take them to the cook?"

The black man made no comment; he just picked up the eggs and walked over to where smoke was rising from the Battery cook.

"Well, there's a turn up for the books," said Hills.

"How would you like yer eggs, sir? Fried, boiled or scrambled?" said Higgins.

"I expect the cook would prefer them to be scrambled, am I right?"

"Yes, I think you're right, sir

"I would like a portion of scrambled eggs with my corned dog and biscuit, please, Higgins."

"And for you, sir," Higgins looked to Julian who was sitting on the side of his bed putting his boots on.

"I doubt if the cook knows how to coddle eggs so I suppose I'll have to join you all in having mine scrambled – with some Rosy Lee."

"Aha, you are a learnin', sir. It'll all be ready as soon as you get yer plates of meat into yer daisy roots."

While the rest of the artillery pounded away at the Boer laager on the north bank, 172 Battery were able to do some urgently required maintenance on the recoil systems of their guns The loss of glycerine oil when they were in action had been very great and the need for replacement oil was getting critical. Peter informed Colonel Eustace that he had to go to De Aar to get the oil, as without it the guns would be useless. He would have to pull a lot of rank to get some action.

As the Battery might well be moved from their present position during the few days he would be away, Peter was worried that they might be used by a superior officer who did not know of the reason for them being in South Africa. He was discussing with Julian what was the best way to handle this problem when he saw Nick Ramsay ride up. He had a small case tied to the pommel of his saddle; he pulled up without any comment.

"Hello, Nick," called Peter, "Everything all right?"

Nick did not answer but dismounted and untied the case from his saddle. It was obvious that something was badly wrong. Peter raised a hand and gestured him over to a quiet place clear of the guns and activity.

Ramsay put down the grip and took off his helmet. "The Colonel is dead."

"Crumpton Smythe?" queried Peter.

Nick nodded. "He went the same way as Hannay."

Peter frowned. "What do you mean 'went the same way as Hannay'?"

Nick looked at Peter "Colonel Hannay, Mounted Infantry. You haven't heard?" Peter shook his head. "Kitchener killed him," said Nick.

"On that first mad day when Kitchener was flinging men around like pebbles, he was furious that Hannay and the MI had not succeeded in an attack so he ordered them to attack again. Like a bloody fool Kitchener actually said they were to charge right up to the Boers and fire their carbines into the laager as though the Boers had spears not rifles. It was a mad order. Hannay queried it as his men had been fighting and travelling for almost two days and were worn out. Kitchener insisted, so Hannay did what he had to do. He sent all his officers away on errands. Then took a thoroughbred, the fastest horse in the Regiment, and asking for volunteers, took ten men on standard horses. He lined them up and charged, as he had been ordered, straight for the enemy. He was soon well clear of his men and almost in the Boer lines when he was shot. All of his men returned as the Boers didn't shoot at them. Hannay's horse also came back. He was a very brave man who decided to die for his men rather than let Kitchener kill them."

Nick stood with a bowed head holding his helmet in his hands. "Old Crumbly had known Hannay for many years and they were very good and close friends. He learned of Kitchener's mad order and what Hannay planned to do, so he joined him." Nick paused to gather his emotions. "Not side by side - but he joined his friend in the end.

"I didn't know about it until my Adjutant brought a young trumpeter who was in tears to me. Apparently Gerard had taken the trumpeter and a trooper to a thorn tree where he could see Hannay start his charge. He sent the trooper back with a message saying that the regiment was to await orders from the Colonel.

"Then Gerard mounted his horse and, when he saw Hannay start off, he told the trumpeter to sound the charge and continue to sound it all the time he could see the Colonel's sword in the air. Then Colonel Gerard Crumpton Smythe drew his sword and rode at the gallop towards the Boers to die in the company of his good friend who was making the ultimate sacrifice for his men."

"I'm so sorry, Nick," said Peter.

Nick bent down and picked up the small travelling bag. "Gerard's wife has been told through the official channels so she actually knows the basic facts. I heard that you might be going back to De Aar for some spares. Is that right?"

Peter nodded. "Yes."

Nick held up the small case. "Will you take this to her at her sister's farm near De Aar. It's got Gerard's personal effects in it. I don't want to trust it to the carriers to get it to her; the contents are very personal. Will you take them to her?"

Peter's heart sank at the thought but obviously he had to do it. "Yes, of course I will." He took the case from Nick and held it at his side.

"I much appreciate it, Peter. She is a fine woman and deserves to be told with dignity."

"Doesn't she know the details yet?" asked Peter.

"I've written but the letter might never arrive. When I find some time to get away, I will tell her the full story but I don't think that will be for some months."

Peter nodded. Nick replaced his helmet and turned back to his horse. He mounted and without turning, rode back to his command.

Chapter 17

A military train carried Peter's party consisting of himself, Sergeant Kirkby and two Gunners, to the rail junction and depot at De Aar which they reached after almost twelve hours of tedious travel.

While Peter was finding out where the RA Quartermaster's Depot was, the Sergeant commandeered a small cart at the station to move the glycerine oil that was presumably in cans.

Peter entered the main stores and went up to a counter that was littered with all types of equipment and clothing. From behind the heaps a Quartermaster Sergeant appeared and simply asked, "Yes?"

Peter ignored the obvious insolence and said, "I'm here for the oil for 172 Battery."

"I can't look for that now. I've got too much to do," mumbled the QMS.

"You will look now and you will look carefully," said Peter. The QMS opened his mouth to give a trite comment but he saw something in Peter's eyes and caught something in Peter's tone of voice that made him think again. "I'll have a look, sir, but I don't hold out much hope. We're getting loads coming in now and masses are going out, with little or no paper work to cover most of it."

"Sergeant, I will come back in three hours' time, if you have not been successful by then, I and my Gunners will come and look for it ourselves."

"I'm afraid that's not allowed, sir."

"Allowed or not, it will happen, so I suggest you find it very quickly."

Peter left the stores; outside he said to Kirkby, "There's an RA mess over there. Get a meal for yourself and the Gunners and be back here in three hours' time. I'll be back about then. If at all possible, I want to catch an evening train back to Kimberley."

"Very good, sir."

Because he rode slowly looking at the countryside, it took Peter over half an hour to reach Dieput where Mrs Crumpton Smythe was staying. On the edge of the road he saw the Doctor's notice board; he turned in and approached the farmhouse. He reined in his horse, dismounted and slid to the ground; Gerard's case was attached to the saddle and he slowly undid the bindings. He was not looking forward to this meeting with the Colonel's widow at all. He tied his horse to the hitching rail and, holding the case in his left hand, walked towards the farm house; he was surprised when a woman, dressed in a white high-necked blouse with a full-length brown skirt came out of a door onto the stoep, and then came down the steps. She was smiling and said, "Hello, can I help you?"

"Hello, I am Peter Rutland and if possible, I would like to see Mrs Crumpton Smythe."

The lady held out her hand and said, "I am Isabella, Georgia's sister. I'm pleased to meet you. She has told me about you." Peter shook her hand but he was even more worried by the comment. "If she is available, may I see her?" he asked.

"Certainly. Come in and I'll call her." Peter walked up to the door and into the main hall. "Please go in there." Isabella gestured to a door. Peter entered and, looking around, saw the room to be an almost perfect reproduction of a London sitting room. "Please wait here and I'll ask her to come."

Peter stood in the middle of the room with his cork helmet under his left arm, which was holding the grip case.

Georgia came into the room; she was wearing a dark green high-necked blouse that had a black armband on her left arm. "Peter, how nice to see you." She held out her hand, which Peter shook gently. She sat down on the settee and said, "Please sit down," as she gestured to a chair opposite.

Peter remained standing. "Mrs Crumpton Smythe," he started.

"Oh no, please - Georgia," she said.

He paused. "Georgia, I think you know of your husband's death and I'm truly sorry. He was a very brave man. Nick Ramsay asked me to bring the Colonel's personal effects from Paardeburg and give them to you." He leaned forward and placed the valise on a low table in front of the settee where Georgia was

194

sitting. She opened it and in silence started to place the contents on the table.

"Thank you for bringing these; they are obviously his very personal belongings." She continued to take the items from the valise while Peter stood to attention opposite her feeling very awkward; he was aware of the love he felt for this woman burning deep inside but he knew that now was certainly not the time to show it.

"I think I should go now," he said and, placing his helmet on his head, he very formally saluted her. He turned and moved towards the door. Georgia felt shocked at this official attitude. "Oh, Peter, please," she said. "Please don't go." He stopped and slowly turned to face her.

"Why did you salute me?" she asked.

Peter took off his helmet and placed it back under his left arm. "I didn't salute you. I felt I had to salute your husband, who proved to be a very courageous and gallant gentleman. I'm sorry if I offended you."

Gently she shook her head, "Peter, please sit down and tell me how he died."

Peter placed his helmet on the table and sat in the chair opposite her. It was a deep easy chair but he sat on the edge and very upright. Then gradually he told Georgia the full story, not only of Gerard's lonely charge but also the reason for Hannay's death charge. At the end she sat with her head bowed, tears falling from her eyes on to her hands.

Peter desperately wanted to take her in his arms and comfort her, to hold her and let her sob out her sorrow for her husband, who she so obviously dearly loved.

"Would you like me to get your sister for you?" he asked softly. She gently shook her head. Peter waited until she had composed herself and taken a kerchief from the cuff of her sleeve to wipe her eyes. "Poor Gerard," she said, "He was all alone but he did have his mistress at the end."

Peter listened in amazement, a mistress! Georgia looked with her tear-filled eyes and said, "Yes, Major, his mistress. I was the Colonel's lady, his wife and we loved each other but the Regiment was his mistress and I came second to her - but I hold no animosity." She looked down at her hands in silence then she raised her head and looked at Peter. "Thank you so much for coming and telling me. It must have been very difficult for you."

Peter rose, picked up his helmet and held it under his left arm. Georgia also got up from her seat and held out her hand. Peter held it in his own, and then slowly he raised it to his lips. "If I can be of any assistance to you in any way, Georgia, please let me know."

"Thank you, Peter, I will always remember that."

He turned, opened the sitting-room door, walked through the hall and out to the stoep. He put on his helmet and walked down to his horse which was tied to the farm hitching rail, mounted it and, without looking back, rode steadily to the road back to the centre of De Aar. He knew he was in love and that, whenever he could, he would return to see her again.

As Peter left, Georgia followed behind him onto the veranda to watch him go. Isabella came out from the kitchen to her side and put her arm through hers. "He's a fine man," she said.

Georgia nodded in silence, her mind in turmoil. As she watched the slowly receding figure riding away, she prayed, 'Please God, don't let him be killed as well – because I love him.'

Peter walked with the two Gunners back to the Royal Artillery store. The Quartermaster Sergeant saw him enter and came over quickly. "I'm afraid there is no sign of your cans of oil, sir."

"Then I and my Gunners will start to search the complete warehouse."

"You can't do that," replied the QMS with a look of amazement on his face.

"Stand back, Sergeant," said Peter, and pulled the counter flap back to allow him and the Gunners to enter.

A Bombardier from behind the stores called out. "I've found it, sir." He staggered over with two large metal cans. "There's supposed to be two more but I haven't found them, yet."

"Excellent, Bombardier," said Peter.

The QMS, who looked very relieved, quickly pulled out a receipt pad and filled in the details. "Will you sign there, please, sir?"

Peter signed and said. "Sergeant, I want the other two cans found and kept very safely for when I return in a few weeks time. Is that understood?"

"Yes, sir." Then the two Gunners with Peter picked up the cans and left the stores. As Peter was walking towards the wagon that would take them to the station, the Bombardier from the stores ran over and said, "Excuse me, sir. I heard you wanted glycerine-oil. I thought it must be for a special gun, so I spent all of the time you were away looking for it. I want to get away from the store; will you take me with you, please, sir?"

Peter looked at the Bombardier, who was smartly turned out and obviously eager to see some action. It was always sensible to have an extra man, especially if he was keen. "What's your name?"

"Dixey, sir, Bombardier Dixey."

"Where is the Quartermaster's Office?" Peter asked.

"Over there, sir, in that low building."

"Stay here, Bombardier," said Peter, and walked over to the wooden building to the side of the main stores. He opened the door to see a Gunner with his feet on a desk, reading a newspaper. The Gunner looked up "Yes?" he said. Peter said nothing but waited. The Gunner, with increasing speed, got to his feet realising that here was a man not to be trifled with. "Can I help you, sir?"

"Where is the QM?"

"Who wants him sir?"

"Where is the QM?" Peter repeated firmly.

"That's his office," said the Gunner pointing at a door marked 'Major Kricksam.' "You are, sir?"

Peter said nothing but walked over to the door and caught hold of the door handle. "You can't go in there," called the Gunner. Peter slowly turned his head to face him. "Sir," added the Gunner.

Peter opened the door. A bleary-eyed man wearing a Major's insignia was leaning back in a chair. Peter's entry had obviously woken him. The smell of stale whisky and cigarette smoke filled the air.

"What the hell do you want?" the Major asked. There was a pause as he looked at Peter's uniform. Then he added with an element of scorn, "Major."

Peter, still wearing his helmet, stood in front of the officer's desk, and said. "I want a transfer posting for one of your men to my Battery."

"You what!" exploded the Major. "Well, you bloody well can't. You blokes, just 'cause you've seen a Boer, think you can come here and get anything you ask for. Well, you bloody well can't. Go away."

Peter stood in silence in front of the desk for a few seconds and then said, very loudly and sharply, "Major Kricksam, stand up!" The inebriated officer looked dazed at this outburst. "What do you mean?"

"I said, stand up! Get up now!"

Kricksam gradually rose to his feet. Peter took off his helmet, placed it on the desk and walked round to where Kricksam was standing. "Move over there," he ordered.

"What the hell do you …?"

"I said move over there." Peter repeated in a tone that was not to be argued with, and sat down in the Major's chair. He took a piece of paper from the desk and wrote -

'172 Battery. 27th February 1900. Bombardier Dixey is to be transferred from the Quartermaster's Store at De Aar to the above Battery as from today.

Signed Lt Colonel P.K. Rutland.'

He handed the paper to Kricksam. "Are you sober enough to read that?" Myopically, Kricksam scanned the paper and said, "I'm not having this."

Peter cut him short. "Yes, you are. You will see that I am a Lieutenant Colonel. If you have any dispute, take it up with Captain Jordan, the ADC to General Roberts."

Kricksam, bewildered and befuddled mumbled, "But…"

"But nothing, countered Peter. He looked round at the untidy office. "Major Kricksam, I'll be returning here in two week's time, by which time you will have made this depot completely efficient. If you do not, I will send a report to General Roberts suggesting that you are replaced by properly trained quartermasters and that you and your staff are moved up country to where the fighting is. Is that understood?"

Kricksam slowly absorbed the bad news. "Yes," he mumbled.

"Yes what?" barked Peter.

The Major again paused and gradually got the point. "Yes, sir."

Peter stood up, picked up his helmet, placed it on his head and walked to the door. He turned. "Kricksam, you are a disgrace to the Regiment. I trust you'll take this opportunity to try and make amends." Peter opened the door and entered the outer office. The Gunner clerk, who had heard everything, was standing stiffly to attention at his desk.

Peter walked out into the bright sunshine and took a deep breath. The hot, dusty air smelt a lot better than that in the office. He waved his hand to Dixey, who came running over. He saluted. "Sir?"

"Get your kit, Bombardier; you are now the NCO in charge of the stores in 172 Battery."

A large smile broke over the Bombardier's face, "Yes, sir. Thank you very much, sir." He saluted and ran off to his bunkhouse for a kit bag that was already packed.

Peter walked over to the Royal Artillery HQ to find out the time of the next military train up to Kimberley and for the return to the Battery. As he entered the door he heard a voice call him. "Major Rutland."

Peter turned towards the speaker and recognised Colonel Bridport, who he had last seen in London. "Good afternoon, sir, I didn't expect to see you here."

Bridport smiled. "The authorities try to keep me in England but I do manage to travel a bit. How are things going?"

"Excellent. These are the guns we need, the fire rate is outstanding. The wheels are certainly too weak for normal conditions, and good maintenance of the recoil system is essential. I've just come back for more glycerine oil because of leakage through the drain plugs. I've just used them in full battle conditions at Klip Drift and Paardeburg and they exceed all our hopes. It's certainly a matter of learning how to use them properly strategically that is the next step."

"How about your men – good enough?"

Peter laughed "Your surprise in posting Hills as BSM was the best news I had."

"He certainly is an unusual man," said Bridport.

"You know him, sir?"

"No." replied the Colonel, "But not many men nearing the end of their military career accept a dangerous posting instead of an easy base posting, and turn down the chance of being as RSM."

Peter was amazed. "Turned down promotion for RSM!"

"Yes, just to be in your Battery."

"Good God," exclaimed Peter. "That man never ceases to amaze me."

"He must think a lot of you." Bridport smiled. "I would like an interim report on the guns whenever you get a chance. Leave it with RAHQ at De Aar for my attention."

"Certainly, sir," replied Peter.

"You can decide when you have given them enough of a trial and want to bring them out of the line," continued Bridport. "There is a great deal more standard artillery coming from England so you won't be missed."

"Right, sir"

"Bobs is impressed by what you have done. He doesn't miss much."

"Where is he now, sir?" asked Peter

"He's in Kimberley, where your Battery is."

On the tedious train journey back, Peter had plenty of time to think and reflect on what had happened over the past few days. Well before the train pulled into Kimberley station he knew what he was going to do. Firstly, he found the RA Transport Officer and arranged a wagon for the Sergeant plus Bombardier Dixey and the two Gunners to take the oil back to the Battery and report to BSM Hills.

Peter then headed for the Army Headquarters and General Roberts.

Captain Jordan led the way to General Roberts' office, opened the door and allowed Peter into the room. Bobs was sitting at a camp desk. He looked up from his writing. "Ah, Major Rutland. All's well, I trust?"

"Yes, thank you, sir."

"Tell me Major. How's your trial coming along?" Peter remained silent but looked toward Capt Johnson wondering if he should repeat secret details in front of him. Roberts smiled and waved a hand. "Paul knows of the background."

Peter faced Bobs. "The guns are excellent, sir. Proportionately light carriages accurately firing 15 pounder shells at up to 15 rounds per minute with virtually no recoil."

"Any drawbacks?" asked Roberts.

"The wheels are not man enough for the rough usage but no actual drawbacks. The recovery recoil system needs regular and careful maintenance because should it fail the gun is an unstable 15 pounder. It really is an excellent weapon."

"That's good news. Now how can I help you?"

"I would like promotion for two men of my Battery. It occurred to me at Paardeburg that should I be killed, the whole success of this scheme will rest on a First Lieutenant. Lieutenant Stevens is a very good and capable officer. I believe he should receive field promotion up to Captain and I also request that if he is left in command, he should be able to report to you direct if necessary.

I'm worried that in the wrong circumstances a more senior officer might insist that he does something that is detrimental to the test."

Bobs started to nod as Peter was finishing. "Absolutely correct, Major. I'll arrange for the promotion and give the necessary written order for him to come under my control."

"Thank you, sir." Peter paused and then started again. "My Battery Sergeant Major has served with the guns since he was a boy. I asked for him to be posted to my Battery because I needed a superior NCO who could control and teach Gunners expertly. He's due for retirement in a few month's time. I've just learned that he gave up the opportunity for promotion to Regimental Sergeant Major in order to serve with me. He is the epitome of all that the Royal Artillery stands for, the stalwart Gunner; he is the essential NCO that all serving officers want at their right hand."

"It sounds, Major, as though promotion is too long overdue," said Bobs. "But, for him to be promoted to Regimental Sergeant Major, he should be serving in a regiment with the ensuing responsibilities," he paused. "I suspect though that he's one of the very few men in the Regiment who know the working and drill of this new gun. I think that your BSM should be promoted to Warrant Officer First Class as a Master Gunner. That makes him the equal in rank to an RSM and I suspect with more standing."

"That's excellent, sir. Thank you very much."

Roberts pointed to his ADC. "Give the details to Capt Johnson and I'll authorise the promotions."

Peter left the Army Headquarters feeling very satisfied and even slightly smug. He walked to the RA Transport office and arranged for a horse to carry him to the Battery.

In the three days he had been away the Battery had been sent back to standing barracks at Kimberley. As he rode into the Battery's new position he was surprised to see Voomby run up to him and take hold of the bridle of his horse. Sergeant Piper was close behind. "I hope you don't mind, sir, but Voomby here wanted to work with the horses."

"No, not at all." Peter smiled. The Zulu looked straight at him and a smile gradually spread across his face revealing his white teeth.

"Good work, Voomby," he said as he dismounted and then gave the man a pat on his arm.

Though the men were still under canvas, the Sergeants and officers were in bunkhouses and there was an actual Battery office for Peter to work from. As he entered the office and took off his helmet, he said to the Gunner sentry, "Will you ask Lieutenant Stevens and the BSM to come here?"

The Gunner ran off to deliver the messages. Peter was seated at his desk when there was a knock at the door.

"Come in, Julian."

Stevens entered and stood comfortably at ease with his helmet in his hands. Peter looked at him. When they first met, Peter thought he was insecure, possibly even weak. How wrong that supposition was. Though in his appearance he did not exude strength of character, it was now obvious that it was there in abundance just below the skin.

Peter stood up and sat on the edge of the desk. "Julian, at Paardeburg I realised two things. The first is that if I was hit and you'd taken over the Battery, you would've had a big problem. This is not just another Battery but, as you know, it is a special venture. It wouldn't be possible to draft in another Major to carry on so it has to be you. I've just spoken to General Roberts and he appreciated the problem. I've asked him to grant you a field promotion to Captain, and said that if I fall, you should report to him for authority to continue in command of the Battery. He has agreed to both of these suggestions."

"Thank you very much, sir. I am very surprised."

Peter continued. "You are an essential part of this operation and have truly proved your value in the past few weeks. I am sure that you and Hills can run the Battery without me."

"I think you might be exaggerating there a bit, sir." said Julian with a smile, "But certainly Hills is the finest of BSMs and one that we can all rely on."

"The best," said Peter.

There was a knock at the door. "Come in." called Peter.

BSM Hills entered and saluted. "You wanted me, sir?"

"Yes." Peter turned to Stevens. "Thank you, Captain that'll be all. I want to give instructions to the new Warrant Officer." Stevens raised his eyebrows and smiled.

"Very good, sir." he turned and left the office. Hills stood with a frown on his face.

"Sarn't Major, when I was in De Aar I met a Colonel Bridport," said Peter. "It was he who, when I was back in England, I'd asked if you could be posted to my Battery. When I saw him recently, he gave me some amazing and embarrassing information. He told me that you gave up the opportunity to be an RSM to join me." Peter paused. "I'll always be in your debt for that action." Hills stood absolutely still but it was obvious that he was feeling most uncomfortable.

"Yesterday," continued Peter, "I had a meeting with General Roberts and asked him to promote Lieutenant Stevens to Captain because of his actions at Paardeburg and his responsibility should I fall." Hills gently nodded in agreement.

"I also asked permission from Bobs to promote you to Regimental Sergeant Major, for your dedication to the Regiment and all that it stands for. He readily agreed that the promotion was long overdue but said that he couldn't promote you to RSM as you weren't serving in a regimental posting." Peter paused. There did not appear to be any disappointment in Hills' eyes; he understood the position.

"However," continued Peter, "The General agreed that promotion was fully justified so, because of your long record and your knowledge of this new gun, he has agreed the appointment of you to Warrant Officer First Class as Master Gunner."

Hill stood with his mouth open in surprise. "My goodness, sir," he gasped.

Peter turned round to his desk and picked up a badge of a large crown with a gun underneath. He stood in front of Hills and handed it to him. "You are the finest Gunner I have ever met. Go and get someone to sew the badge on."

Hills took it and said, "Thank you very much, sir. I'm..." he stopped. "Thank you very much, sir," he saluted, turned and left the office; he was at a loss for words.

Chapter 18

After Cronje's defeat, De Wet knew he had to retire and consolidate his hard-hit forces. He was given command of a much larger Boer force due to the accidental death of General Ferreira, a senior Boer commander. He chose a strong position at Poplar Grove where he was certain he could not only stop Bobs' advance but where he could inflict a damaging blow. He put his right wing on a prominent hill called Leeuw Kop, while he placed his left wing on a range of hills called Seven Sisters; it was an excellent displacement of his forces. He was lucky in that Roberts delayed his advance from Paardeburg in order to reorganise his own forces, so he had time to settle his army in.

Jan and Henk lay in their shallow trench. Henk lay back with his eyes closed; his face was pale, even slightly yellow in complexion. Jan leaned over towards him. "Henk?" he said, "Are you all right?"

Henk opened his eyes. "Yes, I'm all right, just tired," he said and closed his eyes again.

Gently Jan put his hand on Henk's leg. Henk let out a cry of pain.

"Let me have a look at that wound," said Jan.

"No, it's all right I tell you," replied Henk.

Jan put his hand on his friend's shoulder. "Lay back and let me see." Jan took out his skinning knife and gently slit Henk's trousers above the knee. There to Jan's horror he saw a fiery suppurating wound with strong red veins running away up to Henk's groin. The wound from a shell splinter that had hit him at Stinkfontein had, untreated, become life-threatening in its intensity.

"Henk, you must see the doctor."

"Where? In Cape Town?" quipped Henk.

Jan got up and walked away to the rear of the Boer position. Eventually he returned with a man who was a vet; he was the best they had to treat their wounds. The man looked at the horrendous wound and then he smelled it. He took out some clean bandages and bound the leg up to make a neat cover, and said to Henk, "It is very bad. I think you have gangrene in your leg. You must find expert medical help as quickly as possible."

Henk lay back and said nothing. He knew that expert medical help was not even to be contemplated. There was not a Boer doctor within 100 miles from there.

Jan put his head close to Henk's. "Let me take you to the khakis. They have doctors. They will save you."

Henk opened his eyes and smiled, "Never," he whispered. Jan bowed his head; his best friend was dying and there was nothing he could do.

By the time General Roberts' forces had arrived on 7th March, Henk had been dead for two days. Jan had buried him on a south-facing slope of Leeuw Kop where the view stretched for miles across the veldt. It was a scene that Henk would have loved. As Jan dug the grave, the tears ran down his cheeks for his lost comrade. Then he cursed the British guns who had killed him and swore that he would show them no mercy. These faceless Gunners killed and maimed indiscriminately from long distances without having the courage to fight like men, face to face.

General Roberts recognised that the Poplar Grove position was a strong defensive one but he intended to use this strength to his advantage. The Boers would feel confident that they could inflict a great deal of damage on the British force especially if they did their usual frontal attack. But Roberts was going to have the Cavalry sweep in a large circle round to the right and get behind the Boer forces, while his main force attacked again on the right. The left, which was the Leeuw Kop area, was to be threatened so that the Boers would think an attack was coming there.

172 Battery were placed on the left of the British line but set back from the RHA positions; 172 could outrange the RHA but they were slower to move. Their orders were to seek out any Boer guns where possible and give counter Battery fire or cover their trenches.

Peter stood in front of the Battery position that was on a gentle slope above the level of the veldt beyond. There was just one minor hill short of the main range of hills; nothing in front of this kopje would be a suitable position for the Boers to use, only beyond. Though it was late afternoon, it was worth seeing if there were any targets now, rather than wait until the attack started sometime tomorrow.

"Justin, I am going to ride with signals to the crest of that kopje. We will engage any targets with arc sighting."

Justin looked through his glasses at the distant hills and said. "Leeuw Kop isn't that far beyond it, sir. You might be very exposed if the Boers attack."

"Any Boer guns must be in those far hills, so you will be able to defend us if they do attack," said Peter. Julian pulled a wry face in reply.

"Never-the-less," Peter continued, "If we are cut off, your main priority is to safeguard the guns."

"Very good, sir,"

Peter called to the Signals section to mount up and follow him. Ten minutes later they were pushing their horses up the side of the kopje. It was wider at the top than Peter had at first thought. He dismounted just short of the crest and walked forward to see an excellent view of Leeuw Kop. He took out his field glasses and focused them on the hill and the Boer position. He could see areas of disturbed rock and soil which could well be entrenchments.

"Sergeant Line, set up the helio just below the rim and I will tuck myself in beside that rock."

"Right, sir."

Peter crawled towards the edge and slid into the shade of a large rock. By turning his head he could easily call to the Signals section. He pulled out his pad and sketched the line of hills ahead with as much detail as he could. Then he had to judge the range.

"Number 1 Gun ranging High Explosive 4000 yards. Fire." He called out the fire order and watched through his glasses for the result. He heard Sgt Line call out to him. "Message acknowledged, sir." Half a minute later he heard the howl of the shell as it flew over his head on its way to the target. It fell well short, and too far right.

"10 degrees left 5000 yards."

Again he waited until the shell howled over. That was closer.

"5 degrees left, shrapnel, 3 rounds gunfire 5500 yards." As the Battery responded to this order, the noise of the shells flying over them made the horses pull madly at the reins which were held by the Signals horse minders. The result on the far hill was certainly very dusty. Clouds of it rose in the area he wanted to hit.

He peered very carefully to see if there was any movement to confirm that the Boers were indeed there. Yes! A pinprick of reflected light meant that someone had moved something shiny. The area was occupied.

"3 rounds gunfire, 5500 yards."

As he settled down waiting for the Battery to act, he felt a tap on his leg and turned round. It was Sergeant Line; he was pointing to the right of their position. "Boers on horses, sir."

A dozen men in slouch hats were riding in line round the kopje obviously looking for where the guns were. They must have been convinced that no khakis were as close as to be on this kopje.

"Grab the helio and make a run for it. Keep well over to the left and get back to the Battery."

"Right, sir," said Line and scrambled back to the Signals section, who in seconds were up and off. Peter knew he had a little more time so he could wait to see if the Boers caught sight of the Signals. If they did and gave chase, it was certain that Julian could give covering fire to get them away. Peter knew that alone he could slide down with his horse beyond the Boers and, riding like hell be away before they knew he was there.

The Boers spotted the Signals section as they were half way down the slope, and gave chase. Two of them started to fire with their rifles but Line's section was some way off, and they were a moving target.

Peter waited until the Boers were chasing the signals and had almost reached the base of the kopje when he ran to his horse, which was tied to a stout thorn bush. He mounted and then he rode; he rode as he had never ridden before, the ground was hard but in places very uneven and covered with small rocks. The dust he created was quickly spotted by the Boers but he was well clear of them and going for the bottom of the kopje where they would never catch him. His horse jumped, slid and scurried across the crumbled rocks. He heard the Battery fire and knew that they were giving covering fire to the Signals section, who would easily get back.

Then it happened. He was just starting to slow his scrambling horse as they were almost at the bottom - when it fell. One of its legs went into a hole, it rolled and Peter was thrown over its head onto the scree. In the dust he lay stunned; his helmet had rolled some way off down the slope. He raised his head and tried to focus his eyes. Groggily he stood up and looked for somewhere to hide. His horse was up and hobbling down the slope; it was obviously unrideable. Peter slowly scrambled up the hill towards a cluster of rocks but before he got there he heard a call. "Hands up, Englisher!"

He stopped, turned and looked up to see a group of Boers who were holding rifles pointed at him. Beyond them there was no sight of the Battery so they would not have seen that he was captured.

A young Boer slid off his pony and pulled a strip of leather from behind his saddle. He tied Peter's hands tightly together; another man flipped a long rope down that was tied to the leather strip.

The young Boer mounted again and caught hold of the long rope. "Kom" He said and pulled the rope so that Peter walked alongside his horse. The rest of the group moved back down the slope, headed towards their lines.

They rode in single line with Peter, hands tied to a longrope, walking and trotting alongside one of them. They headed back across the open veldt towards the hills of Leeuw Kop. Peter knew that as the attack was going to start in the next few hours, he had to make the most of any attempt to escape. Any delay in his getting away would mean he was further from the British lines.

At the foot of the Kop the horsemen, still in single file, gradually climbed the front face which was fairly steep. The British infantry would find it a tough nut to crack. Near the top they veered off down a small valley towards an encampment where some horses plus basic supplies were being stored.

Peter was untied from the rope that was attached to a saddle. He dropped down on to one knee; he was exhausted after the long journey in the incredibly hot sun.

"Give him some water."

"You do it," was the reply. A mug of tepid water was given to Peter that he readily drank. A stocky man dressed in brown cord trousers and a dusty green jacket stood in front of him. Through a deep beard he said. "Who are you?"

"Major Peter Rutland."

"What were you doing on that hill?"

"Scouting."

"For who were you 'scouting'?"

"I was just looking to see if there were any of your people around when your group surprised me."

"What about the men who were with you?"

"They would signal back what I saw."

"Who did they signal back to?"

"My regiment."

"Which regiment is that?"

Peter said nothing.

"You heard me, Englisher, what regiment was that?"

"I am not obliged to tell you."

The Boer threw back his head and gave a loud raucous laugh. "You pompous donkey – so you're not obliged to tell me. You think we're all stupid. You are a gunner. Your guns are a mile or so behind the kopje. It must be a big group to send out a Major to scout for them."

Peter looked down at the ground and remained silent. The man turned away and walked over to the group of men who were sitting down by the saddles they had taken off their horses. The light was falling and they had started a small fire to cook by and give them some warmth during the cold part of the night.

Occasionally more men would ride in and hobble their horses before joining the enlarging group round the fire. One figure appeared, a youngish man with the usual slouched hat, but Peter thought he resembled someone he knew – then it dawned on him – it was Jan!

Sitting there with his hands tied, he could not do anything, but he decided not to acknowledge Jan in front of the Boer group. It might be a bad point against Jan if they knew he had a Rooinek as a relation. The leather strip around his wrists was tied with expertise; it was tight, very tight but it did not cut off the circulation to his hands. He tried stretching them but he could just feel them cutting into his flesh.

A Boer rose from the group and walked over. "Get up," he said. Peter rose stiffly and stood upright.

"Go over there," the Boer said pointing at the group of men by the fire. He walked over and stopped in the area of the fire light.

"Will you tell us more?" asked the Boer who had questioned him.

"There's nothing more to say. I was scouting and I got caught." He could see Jan on the edge of the group and it was obvious that Jan knew who he was.

The Boers talked amongst themselves. They obviously did not know what to do with him.

"He's not going to tell us any more."

"Send him back to the General."

"It's a waste of time."

"Yes, shoot him now. We don't want damn prisoners around us."

"I agree. They shoot our men who are taken prisoner so let's do the same to him."

"No," said the stocky bearded Boer. "I won't have his blood on my hands."

"I'll do it then."

"No you won't. He is going back to De Wet and he'll decide what's to happen." He gestured to Peter "Lie down by that rock. Now one of you will have to guard him."

"I'll do that," said Jan. He came over and roughly pushed Peter back to where he had first been sitting.

"Sit down there," ordered Jan. "Make one move to escape and I will shoot you – with pleasure." Peter slumped down against the rock and watched very carefully what was happening. It was obvious that he was in great danger; some of these men were very willing to kill him and so dispose of a problem for them.

Jan brought his blanket and saddle and laid it out for sleep just a few feet from where Peter was sitting. He pulled out a horse blanket and in silence gave it to Peter.

"Leo," he called out, "Bring me some of that stew will you, and a bowl for the khaki."

Leo came over with two bowls that he put down by Jan's saddle. "Otto wants to kill him now," said Leo quietly. "It's wrong; we mustn't let him do it."

"Don't worry, he won't. This Rooinek is going back to De Wet," replied Jan.

Leo went back to the fire; Jan bent down and gave a bowl to Peter. "For the time being you are safe but don't try and make a run for it. They will certainly shoot you if you try."

Peter looked at Jan who gave him a wink. "Just now you're a damned nuisance to all of us," he said and gave a small smile. Peter nodded.

They both ate their food. Then Jan said loudly and firmly, "Lie down and sleep. Keep still or I'll kill you."

Peter lay down and pulled the horse blanket over his shoulders. Though he was very tired, sleep did not come quickly. He thought about the past few hours; it was terrible bad luck to be caught but he could have been killed then or surprisingly just now. Eight hours ago he was a Lieutenant Colonel in charge of a Battery of revolutionary new guns – and now he was a prisoner, and very grateful that he was not going to be shot. Eventually weariness overcame him and he slept.

He felt the gentle pressure of a hand on his leg. He opened his eyes; it was very dark but there was some moonlight. A hand was laid across his mouth to ensure he was silent. He turned his head to peer through the darkness and slowly made out the black face of – Voomby! Peter nodded. Voomby slipped a sharp knife across the leather bindings on his hands which fell away. He moved around Peter's legs towards where Jan was sleeping, his knife held ready to kill the sleeping man.

"No!" said Peter in a loud whisper.

Voomby turned his face to Pete, who shook his head. Voomby pulled back and Peter looked towards Jan. He was awake and had his rifle lying alongside his body.

"Tot siens," said Jan. "Voor spoed - good luck." Peter reached out and touched Jan's hand, then silently followed Voomby away from the Boer camp.

Jan watched the two shapes disappear into the darkness. There would be trouble tomorrow morning - but the prisoner had been too clever for him – anyway they didn't know what to do with him and now the problem was solved. He rolled over under his blanket and instantly went to sleep.

Peter ran in a crouch to catch up with the fast moving shape of Voomby, who seemed to be able to see in the darkness. Peter followed his every move and stayed as close as possible. Gradually they came off the hills and scrambled down the sides of dongas leading to the flat land that separated the Boers from the British. When they were on flattish ground, Voomby started to trot, not fast but relentlessly. Peter had a great deal of trouble keeping up. Then suddenly the Zulu stopped. Peter bumped into him but remained silent. Voomby held his hand up to keep Peter quiet and moved slowly sideways to a clump of scrub. He gestured to Peter to get down and stay there. Then he turned and disappeared into the gloom.

"Bloody hell," thought Peter. He had no idea where he was, nor if the Zulu did not return by daylight, what he should do. He looked up at the sky to see if he could recognise any stars to be able to find either north or south but without success. Then he worked out that as they had come down off the ridge of hills, which must have been Leeuw Kop, they must have been travelling across the flat area towards the British lines. He decided to wait for about an hour and then, if Voomby did not return, to start walking hopefully in the same direction that they had been travelling.

A scuffling sound made him freeze. Then he saw Voomby, and another figure who seemed to be in Army uniform. "Who are you?" the figure asked.

"Major Rutland," replied Peter. "Who are you?"

"Sergeant Blaze of the Canadian Royal Regiment Mounted Infantry. We're the Machine Gun Section."

"What are you doing here?" asked Peter.

"Actually, sir, we're lost."

"Take us to your section, Sergeant. Maybe the Zulu guide can show us the way back."

"Right, sir, we're down in this gulley."

Chapter 19

Peter, with Voomby behind him, followed the Sergeant down the sloping edge of the donga. As he slid down into it, he became aware of a number of shapes that he gradually made out as horses with a number of men standing beside them.

"We left our lines to swing round to the left of the Boers, but night came sooner than we expected, and we were lost before we knew it."

"Where's your officer?" asked Peter.

"With the other machine gun, but we lost contact with him a long time ago."

Peter had no idea where they were, or even where north or south was. "Have you a compass?" he asked.

"No, sir"

Peter turned to Voomby, "Where are our guns?"

Without a second's hesitation he pointed over Peter's shoulder. "Long walk."

"You lead all of us there."

Voomby shook his head. "Too many enemy near. You and I pass through but with soldiers too much noise. We wait."

"Wait! What for?" asked Peter with surprise.

"The battle will come soon. Then we go." It had an element of sense but Peter would rather have tried to get further away in the darkness but only the Zulu knew the way so they would have to wait.

Peter spoke quietly to the Canadian. "This guide says that we are in the middle of the Boers and that we should wait until daylight and when the battle starts to make a run for it."

"If you say so, sir."

"I think it's the only way, so get your men to settle down as quietly as possible and wait for dawn. It can only be two or three hours to go."

The Sergeant moved among his men giving quiet orders, and then came back to Peter. "I've posted four sentries so that the rest can get some sleep, sir"

"Well done. Get some rest yourself. I'm going to try and sleep as well."

Peter lay back against the side of the donga, feeling weariness sweep over him. He looked around for Voomby but he there was no sign of him. Peter's head slumped forward and instantly he was asleep.

He woke when he felt his shoulder being shaken; it was the Canadian Sergeant. "The sun's well up, sir, but there's no sign of your native."

Peter shook his head to wake himself up fully and stood up. The Sergeant had let him sleep on for about one hour past dawn. Peter looked around the donga and then carefully crept up the side and peered over the edge where there was a small bit of scrub. All he saw was flat veldt and Leeuw Kop horribly close. He slid back down and said to the Sergeant, "We must wait a bit longer. I'm sure the guide won't let us down. If your men have any food and water, I suggest you let them have some now as there might be little chance later on."

"They've already had some food, sir. Would you like some?"

"Just some water if you can spare it." A water bottle was offered and Peter took a couple of mouthfuls.

"Here he is."

Voomby, crouching low, was coming down the donga. He came up to Peter. He waved his arm towards the rising sun. "Cavalry over there."

"British?" asked Peter.

Voomby nodded. "We wait." He silently moved away back up the donga.

The waiting was nerve- wracking, and seemed to last for hours. At last Voomby reappeared in a crouching trot, and waved his arm to gesture them to follow after him. Surprisingly he went deeper into the donga with absolute certainty as to where he was leading them. The Canadians quickly walked their horses behind him, occasionally having to trot to keep up. Peter scrambled to the head of the column just as Voomby signalled them to stop. He moved off a short way, slowly climbed the donga side, and after a minute he waved to Peter to come and join him. Peter crawled up and peered over the edge to see an amazing sight. Some 300 yards away was the end of a line of Boers, all lying down ready to fire at the advancing British. Voomby looked at Peter and smiled. He pointed to the Canadian machine gun and then to the Boers, who were a perfect target as the gun would be shooting at them from the side and would take them in enfilade.

Peter slid back down to the Sergeant and explained the situation.

"We can unload the gun from the horses down here, and mount it together up there in a minute," the Sergeant said.

Peter nodded; the Sergeant gave whispered orders and the men went through their well-practised drill. They stood ready to run up the side of the donga, plant the tripod stand and mount the Armstrong machine gun; ammunition belts were at the ready and they would open fire instantly.

Peter, who had returned to be beside Voomby, looked down at the gun crew and waved his hand. They scrambled up the slope, two men heaved the base into position - the barrel was seated and the belt fed into the feed slot. The action was cocked - and again Peter nodded.

Rat-a tat-tat-tat. The first burst flew high over the nearest Boers' heads, but they instantly saw what danger they were in and started to scramble and run as fast as they could.

Rat-a tat-tat-tat. The next burst was in amongst them and they started to fall. One raised his rifle to fire but was immediately cut down. The rest were now almost out of sight, back with their horses and retreating in disorder.

"Fire well beyond this line," suggested Peter, "There might be more beyond."

The Machine Gunner edged his gun higher and let forth a long burst.

Peter and the Sergeant peered carefully towards the enemy but could not see any further movement. Then both of them heard, in the very far distance, a cavalry trumpet sounding the charge. It must be General French sweeping round to the Boer left. Both men and the Zulu scanned the area in front but saw nothing other than dust coming from the right where the Boers were fleeing helter-skelter from the battlefield.

Peter looked at Voomby. "Do you think we can go back to the guns now?"

Voomby smiled, "Yes, mJor."

The British Cavalry had indeed swung round the Boer left and threatened to cut off their line of retreat, while the Royal Artillery had thundered at them in the centre and right to break their will. The Boers were in full flight. Cronje's defeat and surrender at Paardeburg had unnerved them and they were not going to be similarly surrounded - so they retreated. De Wet could not stop them until a long way further back, at the farmstead of Driefontein.

Jan was sickened by the British success which he felt was mainly due to their damned guns. As he saw the men of his commando leave their excellent defensive position he decided to do some hunting on his own. He was going hunting to avenge Henk's death. He was going to find some of those 'Verdomp' guns and fire at them from a great distance where they could not see him but he would be sure of hitting some of them to give them a taste of their own medicine,

From the commando ammunition wagon he took two extra bandoliers of rifle bullets. Then, leading his pony by the halter, he left the commando camp, not going east with the retreating Boers but west towards the Khakis and their damned guns.

Coming off the hill of Leeuw Kop, he went where he knew that the land was flat except for a hill a mile or so away. He did not make directly for the hill but found a donga which took him around it and then through further gulleys to get him close to the British Following these dongas he would repeatedly stop, tie his horse to scrub and scramble to the edge to find out where his enemy was. Eventually he saw them. Guns, less than a mile away on a slope just above the flat level of the veldt - but there only seemed to be two. It must be a small section. All the better, if I can knock out a couple of the men, they will be worried in future.

Leading his horse he found a good position that he reckoned was about 1000 yards short. He could clearly see the men, guns and limbers. He decided to aim at a limber well clear and to the left of the position. He could watch for the puff of dust that his shot made as it fell and then he could get the range reasonably accurate for when he shot at the men themselves. He put his sights to 900 yards, aimed at the limber and fired. He watched carefully and saw dust spurt up well short. He lifted his sights to 1000 yards and fired again, this time to the side of the limber, and was pleased to see dust rise just beyond it.

So he knew the range; there was almost no wind so now he wanted a target. He watched carefully to see if his sighters had caused any consternation to the Gunners, but they did not seem to either notice or care.

There were some Rooineks there but he knew he had to wait until there was a cluster of maybe half a dozen and then fire off at least five shots. Then he had to get out quickly before they saw him and turned their guns on him.

One man was leaning against a tree using field glasses; then Jan saw four men near the right-hand gun. They would be his target. He adjusted his position so that he could aim comfortably and also be able to work the bolt of his rifle quickly without coming off the aim too much. He firmed the butt into his shoulder, took up first pressure, then fired, reloaded and fired again and again. Five shots were let off then, with a glance, he saw that at least one of the men was down before he slid down the side of the donga. That's for Henk he told himself as he led his pony away back to find his commando – wherever it was.

Peter leaned against the tree and, using his field glasses, scanned the empty veldt. The Boers had run, presumably the Battery would be told to move up fairly soon.

Wizz. Crack. Wizz. Crack.   Rifle shots flew close by him. Wizz. Crack.

He scanned the ground for the riflemen and yelled to the sentries, "Watch for shots and fire."

Wizz Thump. Wizz Crack.

The different sound told him that someone had been hit. The sentries fired a couple of shots at nothing.

"Cease fire," Peter called. Then he heard a groan and he turned

Hills was lying on his back. There was a bloody hole in his chest on the right side of his uniform, blood seeping from the corner of his mouth.

"Oh God, no!" Peter ran over and, with a terrible fear tearing at his stomach, he knelt down beside the body. He touched Hills' face – an eyelid fluttered.

"Alfred!" Peter called. "Come back!" Gently Peter turned Hills onto his side so that the blood running from his mouth did not choke him.

"Alfred!" called Peter again, a desperation swamping him because of his inability to do anything. "Fight. Don't go!" Peter looked round, he needed help – now! He saw three Gunners by the spare ammunition of Number 2 gun.

"You three, over here at once." The three Gunners sprinted over.

To the first he said, "Tell Captain Stevens that the Master Gunner is seriously wounded and we must have a doctor."

To the next he said, "Get a stretcher from the spare ammo cart and come back with another Gunner."

To the third he said, "Get a canteen of water and some blankets and field dressings."

With all three men running to his orders, Peter was alone with Hills. "Alfred, you must live. You can't die now, not after all this time and all we've been through." Peter lifted Hills' hand and felt for a pulse in his wrist - but he could not feel anything. He moved his fingers and tried again - but there was nothing.

"Excuse me, sir." A RAMC orderly gently pulled Peter away and pushed his fingers into Hills' neck.

"What are you doing?" asked Peter.

"I'm feeling for a pulse. Yes, there is one but it's very weak." He rolled Hills onto his back and unbuttoned his jacket. A large bloodstain oozed over the shirt. The orderly cut the shirt open to reveal a round wound in the right chest. He took out a field dressing, put it on the wound and said, "Will you press firmly on that sir; it will slow the bleeding, I must clean his mouth and throat."

Peter held the dressing against Hills' chest but he felt a terrible anguish inside. He knew this was a fatal wound; any shot in the chest would kill within a few hours.

"He seems to be breathing all right," said the orderly, "and there's not much blood coming from his mouth. Maybe he's not hit in the lungs."

The two Gunners with a stretcher arrived. "We must lift him very carefully and keep him on his side," said the orderly. "Put the stretcher alongside him."

The Gunners and Peter knelt along Hills' body and then gently lifted him onto the stretcher. The orderly rolled up a blanket and used it as a backrest while Hills' head was rested on another folded blanket.

"Lift him steadily." The two Gunners walked the stretcher slowly back to the guns area and under the shade of a thorn tree

"Where is the nearest Field Dressing station?" asked Peter.

"It's about a mile away, sir. I think he'll do best to wait in the shade here, and I'll get some Indian dooly bearers to take him there."

"Will he be all right while you are gone? Is there anything we can do while we are waiting for them?"

"I'm afraid not, sir. He'll either make it back to the post or he won't. If he can make it there he stands a fair chance. I'll be as quick as I can."

"Take a horse," said Peter.

"Oh, I don't ride, sir"

"Sergeant Kirkby," shouted Peter. "Here with your horse at once."

Kirkby ran over with his horse already saddled.

"Get mounted," said Peter "and take this orderly to the first aid post. Make sure they send a dooly back here at once."

"Right, sir," he mounted and leaned over to pull the medical orderly up behind him. "Hold on, sunshine," he said and they were off at a smart canter.

Peter went over to the stretcher. He knelt down and taking out a handkerchief he wet it with water from a bottle and gently wiped Hills' lips. He vaguely remembered that you must not give water to a man who is wounded in the chest, or was it the stomach?

"God, I don't know what to do." He took off his helmet and ran his hands through his hair in a gesture of desperation. He felt a hand on his shoulder. It was Julian. "I have just heard; how is he?"

Peter found he could not reply; he simply shook his head. He felt Julian squeeze his shoulder in a silent response of understanding.

"There're a couple of riders coming back, sir," called a Gunner.

Peter looked up. Two horses were cantering back towards the gun site. One was Kirkby, the other looked like an officer. They both halted and the officer dismounted and, holding a satchel bag, came over.

"Lieutenant Webster. I'm the local MO. Let's have a look at him," Webster knelt down, took away the rolled blanket and rolled Hills onto his back.

"Well, he's breathing." He took out a stethoscope and used it to listen to Hills' chest. "Yes, he's breathing without too much fluid down there." He listened again and said, "His heart is going steadily." He took off the stethoscope, thought for a few seconds and said, "He'll do better slightly sat up. Have you a couple of blankets?"

Peter turned to order them but a Gunner was there with a number of blankets all ready.

Webster folded one up and said "Lift him up gently and I'll put one under his back and the other two under his head."

Hills opened his eyes. Peter leaned over him.

"You've been hit in the chest but you are going to be all right. Just relax. The medical orderlies are taking you to the main hospital."

Hills tried to sit up "But…"

Peter put a hand on his shoulder. "Lie still. Everything will be all right. You will be back here very quickly."

Hills gradually relaxed, laid back and closed his eyes.

Peter stood up and said to Webster. "Will he be all 'ght?"

Webster shrugged. "I really can't say, it's a very bad wound, but we'll do our best." He looked towards the medical post and said. "Here come the dooly orderlies. They'll take him to the post and there we will be able to examine him better and then get him back to the hospital."

Four turbaned Indian bearers arrived and laid out a large dooly stretcher on the ground. Hills was gently lifted and placed onto it. The dooly was suspended from a carrying pole by ropes at each end; it would be a smoother ride than a normal stretcher. Two of the bearers lifted the pole, placed it on their right shoulders and with even steps started the long walk back to the medical point.

Peter watched them go with a feeling of despair and then he walked over to where he was standing when Hills was hit. He looked through the shimmering mirage sliding across the veldt to where the shots must have come from. Was the rifleman still there?

"Where are you?" Peter murmured. "I'd kill you with my bare hands if I had you now." He felt a sudden surge of hatred that he had never felt before against any of the Queen's enemies that he had ever fought before.

"If Hills dies I'll …." He shook his head. No - he must be rational otherwise the Battery would suffer, but he could feel the deep wound that was inside. He turned back to the guns. Julian had ordered the stand down and was starting to do essential maintenance. Both guns had been used hard and they badly needed expert care to get them ready for their next part in this conflict.

"Captain," Peter called to Julian.

"Yes, sir." Julian walked over and Peter turned with him to make sure they were out of earshot of the men working.

"Julian, we must reorganise. Without Hills we must have someone to take up some of his duties."

"A BSM, sir?"

"Yes, I think McCann will be right for that job if he stays on the guns but we need some one to look after the back-up supplies. I think that Dixie would make a Sergeant to keep the supplies and wagons in the Battery back-up position."

"Good idea."

"I'll tell them at once," said Peter

"We've got a big problem with the recoil glycerine oil again, sir. There's still dust getting into the channels and we can only salvage so much of the oil in use. There is under half a can of the clean spare oil left.

"Damn. I'll have to go back to the De Aar stores to get the rest, if it's been found." Peter took off his helmet and wiped his sweating brow, "I'll ask the CRA for permission to go."

"We also need filters to clean up the oil for reuse. Without them and the extra oil, sir, we're finished."

"You're right, Julian. Do the best you can with what is left and if necessary, we'll only use one gun. It sounds as though our trial is coming to an end."

Colonel Eustace the Commander Royal Artillery said that Peter could go back to De Aar but not for at least a week - just in case the full artillery was wanted.

Peter visited the Field Dressing Station and spoke to Lieutenant Webster, who told him that though Hills was not in immediate danger, he was very weak from shock and loss of blood.

"There's certainly a bullet in his chest but it doesn't seem to be against any major organ. If they can get it out, and they can clean the wound and he can stay clear of infection, he stands a reasonable chance of making it."

"Where is he now?" asked Peter.

"We saw him to the Mobile Field Hospital and I hope by now he is safely in a hospital in De Aar, or even further back towards Cape Town."

At this news Peter had a wry smile to himself. He would get the oil and, if Hills was in De Aar, he would visit him at the same time.

Chapter 20

It was six days before the CRA gave Peter permission to leave the Battery gun site.

He decided to take four Gunners and Sergeant Dixey so that he would have men to search the stores if necessary, with Dixie being the man who would have the stores knowledge to hopefully find the other two cans.

It was a slow and painful train journey of 18 hours to get to De Aar. Then, with Dixey alongside him, he walked into the RA Quartermaster's Stores that he had been to only a few weeks ago. To his surprise, the same QM Sergeant that he had seen before came smartly to attention as he entered the stores.

"Can I help you sir?"

"Yes, I want the …"

"The other two cans of oil. Yes, sir. We found them and we've got them stored safe like." He walked over to a metal cupboard and opened the doors. He leaned down and pulled out the two cans of glycerine oil. He stood up with a smile.

"Well done, Sar'nt. Very efficient I must say. I expect you want me to sign for them?"

"If you would, sir," and he held out a signature pad.

As Peter signed the pad, he said. "Is Major Kricksam still here?"

"No, sir. Major Ryle is the new QM, and we're a very happy team sir." replied the QMS.

Peter smiled, then said to Dixey, "Sar'nt Dixey, two cans here for the railway station."

Peter left Sergeant Dixey outside the RA stores with instructions to remain at the Royal Artillery Depot until he came back from the hospital.

While the actual hospital was not difficult to find, to discover exactly where Hills was, was a different matter. Eventually he found a nurse who suggested he looked in a long marquee where a number of RA casualties were. Peter walked down the line of beds feeling very depressed at the sights he saw. He passed a bed with a man lying flat when he heard a weak voice say, "Major Rutland."

Peter turned and saw Hills trying to lift himself on his elbow. He looked terrible with sunken eyes and a sallow complexion.

"Lie still," said Peter. He looked round and found a folding chair that he pulled up to Hills' bed.

"How are you?" he` asked. He expected a noncommittal 'Oh I'm all right sir,' from Hills but he was amazed when Hills said, "I'm reasonable, sir, but I must get out of here."

"Why?" asked Peter.

"It's the endemic fever, sir. It started here last week. Men are dying, even one of the nurses died yesterday. Can you take me back to the Battery? Please get me anywhere but don't leave me here."

Peter was horrified at this outburst. "How is your wound?" he asked.

"That's coming on all right, sir. I'm weak but I'll be all right as long as I get away from here."

Peter looked at Hills' gaunt face; it was filled with – fear. There was no other word for it; Hills was terrified that he would die of fever here in a hospital.

Peter stood up, "I'll go and find your doctor and have a word with him."

"It's Doctor Griffiths you want, sir."

"Right," said Peter and walked back down the ward. He saw a nurse and asked where he could find Dr Griffiths. She showed him where the Medical Officer had an office.

Peter knocked at a door marked 'Captain D. Griffiths MO'.

"Come in," came a reply. Peter opened the door and walked in. A man of thirty odd years was sitting at a desk. He looked worn out with dark rings under his eyes. "What can I do for you, Major?"

"Major Rutland, Captain. I have come about my Master Gunner Hills, who is in the RA ward. He is recovering from a chest wound."

"Ah yes. God, he was lucky. That bullet was just about spent when it hit him. I managed to get it out of him whole, and though it had slipped between his ribs, it had only just hit the lungs. Still, he's strong so with luck he'll pull through."

Peter sat down on a chair in front of the desk. "He wants me to take him back to the Battery," he said.

"No," replied Griffiths. "That'd kill him. He must not be moved as any physical jerking could open the wound and may tear the lung. No, he must stay as still as possible."

"He's very worried about the enteric fever coming to the hospital," said Peter.

Griffith nodded. "He's right to worry. It's a potential nightmare for us."

"Can't I get him away at all?"

Griffiths shook his head. "The hospital ship in Cape Town was filled up and has just left so I'm afraid there's nowhere for him to go. The next ship won't be back for two to three months."

"Captain, I am in fact a Lieutenant Colonel. Can I pull rank and get some action?"

"Even if you were a General, I'm afraid I could do nothing, unless you can get a new hospital with all the services moved further out into clean country. I'm sorry Colonel, but your Master Gunner will just have to take his chances with the rest of them."

Peter stood up; there was obviously no point in trying any more. Hills couldn't be moved and the fever was coming. He felt so very depressed as he left the Doctor's office and slowly made his way back towards the RA ward. He had just crossed the corridor towards the ward when he heard a voice call "Peter!"

He turned round and saw Georgia Crumpton Smythe running towards him. She caught hold of both of his hands and with a great smile asked, "Why are you here?"

Peter looked into her large brown eyes and said, "I've come to see my Master Gunner."

"Oh yes, of course, Alfred Hills," she said.

"How do you know him?"

"I wrote his letters home for him when he was too ill to write, and he mentioned you. In fact, he thinks a great deal of you," she said.

"But what are you doing here?" asked Peter, "I thought you were with your sister."

"I am with Izzie but I help here during the day. They're very short of nurses and general helpers."

"Hills wants me to take him back to the Battery."

"Oh, surely you won't do that. He is still very weak – it could kill him."

"I know, Doctor Griffiths has just told me but Hills is so worried about the enteric fever that's starting to spread here. I must get him away from here; he is so weak and vulnerable."

Georgia, who was still holding both of Peter's hands, gave them a pull. "He can come back to the farmhouse. I'm sure that as long as he stays still, all he needs is some gentle care and good food."

"Could he really stay there?"

"Of course," she replied.

Peter looked down at her and, on an impulse, he kissed her on her forehead.

Georgia smiled up at him and said, "Let's go and see poor Dr Griffiths."

As they walked back towards the Doctor's office, Peter said, "Why poor Dr Griffiths?"

"Poor man, he is worked off his feet with little or no help and so many sick men to worry about – and he does worry about them."

Peter knocked at the door and they both entered. "I'm sorry to bother you again, Doctor, but could I move Hills to Mrs Crumpton Smythe's farmhouse, where she would look after him?"

The Captain leaned back in his chair. "That'd be the best thing for him without a doubt but, damn it all, Colonel, you are taking one of my loveliest and most cheerful helpers."

To Peter's amazement, Georgia went round the desk and ruffled the MO's hair. "Don't worry Frank I'll still work here for you."

He smiled. "Thank God for that. I'd have a mutiny if the men thought you'd left. Take great care of Hills. He'll be very frail for the next couple of weeks though I'm sure fresh air, good food and clean water will work wonders. Good luck."

"Thank you, Captain," said Peter, then he and Georgia left the room.

Outside Georgia said, "Colonel? Have you got a secret?"

Peter laughed, "Yes, I'm a Lieutenant Colonel but not while I am working with my guns. It's a long story. Let's go and see Hills."

In the RA ward Georgia walked up to Hills, who was lying flat on his bed. "Hello, Georgia," he said.

"Hello, Alfred,"

Peter looked surprised. "Georgia?" he said.

"Yes, Georgia," said Georgia.

Peter smiled and said to Hills, "This is Mrs Crumpton Smythe."

A look of amazement flashed across Hills' face "Crumpton Smythe, the Colonel who..?"

"Yes," said Peter.

Then Georgia said, "But to Alfred here I am Georgia."

"Oh, no, madam," said Hills, "I couldn't."

"Oh yes, you can and your Colonel has just got permission for me to have you at my sister's farm just down the road. We'll have you in a bed and we'll get you well in no time at all."

Hills struggled to sit up. "That's marvellous, sir."

"You lie still," said Peter, "I'm going to get transport for you."

"I can walk, sir."

"No, you can't. I'll get a stretcher for you." said Peter and rose to find the necessary ambulance.

Hills lay back on his pillow, while Georgia stayed at his bedside. Hills closed his eyes and said quietly as though to himself, "Strange that the Colonel's wife nursed me when I was wounded in Afghanistan, and now his friend is looking after me. I'm very lucky."

Georgia smiled, "Yes, Alfred, so am I."

Peter found an ambulance with ease as there were plenty around, so he chose a large eight berth one with very good springs. Hills, lying on a stretcher, was placed in the rear of the ambulance carriage. A nurse and an orderly accompanied him on the very slow trip to the farmhouse.

Peter and Georgia rode in the Cape cart that she used every day, to arrive ahead of the ambulance. Georgia asked Isabella if Alfred could stay with them and, as she expected, Izzie said, "Of course he can, the more the merrier."

Alfred was put into a large double bed in a bright airy room overlooking the garden and the hills beyond. Though he was still very weak, his attitude was almost buoyant.

"This is marvellous, sir." Then he looked at Izzie and said, "Thank you so much, ma'am. I know I can get well here and be out of your way very quickly."

"Alfred, you can stop this 'Ma'am' stuff right now, I am Izzie and my husband is Franklin. He is in charge here, especially with the sick inmates of which you are the only one." She tucked the sheets in around him, "And you don't leave here until Franklin says you are completely fit. No argument!"

Alfred smiled and settled back onto the pillows piled behind him. "Thank you. I think I'm going to enjoy myself here."

Izzie leaned over and stroked his forehead. "Now get some sleep," she said and hustled Peter and Georgia out of the room.

Sitting out on the stoep with a glass of cold lemonade, Peter said to Izzie and Georgia. "I am very grateful to you both. I don't know what I would have done without you. I owe a great deal to Alfred, and to have left him in that hospital would have killed him, and destroyed me."

Izzie smiled at him. "You are a great big softy – but don't worry, I won't tell anyone, and we'll keep Alfred here until he is properly fit. Will he then go back into the action?"

"No! Emphatically no. He came out here especially to serve with me; he is due for retirement and I'm making damn sure he goes straight home to England."

"Well, there's no arguing with you, then," laughed Izzie. "Alfred goes home to England!" she said in a gruff voice. All three of them laughed at Isabella's parody of Peter.

"God, he's a lucky man to come here," said Peter.

"He said that your wife nursed him in Afghanistan," said Georgia.

"He was wounded in the thigh while he was saving my life. Bea stitched him up and dressed the wound until he was fit. He was always so embarrassed when he had to take his trousers off for her to examine it."

Isabella stood up. "I'm going to get the children's tea and something for Alfred. Why don't you two take a walk down to the stream?" She collected up the empty glasses and went into the kitchen.

Peter stood up and Georgia followed. They walked down the steps and into the shade of the trees around the house. Georgia put her arm through his as they strolled along. He held her hand, then stopped and turned to face her.

"Georgia," he paused, "when I was last here I brought terrible news to you and I felt .." She turned and lifted up her face to look at him.

"Georgia, I love you. I knew it then and I know it now. It's so soon after Gerard's death I shouldn't be saying…"

She lifted her hand and gently pressed her fingers against his mouth.

"You don't have to say anything more – because I love you."

He leaned closer and kissed her gently. She put her hand behind his head and they kissed passionately. They stood holding each other tightly, then kissed again.

Isabella saw through the kitchen widow the two embracing and kissing. She felt an inner warmth at the sight; they were right for each other, and they needed each other after their own personal losses.

Peter and Georgia strolled through the dappled shade of the trees towards the small river.

"How much longer do you think this war will last?" asked Georgia.

Peter slowly shook his head. "In military terms we've almost won. One last push and we will have taken Bloemfontein. That's their capital city. They've no large centre to retreat to and use as a base so we've won – or have we? I think they have an inner strength and such great tenacity that they'll fight on. They could well break up into two or three armies and continually harass us. I truly have no idea – except that I am sure at some time both sides have got to sit down and talk."

"So you'll be here for some time to come?"

"No. I'm on a special project and I think it's almost at an end." He turned to face her. "When that time comes, will you come home with me?"

She lowered her head and pressed it against his chest. "Yes. I would like that," she replied.

He put his hand under her chin and gently lifted her face and kissed her.

"The hospital," he said. "I'm worried about you working there. The enteric fever will come. There is no doubt."

"I shall be all right."

He hugged her tight and said, "No, Georgia, please don't go back. I couldn't bear to lose you."

She lifted her head; she looked at him and saw the deep concern on his face. He feared losing a second love to dedication to the needy, and the ensuing disease.

"You won't lose me – but I'm needed there. You showed me that when we had dinner in Cape Town. In fact, it was your Beatrice who showed me that. For once in my life I am actually needed – I must go back."

He hugged her again and, placing his lips on her hair, he kissed her; this time it was his turn to feel terrible anguish at their parting.

Chapter 21

Two days later, after travelling on basic military trains, Peter and his party reached the Battery position. It was starting to get dark by the time they actually arrived, but there were no tents erected and all seemed to be packed into wagons and ready for moving off.

"What's the situation?" Peter asked Julian.

"We're to be ready to move either tonight or early tomorrow morning. The Boers have set up a defensive position just a few miles away. It could well be the last defensive battle they'll fight before we enter Bloemfontein."

"Are we fully equipped and provisioned?"

"Yes, now that we've got the spare oil, we're truly ready for action, though I don't know how long Number 2 Gun's going to last with the improvised washers. The recuperator no longer leaks when on the road but it does when being fired. I had a test with it yesterday and after just a few rounds the oil started to dribble out."

"If this is supposedly our last battle," said Peter, "we can use Number 2 Gun till it finishes and just rely on Number 1."

"One other thing, sir, the wheel hubs on guns and limbers are very worn; they are getting very weak and wobble badly on uneven ground. I've put the best wheels on the guns but the limbers are in poor shape."

"Well, we'll do our best. If we lose limbers that isn't too bad, but the guns must be brought back."

Julian nodded. "How is Hills?" he asked.

Peter smiled. "When I saw him at first he was desperately weak and very worried about the enteric fever which was coming into the hospital. But as luck would have it, I met Mrs Crumpton Smythe, the Cavalry Colonel's wife, and she said that Hills could stay at her sister's house while he convalesces."

Julian smiled. "That's a load off our minds then."

Peter nodded, but at the mention of Georgia and the enteric, he felt a wave of gloom sweep across him.

"Where's my kit?" he asked.

"Higgins has got it on the third wagon, sir."

"Thank you. I will report to the CRA and get our final orders."

The details that Peter received from the CRA were that the whole column was leaving at dawn next day and that 172 Battery would simply march to the right of the line of the attack. There were no special orders for them because, now there were plenty of field gun Batteries to cover all the artillery support that was necessary, 172 would be kept as a reserve, or for any special duty.

Peter was not sorry about that. He was hoping that with just a moderate amount of shooting, the Battery could be withdrawn and the guns could go back to England – then he could take Georgia out of the hospital - and home to Surrey.

De Wet knew that his next battle with the British would be the last one to defend Bloemfontein. If they failed, then the capital would be lost to Roberts. De Wet chose an area to the south of the town close by the farm at Driefontein. It was well suited to defence as the dongas gave plenty of cover for his men and also protection against flanking attacks or even head-on cavalry charges. He had defence in depth.

Bobs equally knew that this was the last fight before Bloemfontein. He also knew that he could not outflank the Boer without having to go many miles into inhospitable country and then fight on the Boer's terms of fast movement. Bobs decided that it would be a matter of pounding away, and he was certain that eventually the Boer would retreat.

It was late that afternoon when a Major from General Roberts' staff came galloping up.

"Major Rutland?" he asked.

"Yes," called Peter.

"I'm Major Raikes." He quickly dismounted and pulled a map out of his map case. He opened it and pointed. "We're here. The Boer are fighting stubbornly in trenches here but we will eventually wear them down, possibly by dusk. But the trouble is that we've seen a number of wagon trains moving back over here on the right of the action. There are so many damned dongas criss-crossing the area that we can't see which they are using.

"The CRA is using all his firepower in support of the infantry attack but says you're free to swing round this right end to have a go at the supplies.

"There's a sizeable kopje over there." the Major pointed to the right front of the Battery position. "It's here on the map." He put his finger on the map and said, "You can see that if you could put down as much fire cover as you can along this line, Mr Boer might think there are many more guns here and give up this escape route."

In silence, Peter looked carefully at the map. "If we can get halfway up the back of the kopje here, then split the guns to go around either side, we can bring down one hell of a lot of gun fire on the area below."

"If you can do that Major, General Roberts wishes you to start as quickly as possible. He really wants to stop the supplies getting away," said Raikes.

"At once, Major," said Peter and shouted out, "Battery limber up!"

Major Raikes mounted his horse. Peter called out, "We will be in action in about half an hour." Raikes saluted and, putting spurs to his horse, galloped away.

Within a few minutes 172 Battery, consisting of two guns and only four limbers, plus Sergeant Dixey and three supply wagons was trotting towards the large kopje. Julian rode up alongside Peter at the head of the line.

Peter pointed at the side of the kopje. "Do you see that gulley with the patch of trees just half way up?"

"Yes," acknowledged Julian.

"Well, I think it looks fairly flat about one hundred yards to the left. When we get there we'll split the guns and go either side of the hill until we can see Boer activity. Then it's just a matter of blazing away to either hit or scare the wagon trains. We'll leave Sar'nt Dixey and the wagons at the bottom of the main slope to make our base camp."

The start of the hillside was reasonably even and quite steep but the guns fairly bowled along. Peter was right, there was a flat area close to the gulley that was a donga cut into the hillside and quite overgrown with trees.

When the Battery arrived, dusk was only an hour or so away.

"Julian, you take Number 2 Gun and the two limbers to the left. I think that'll be the shortest track for you to see the Boer. I'm going to the right and try and get higher. That'll take me longer, but I'll start firing the moment I arrive. When you've used all your ammo come back here and wait for me. There's a chance that I might not make it back before night time. If it's too dark wait here until I come back in the morning."

"Very good, sir," said Julian, who turned to his gun crew.

"I'll take Voomby with me to help with finding a track," Peter called out. Julian raised his hand in acknowledgement.

De Wet had entrenched his men well. Bobs was being held back but De Wet wanted to make sure that when he had to retire, the line of retreat would be free. They had to make sure that the wagons were able to get the supplies away. He waved his arm to a number of men in Jan's commando. "Come on, Kerels, let's help the wagons," he called.

Jan kicked the ribs of his pony and headed towards the cloud of dust that was the sign of the wagons moving. There were many dongas and spruits to cross before the land flattened out, and that made it so difficult to move the supplies. The good thing was that the Khakis would have difficulty as well. Their beloved railway was some way off.

At one donga he saw a small wagon with two horses struggling up the far slope. He threw his rope towards the men pushing the wagon and they tied it on the front axle. Then, with an extra horse pulling, they managed to get the wheels turning and gradually it cleared the steep side and reached the flat ground above. He wound his rope back and went looking for more wagons to assist. Dusk was less than an hour away; when that arrived they would get away and the Khakis would bed down for the night.

Then he heard the British guns start shelling. The explosions were well off to the west; maybe they can't see us, he thought.

Number 1 Gun followed a track up the kopje that was clear but steep then, just as Peter was beginning to despair, he saw the plain spread out before him. The ground below was veined with gulleys, some wet but mainly dry. These dongas, invisible from the lower ground, were so visible from this height as they veined across the veldt. Some were up to fifty yards wide while others were very narrow. There was also the swirling dust rising in a fading cloud; it came from the lines of wagons streaming away. He heard a gun fire – it was Number 2 Gun opening up. Then its shells started to fall fast and furious into the dust cloud over to the left.

"Action right!" shouted Peter. It was going to be very difficult to get the gun into action on such a small flattish area. The two limbers would have to be in-line rather than at the gun's side.

The dust from the wagon train was certainly a long way off; Peter guessed at 5000 yards and gave a Fire Order. A High Explosive shell howled away. Peter watched its flight towards the line. It fell well short in a pimple of dust.

"5700 yards 3 rounds gunfire."

He could still hear Number 2 Gun banging out its shells. They were raising even more clouds of dust well over to the left of the dongas.

Peter decided to aim as far up the column as possible. The shells fell around the lines of wagons but it was very difficult to see exactly where they exploded. He peered through his glasses and decided to fire a large number of shells at slightly increasing ranges.

He was about to give a fire order when he realised that Number 2 Gun was no longer firing. Maybe Julian was pausing as well.

"5 rounds gunfire. 5750 yards."

The Gunners fed the Ehrhardt swiftly, and quickly completed the order.

"5 rounds 5850 yards."

Again the five shells flew out with amazing speed to add dust and presumably confusion in the wagon train.

"5 rounds 6000 yards." As they started firing again Peter decided to reduce the range and cover the area again.

Suddenly a large red and yellow flash appeared, followed by a tall swirling column of smoke and dust that rose into the darkening sky. "Wow. That must've been an ammo wagon."

He scanned the area of the explosion as the smoke cleared. It was right in a donga, and there appeared to be a large thorn tree a few yards from the edge.

Peter called out to BSM McCann "How many rounds have we left?"

McCann would be counting them one by one. "Seventeen, sir. Five shrapnel, twelve HE."

Peter acknowledged with a raised hand. Then once again he noticed that there was no sound coming from Number 2 Gun. They had about the same number of rounds but they seemed to have stopped already. Maybe the oil plug had failed.

He walked over to the BSM. "Sarn't Major, fire off the shrapnel at 6200 yards, then all of the HE starting at 6100 and dropping 100 hundred yards every three rounds until they are all used up. It will be completely dark by then."

"Very good, sir."

Five minutes later BSM McCann reported. "Fire order completed, sir."

"Thank you, Sar'nt Major. Limber up."

Jan's little pony was sweating and showing signs of fatigue. Jan had helped with the moving of a large number of wagons of all sizes that had now passed down the track leading to the road to Bloemfontein – then more of those damned guns started firing and they were close.

An artillery team had just dragged the 2 pounder pom-pom gun up the slope but the ammunition wagon that followed was well in the mud and one front wheel was slipping off the axle. With four mules pulling and seven men pushing it was only just moving. Yet it had to be got out of the dongas to clear the way for the other wagons behind.

Jan rode to edge of the donga and threw his long rope down to the men below. They tied it to the front axle while Jan wound it round a large thorn tree at the top of the donga and then to the pommel of his saddle. This way he could get the pony to pull while he could also lend his weight to the rope.

He yelled to the men below and smacked the pony's rump, then the whole team of men, mules and horse all pulled together. He looked over the edge and saw that slowly, very slowly, the wagon was moving - but he also heard the shells getting closer. He yelled at his pony again and, with his hands torn and bloody from pulling, he threw his weight against the rope once more.

The shelling had stopped a few seconds before. Then he heard the howl of more shells flying towards them. The first one smashed into the donga just behind the wagons - the next shell he did not hear or see – he was just aware of a bright yellow sun that faded to blood red as he was lifted up to oblivion.

Jan was thrown through the air back on to the veldt, a lifeless form. His body slammed to the ground; it fell on to its right side as though he was in a position of sleep, but the crushed chest and the blood running from his mouth belied the image that he was just resting.

As the Gunners worked at coming out of action, Peter looked around the gun site – again the detritus of battle was all around him in the shape of brass cartridges and shell wrappings, but thank goodness, this time none of his men's blood. With a lot of difficulty, the Gunners just managed to turn the gun round and limber it up in the small space and in the deepening gloom.

Peter walked over to Voomby. "Can we get down now or should we stay here till the morning?"

Voomby instantly replied. "We stay here. Too dark to go."

Peter nodded. "Sar'nt Major, we'll stay here the night. Post sentries and we'll be off at first light, so wake the men at 4 a.m. It'll still be dark, but dawn will be close and we can move the moment we can see where we are going. No fires tonight so its cold victuals all round."

"Right, sir," acknowledged McCann.

The horses were hitched to a long line and given what food and water was available, which was not much. The Gunners had their iron rations of biscuit and bully beef plus some water. With the gun limbered up ready to move, and the horses hitched for the night, the gun crew settled down to wait for the dawn.

Peter lay on a reasonably flat piece of ground closed his eyes and, before sleeping, he let his mind wander.

This was obviously the end of the trial. Limber and gun wheels were in bad repair. Number 1 Gun was still working but there was very little glycerine oil left. Number 2 Gun was probably dry of oil by now. It was surprising that it had not been firing for longer though. Still, it was all coming to a very satisfactory end with both guns safe. A shudder went down his spine at the thought that a gun might have been lost at any time but both were going back, whatever the condition.

He knew that Voomby was sitting against a rock close by. He was never far away. What are we going to do with him?

Gradually sleep overcame him.

Chapter 22

A hand was gently shaking his shoulder. It was Voomby. "Shots."

Peter sat up and listened. It was still quite dark but dawn was not far away. He heard a scrambling coming closer to him. It was McCann. "The sentry heard shots over to the west, sir."

"Wake the men and try and get the horses hitched up. We'll leave as soon as we can."

He turned to Voomby. "Where were the shots?" Voomby pointed towards the rear of the kopje.

"From where we are meeting the other gun?" asked Peter. Voomby stood in thought, then he nodded.

"Can you lead the men in this light if we walk?" Voomby nodded again. "Yes, mJor."

Peter walked to where the BSM was checking the gun and limber. "Sar'nt Major, there might be trouble back at the base camp. Leave three men with the gun and one man with the limber. They are to come down the track as soon as they can see their way. The rest of the men will take their rifles and we will follow Voomby down."

"Right, sir." He ran over to the gun and after giving instructions returned with the remaining nine men all with rifles held at the high port.

Peter spoke to them. "I think there's some trouble down at the base camp where we left Captain Stevens. Voomby is going to lead us down there. Now I don't want any shooting unless it is obviously necessary as we might hit some of our own men. Voomby will lead; watch carefully, be ready but be cautious."

He turned to Voomby, who started to trot down the track they had previously come up. Though the light was poor, it was getting better every minute. Peter followed Voomby but did not allow him to go too far ahead. There was no point in arriving without all of the men.

Voomby led them along the track and then to Peter's surprise he turned uphill. The Gunners all followed as he turned into a donga that fell down the hillside.

They scrambled along until Voomby stopped and slowly crept out onto the track again. They had cut across the hill and shortened the distance considerably. Peter could just make out in the improving light the area where he had left Julian the previous evening.

Voomby crouched and slowed to a crawl – then he stopped and with a slight arm movement gestured to Peter, who crept alongside. Voomby pointed. There in the gloom Peter could see a limber standing without horses. Voomby gestured for him to stay still while he then crept towards the position. Peter could see him clearly but there was no one else about. After a few

259

seconds Voomby stood upright and waved an arm for them all to come down.

When Peter arrived, he saw a limber and an amount of kit that had been strewn about. Voomby pointed across the track and walked over.

Two wounded Gunners were lying beside a rock. They were obviously in a bad way but surprised to see the other party.

"Sir!" called one.

Peter went over to him. "What happened?"

"The Boers caught us and have taken the gun with the rest of the crew."

"Bloody hell," Peter exclaimed. "How did they get the gun away?"

"They tied their ponies to it and dragged it off."

Peter stood up. Could they catch up with the Boer party?

"Major Rutland, sir." It was Sergeant Piper. "The Boers have taken the gun, sir."

"And the horses?" asked Peter.

"No, sir, Captain Stevens had the horses put in the gulley over there to keep them sheltered. I went over last evening and stayed there with them but heard the firing when the crew were captured."

"How did the Boers manage to take the gun away?" asked Peter.

"When I heard the firing, I crept up and I think the Boers wanted to blow up the gun and then they decided it'd be too noisy, so they decided to drag it back to their camp. Captain Stevens told them that there weren't any horses because you'd taken them all. They hitched the gun up to a limber then, with their long ropes attached to four ponies in front and two behind as brakes, they dragged it off down the track over there. The limber is full of ammo. All the gun crew were captured but they can't have got too far ahead as they were going very slowly with the ponies and the gun."

"How many Boers were there?"

"About ten, sir."

"And you've got a team of horses down in the gulley?"

"Yes, sir."

"Well done Sergeant."

Peter turned to his Gunners, who had gathered around him.

"Voomby, can you see where they've gone?" The Zulu nodded and pointed down the track. "We'll take the horses and catch up with the Boer party," said Peter.

"No horses, mJor," said Voomby. "We catch them on foot."

"On foot?" queried Peter.

Voomby nodded "We catch them. They go on track."

Peter looked at the Zulu who seemed very confident. He had got here by a short cut. Maybe he knew of another.

"Sar'nt Piper, we are going after the gun. Voomby is sure we can cut them off. Number 1 Gun will be down here shortly with a spare limber. Are there any shells in that limber?" asked Peter pointing at the one on the track.

"Yes, sir. We only fired off half of them when the oil washer on the draining bolt failed. We fired two more rounds but we couldn't control the piece, so Captain Stevens brought it back with both limbers."

"When Number 1 Gun gets here put some shells into its limber," said Peter. "Come down the track with the four Gunners. Don't get too close to us if we are in trouble. If we lose Number 2 Gun, it will be bad, but it'll be a disaster if we lose both of them – so be ready to run for it. Leave us and save the gun. That is an order!"

"Right, sir. What about these wounded men?"

"We can't do anything now – let's hope we return and then help them."

He looked at the other Gunners. "The rest of you, we'll follow Voomby and then attack the Boers when we catch up with them. They can't be too far ahead, and they've got to tow a gun. Who have got their Marksman badge?" he asked. Three Gunners raised their hand.

"You three stick with me. When we reach the tail end of the column we'll shoot the back guards. Aim carefully for the middle of their backs. Don't just let it fly. Make sure you hit. Understand?"

The three Gunners nodded. "The rest of you stay close to but only open fire when we are all shooting. I don't want a lot of loose firing. Remember your mates are down there and we don't want to shoot them - so be careful."

He turned to Voomby and nodded. The Zulu started off at a moderate trot; the rest of the Gunners followed clumping along in their boots behind the almost silent native.

After several minutes Voomby stopped, then led the party down a small donga. Scrambling along, tripping and scraping they followed.

Again Voomby stopped. He crept up to the edge and gestured to Peter. There, just one hundred yards away, were three Boers on ponies at the rear of the line with some of Julian's Gunners walking in front of them.

Peter waved up the three marksmen, and spoke to the rest of the Gunners. "Stick with me. We'll shoot the tail end men and then all of us will charge at the gun."

The four men clambered out of the donga and Peter waved the rest to follow. The Boers did not look behind them as Peter and his men gradually closed up on the line of men and gun.

When a bend came in the track, the gun was not in sight but Peter could still see the last three Boers. He lay down and aimed at the left-hand Boer rearguard. His marksmen followed suit. Peter fired. One Boer instantly fell off his horse as the other Gunners also fired. One more Boer was hit and fell but the third turned and kicked his horse on to get to the head of the column.

"Now!" shouted Peter. "Charge!" All of his party ran forward shouting. It was a mad scramble over the last hundred yards towards the gun where the other Boers could be seen with Julian's Gunners. All of them looked round to see what was happening.

"Get down!" shouted Peter at Julian's party. His own Gunners started to fire at the Boers who had been towing the gun as they loosed the long ropes but Gunners are notorious for being bad marksmen. A number of the Boers started to fire back to give cover to the rest of their commando as they detached themselves from the Ehrhardt.

The Boers to the left of the gun were scrambling to get away but they were still firing at the charging

263

Gunners. Peter saw two of his men fall, hit by the covering rifle fire from the retreating Boers. He knelt down and resting his left elbow on his knee, aimed at one of the horseman. He was about to fire when a sharp blow struck him on his left arm; a Mauser bullet had smashed into his forearm, its blow knocking him over. Slowly he got onto his hands and knees - his left arm pouring blood.

Holding his left arm up to his chest and dragging his rifle, Peter scrambled down the slope to be between two rocks. He lifted his head to see his Gunners were still firing at the retreating Boers but with little effect.

Julian, with a number of his Gunners, slithered and crawled their way back to where Peter's men were firing.

"Peter, you're hit!" he said.

Peter nodded, "I'm all right. Sergeant Piper is ….."

A crackle of shots slammed into the group of Gunners. The firing came from a group of Boers further down the track who had turned to cover the retreat of the rest.

Very few of Peter's Gunners remained and were able to return any fire. The Boers were running but they had nearly wiped out the Battery and the gun was almost their's for the taking.

"mJor! mJor!" Voomby, who was in some rocks over to the right, shouted to Peter and pointed up the track. A couple of hundred yards away was Sergeant Piper bringing down Number 1 Gun.

"Oh God!" Peter cried out.

"Voomby!" he shouted. "Tell Sergeant Piper to get away. Leave us and save the gun!"

Voomby slid out of sight as he tried to work his way to Number 1 Gun.

"Julian," said Peter. "Try and get to Piper and get the gun away. What's left of us will give you some covering fire."

Julian knew it was the right decision; he turned to call his men when a volley of shots slammed into the small group. The fire came from above them!

Julian peered round a rock and said. "They're up the hill near that crag."

"Bloody hell! We're sitting ducks here."

"I'll take a couple of men and try to get the gun away," said Julian.

"No," ordered Peter. "It'd be certain death. Stay here. I might be able to get some of them from this position."

He poked his Lee Enfield around the rock and up at the crag. He saw a movement up there. His left arm hurt like hell but pushing it forward he rested his rifle on it and managed to get a reasonable target. He squeezed the trigger and fired a shot. As he peered up at the crag again, a Mauser bullet slammed into the rock beside his head, sending dust and splinters stinging into his face.

"It's no good, Julian." He twisted his head round – but Julian had gone.

Peter slid to the side to where he could see Number 1 Gun on the track. He could hardly believe his eyes - Piper was bringing it into action! It was only 100 yards from the crag. Peter saw a Gunner take a round from the limber and immediately fall down as a bullet hit him. Another man picked up the round and loaded it. At incredibly short range Piper fired the gun but the round sailed over the top of the crag and slammed into the hillside hundreds of yards away.

Again the Gunners loaded, but by now another man was down. The breech slammed shut and again Piper fired – this time the shell hit true. The High Explosive shell exploded just under the crag which seemed to lift into the air and then swiftly disintegrate into a mass of boulders, rocks and dust.

Peter dropped his rifle and scrambled to his feet yelling to the few men left. Now was the time to charge for Number 2 Gun as the Boers on the crag were wiped out. The avalanche of rocks bounded down the hill, one flying past Peter's head; he ducked and stood upright to shout at his men again.

It was as he stood there that a football-sized rock slammed onto his helmet, smashing it to pieces and tearing into his scalp. He was thrown back down the slope, cracking his head against a flat rock, and instantly lost consciousness. He lay with his head down the slope and his left leg twisted underneath his body. Blood poured from the head wound across his eyes and mouth while loose rubble continued to slide against his body until he was almost covered.

Julian reached Number 1 Gun just as Sergeant Piper fired the second round.

"Load again, Sergeant!" he shouted. The Gunners acted in a daze and then, gasping and sweating, stood ready.

The dust from the collapsed crag gradually cleared but no more Mauser bullets flew their way. Had the Boers gone? Julian and the small number of Gunners stood and waited – but, other than the cries of the wounded, nothing moved.

Julian looked around for Peter. "Major Rutland," he shouted ."Major Rutland!"

Then with some anxiety he again called out, "Has anyone seen Major Rutland?" But there was no response.

"Oh God – no," he murmured.

"Sergeant Piper unload, then limber up the gun," he ordered. Again he shouted out to all the Gunners. "All of you look for Major Rutland."

Further down the slope Bombardier Smith, holding a field dressing to his upper leg called out. "He's down here, sir." He paused, then he added, "I think he's dead."

Julian ran and scrambled down the slope. Peter lay covered in the scree dust with blood still flowing across his face. Julian pulled him round, straightened out his legs and with a field dressing wiped the blood from Peter's face. He pushed his hand inside Peter's jacket and shirt to feel for a heartbeat. Yes, there was one.

Julian stood up and shouted, "I want some field dressings and two Gunners for the Major."

The first to arrive was Voomby. He uncorked his water bottle and gently poured water over Peter's face to wash away the blood from his nose and mouth.

Gunner Adams slithered down the slope with some field dressings. Julian took one and said, "Go and get a stretcher."

"Where from, sir?" asked the Gunner.

Julian looked up at him. "No. We haven't got any. Hell!"

"We could carry him down, sir" suggested Adams.

Julian looked around for any idea of how to get Peter down to the Battery camp at the foot of the hill.

"I carry him," said Voomby. Julian looked at the muscled chest of the Zulu; he was a strong man, he should be able to carry Peter in his arms down the slope where two men could not manage.

"Right," said Julian, and then he shouted out, "Bombardier Gantry!"

Gantry ran across the slope holding a rifle. "Yes, sir."

"Voomby is going to carry the Major down to the base camp. You go with him and help him as much as possible. It is going to be a hell of a long trip for him holding Major Rutland in his arms all the way. Take a canteen of water and keep a sharp lookout for trouble. Boers might still be this side of the hill. When you get down there, tell Sar'nt Dixey to get the Major to the Field Dressing Station at once. Make sure that Higgins goes with him. Come back with as many men as possible carrying all of the stretchers. The Sar'nt might even be able to get a small wagon up here. See what he can do."

"Right, sir," said the Bombardier.

"Now go, and go quickly," said Julian. He bent down and helped Voomby pick Peter up and settle him into the Zulu's arms with Peter's head resting, red with blood, on the black shoulder.

Voomby turned to face the slope and started to walk and slide down the scree. Julian watched as the three of them moved down to the base camp. Then he turned and started to organise help for the rest of the wounded; at least Peter would be with the medics shortly and then in a hospital.

Chapter 23

Peter heard someone whistling and opened his eyes. Two men were bending over side by side at the end of his bed.

"Who…?" he murmured.

"Gor blimey," the two men said, "Now you lie still sir, I'll get the MO," and they disappeared.

Peter blinked and looked up at the ceiling above his head; it was a dirty white and appeared to be gently moving. His head hurt like hell; he moved his arms and felt a sharp stabbing pain in his left forearm.

He saw the ceiling move sharply and two men stood beside his bed. "Glad you're back with us," they said. "How do you feel?" they asked.

"Where am I?" asked Peter.

"Number 18 Field Hospital, just south of Bloemfontein – in a rather special ward. Now, how do you feel?"

"I've got a terrible headache and my arm hurts – but why are there two of you?"

"Ha," snorted the men. "I'm Captain Cheney. You have had a bad blow to the head, you've been in a coma for the past few days and you are suffering double vision from concussion. Now, I want you to stay quiet and as still as possible. I'll get some morphine for the pain; otherwise everything will come right with the help of God and your batman, who's a right bloody nuisance."

The two men turned and spoke to someone else. "He will be all right as long as he's kept quiet, and he must not move about. You are in control."

"Very good, sir. I'll make him behave." said a voice that Peter felt he recognised.

"I'm damn sure you will," replied the other two men.

A few minutes later Peter felt his lips being parted and a sweet liquid dripped into his mouth; the pain gradually faded away and he slept.

When he awoke again, once more it was to the sound of whistling. Without moving his head, he said, "Who's there?"

"Only me, sir, 'iggins."

"Oh yes, Higgins." The Gunner stood at Peter's bedside, and to Peter's relief there was only one Higgins.

"Can I get you anything, sir?"

"I'd love a whisky and soda."

"Gor blimey, sir. I don't know about that. I'll ask the MO."

"If I can't have a whisky I'll like some water."

"Right, sir," and Higgins disappeared from Peter's vision.

When he returned, he brought a mug of water and a second figure came in behind him.

"How are you, sir?" said Julian.

"I feel rather battered actually."

"Not surprising. You have a torn scalp, a badly bruised head, concussion, a bullet through your forearm and a sprained ankle."

Peter gave a wry smile. "How's the Battery?"

"Do you realise you were wounded five days ago?" said Julian.

"Five days!" Peter exclaimed

"And in those five days a great deal has happened." Julian pulled up a camp chair and sat beside the bed.

"We got both guns off the hill and three limbers, We lost three Gunners and Sergeant Kirkby killed. BSM McCann has had his leg amputated but seems to be recovering. Five more are wounded and in hospital – and of course you."

"God, it was bad then."

"It was very bad. If Sergeant Piper hadn't turned up and used Number 1 Gun, we'd have lost the lot." Julian lowered his head and added, "I think we should put Piper up for a commendation of some sort."

"I agree; his decisive action saved the day."

"We managed to get the guns and the wounded down and back to the Battery site. You and the rest of the wounded were transferred to a Field Dressing Station and then on to this Mobile Field Hospital. I sent Higgins to be with you, and the next day a bomb exploded in my tent."

"A bomb?" said Peter weakly.

"Higgins came back from this hospital in an absolute fury. He told me in no uncertain terms that you were in unacceptable conditions or as he put it - I quote, 'It ain't bloomin' right. The Major's ward's in a right old four and eight', which means a terrible state.

"I came down here and saw that the medicos were well overstretched and hadn't enough room, so I said we would erect a tent for you. 'Oh, no, you won't' was the reply. 'Yes, we bleedin' will' says Higgins. Then he and Voomby had a tent up before the MOs could move. They mumbled that it would have to come down later.

"While all this was going on, I got the guns back to the Artillery park and reported to Colonel Eustace. I said that the trial was over and so they should go back to England. He was not best pleased but I told him that the guns were damaged and now virtually useless. He wanted all the spare Gunners transferred to active Batteries. I told him that there wouldn't be many as I wanted those that were still fit to handle the guns in transit and also I wanted to keep all Bombardiers and Sergeants who had knowledge of the guns.

"Then I had a stroke of luck. Just after the Higgins explosion, I met Colonel Bridport. I told him everything, suggesting that the guns should now be sent back to England with the NCOs. He completely agreed and told me that I could say that, through him, Bobs agreed to you having a private tent ward. After that everything was easy."

"Where is Voomby now?" asked Peter.

"Higgins was furious when the MOs told Voomby he couldn't stay in the hospital lines, but there was nothing we could do, so Voomby encamped just outside the area in a position where he can keep an eye on the tent. After my meeting with Colonel Bridport, Voomby now stays just outside your tent door and only sleeps inside if it's raining. Higgins and he have a good working relationship – you are covered from all angles."

Peter smiled. His head and arm ached but the pain was bearable.

Julian moved his helmet in his hands as though he was nervous. "I feel I have done all that I should within my duty to the Regiment."

Peter slightly lifted his head and frowned. "Julian, you have been excellent. Why are you worried?"

"I've done something that I was not empowered to do. Higgins asked me what will happen to you when you can move about." Julian paused and twirled his helmet again. "I decided that you shouldn't stay here because of the enteric fever – so I telegraphed Mrs Crumpton Smythe, who is looking after the Master Gunner. I gave her the basic details and asked if you could be moved down there to recuperate. I hope I did right, sir?"

Peter smiled and said quietly, "Yes you did right, Julian. What was the answer?"

"Well it wasn't what I expected having wired Mrs Crumpton Smythe. The reply simply said 'Izzie says the more the merrier.' Which I assume is a yes."

"It is." said Peter. "Thank you, Julian." He closed his eyes and lay back onto the pillow - when he opened them again, Julian had gone.

After a couple of days Peter was able to get up and walk around, but it was a further four days before the MO said that he could leave for De Aar.

Accompanied by Higgins and Voomby, he boarded the train that would take him away from the conflict, away from his guns, away from the next phase of the war. This rail journey was to be his first step on the road back to England.

At the main junction station at De Aar, Peter slowly climbed down the steps from the train and, leaning on a stick, limped across the platform followed by Higgins and Voomby, both of whom carried the small amount of baggage they all had. A Cape cart and a two-horse wagon, with Franklin in the driving seat, were waiting for them. Georgia came running across the road to Peter and threw herself into his arms.

"You look terrible," she said.

Peter threw back his head and laughed. "Thank you for those kind words."

' But you are alive and here," Georgia added. "Oh, it's so good to see you. I've been so worried since we received Julian's wire message." She buried her face into his jacket front and hugged him tight. Peter could feel her crying. He put his hand under her chin and lifted her tear stained face, "I only came back for you," he said and kissed her.

"When you folks have finished a-huggin and a-kissin', we'd sure like to be gettin' home." Franklin's southern drawl swept over the two and made them laugh.

Peter and Georgia walked over to the Cape cart while Higgins and Voomby put the baggage on the wagon.

"Right, let's head for the farm. Up y'all get." Higgins climbed up alongside Franklin but Voomby stood at the side of the wagon.

"Up you get," repeated Franklin to him.

"No, me not ride."

"Oh hell, you do. I ain't havin' you run alongside o' me. Up you git or I am a-coming down there with you." Voomby smiled and climbed on board behind the two men.

"Now if you two love birds will move your rumps," he called to Peter and Georgia, "We can git movin."

Georgia tossed the reins and the small convoy started on the short trip to the farm.

As they arrived at the lane entrance to the farm, Izzie plus the two children and their nanny came running over.

"Oh, Peter, it's lovely to see you," said Izzie and gave him a hug, then she put her arm around Georgia. "This moonstruck female has been utterly useless while we have been waiting for you." She took Peter's arm. "Come on inside you look as though you could do with a rest or a stiff drink – or both."

"Thank you so much, Isabella, for letting me come," said Peter and kissed her cheek. "How's Alfred."

"See for yourself."

There on the stoep sitting in a chair was Hills. He slowly got up as Peter and Georgia walked towards him.

"Very good to see you, sir."

"And to see you, Sar'nt Major." Peter smiled as he shook Hills' hand and then put his free hand on his shoulder.

Izzie gave a snort of disgust. "Does this mean we've got to call him Sergeant Major and you Colonel now?" she asked. "Or can we be normal and be Peter and Alfred?"

Peter looked at Hills and said, "You know, Alfred, I've seen some very bossy Sergeant Majors but our hostess beats them all. You and I are certainly outranked."

"Nope, I'm the General here and what I say goes," said Franklin. "You, Peter, are going to have a light meal and then you're going to bed. You're as weak as a kitten. Now git to your room. Food will be there shortly."

It was next day after lunch that Peter with Georgia, Izzie and Franklin were sitting in the shade of the large thorn tree.

"Georgie," said Izzie, "could you get us all a glass of cold lemon juice, please?"

"Of course, I'll bring a jug and glasses," said Georgia.

Peter, looking at the majestic view, felt Izzie move closer to him. "Peter, if you love Georgia, you must sweep her off her feet and take her away. If she stays here, she will be working in that hospital and she'll get enteric," she said. "Isn't that right, Franklin?"

"If I was running that hospital I'd sure want someone like Georgie there to help, but Izzie's right. If she keeps agoin' there, sure as God made little green apples, she'll get the fever."

Izzie went back to her chair as Georgia arrived with a tray with glasses plus a clinking jug of iced lemon juice.

As she poured the drinks out, Peter said, "I owe a great deal to Voomby but I don't know how I can help him." He took his drink. "What am I going to do for him? I can give him money, but I don't know if that will help."

"Well, I think actions have happened already to answer that question," said Franklin. "I think he's already bedded Hannah our nanny. I saw them both this morning. He had a very satisfied look on his face while Hannah was giggling like a new bride."

Georgia and Izzie both put their hands up to their faces in surprise, and laughed. "That quickly?" said Izzie.

"Yup," said Franklin. "That quickly."

"Look Peter," he continued, "I want to raise some more cattle here so I will be needin' a good stockman. Let him have some money to buy cattle then he can have some of his own and settle down here with Hannah."

"What happens to Higgins?" asked Georgia.

"'iggins and 'ills are coming back with us," said Peter.

"With us?" exclaimed Georgia.

As though by a secret order, Izzie and Franklin stood up and, apparently on an important errand, they walked towards the kitchen.

Peter stood up also. "Let's walk down to the river," he said to Georgia.

Arm in arm they walked past the shrubs towards the shade of the trees growing alongside the stream.

In the shade of the old thorn tree, Peter stopped and turned to face her. He put his arms around her and looked down into her large brown eyes. "Mrs Crumbly Smith, will you please change your name to Mrs Rutland?"

Georgia smiled, gave him a hug, and laid her head on his chest. "That would give me great pleasure, Colonel Rutland. I always wanted to be a Colonel's wife," she replied. "I would like to see your England before I take you to see Vermont."

Epitaph

In the country around Petrusburg in the Orange Free State, close to a farmstead called Driefontein, a strong steady wind blew across the arid ground. A faded, brown slouch hat was rolled across the veldt through the dust; a sudden gust of wind lifted it into the outer branches of an ancient thorn tree that was growing on the edge of a wide donga. The worn old hat became lodged deep in the small branches and thorns, almost hidden to any passer-by; there was only one thing on it that might catch the wayfarer's eye, and that was the tulip-shaped badge pinned on the crown.

Fixed firmly in the branches, the old hat with its sweat-stained brim would remain in the aged tree for many seasons– through the leafless twigs of winter and through the sweet scented blossoms of summer. There it would stay to be the only visible but hidden memorial of Jan Pieters, a South African, who so loved the beauty and grandeur of this his homeland, that he gave his life for it. He lies in an unmarked grave somewhere nearby – known only to God.

Historical note

It had been realised for some time that the Royal Artillery were relying on old technology artillery pieces.

In October 1899 Sir Henry Brackenbury was appointed Director-General of Ordnance. He sent experts to the continent seeking the best in Field Guns and found the Ehrhardt Gun made by a German firm in Dusseldorf.

It fired a 14 pound shell from which the whole of the recoil was taken by a recoil carriage that left the carrying carriage absolutely steady when the gun was fired.

The barrel was attached to the cradle by a track, which it slid along on firing. This cradle contained a hydraulic buffer filled with glycerine, and a spring recuperator.

When the gun was fired, it recoiled along the track, forcing the glycerine through grooves, thus absorbing the energy of the recoil. As the barrel recoiled, so it compressed the bank of recuperator springs within the cradle. These then returned the barrel to its original position.

This meant that the layer could remain seated when the gun was fired. The sights were on the stationary carriage, so relaying could be done while the gun was still recoiling. The breechblock was a slightly tapered interlocking cone hinged to swing to the right-hand side.

The Ehrhardt could fire 20 rounds per minute against the standard 15 plunder's rate of five or six rounds per minute.

The British Government secretly placed an order with the Ehrhardt Factory for 108 complete guns, plus wagons, stores and spare parts. Only half a dozen men knew of the transaction. Customs examinations were dispensed with. All this equipment was packed in cases marked 'Machinery and Explosives' and sent direct to Woolwich Arsenal.

The gun had a calibre of 3 inches and fired the standard '15 pounder' shell, to a maximum range of 7,000 yards, with a time fuse of up to 6,600 yards. It had a gun crew of ten men. This revolutionary Quick Firing Gun was introduced to the Royal Artillery in June 1901.

This gun was not actually used in the Boer War but a number of artillery experts were withdrawn from the conflict to be able to assess the new weapon. The government adopted the system and then adapted it to be used in a slightly heavier gun. This was the basic design of the 18 pounder used by the Field Artillery, which fired over 100 million rounds in the First World War.

There is no known example of an Ehrhardt Gun left in existence today.

The Boer War

The British Army had a nasty shock when it came up against modern rifle fire with smokeless powder for the first time. They had already decided that khaki was better camouflage than scarlet jackets. France and Germany did not take any notice of the lesson that the British had learned and only found out to their cost in the first few weeks of the First World War. Germany sent crowded masses of men against entrenched British soldiers at Mons and paid a terrible price, while the French were acting in a similar manner, dressed in conspicuous blue coats and red trousers.

....

The Boer war was the last war fought by Britain where more men died of disease than were killed by enemy action. Enteric fever and cholera were the two main killers.

The first book published in the Rutland series is – **'Rutland's Curse'**.

Peter Rutland fights his way through Afghanistan in 1878, while serving under General Roberts or 'Bobs', who made his name in this small Victorian War with his famous march from Kabul to Kandahar.

Based on the 1878 campaign, this young Artillery officer embarks on a hazardous mission to return a holy relic, despite inside treachery and a long-standing curse, whilst fighting a noble enemy and a personal war on Afghanistan's bloody plains, where to his surprise he finds great loyalty and also love

Afghanistan 1878 – A bloody conflict is being fought to keep the advancing Russians out of India. Peter Rutland, newly commissioned into the Royal Artillery, has been posted to Kurram. He is eager to follow in his father's footsteps, a retired Major who served with the Guns in Afghanistan in 1840. Peter is puzzled and disappointed at his father's request for him to resign his commission and work in the family business. Peter is undeterred on discovering the reason for his father's opposition to the Afghanistan posting - the 'curse' on the Rutland name – 'When your blood returns here it will darken the stones of our valley.'

This courageous and inexperienced young officer embarks on a hazardous mission to return a precious holy relic to its rightful owners – the religious authorities in Afghanistan.

'**Rutland's Curse**' vividly brings to life the explosive action on the battlefields in the hostile terrain of Afghanistan, where cultural misunderstandings, treachery and revenge become a personal war.

Roger Carpenter is currently writing a novel called '**Rutland's Blues and Greys.**' based on the American Civil war.

For more historical details you can visit his website – www.roger-carpenter.co.uk